ACCORDING TO THE EVIDENCE

ACCORDING TO THE EVIDENCE

Bernard Knight

This first world edition published 2010
in Great Britain and in 2011 in the USA by
SEVERN HOUSE PUBLISHERS LTD of
9–15 High Street, Sutton, Surrey, England, SM1 1DF.
Trade paperback edition first published
in Great Britain and the USA 2011 by
SEVERN HOUSE PUBLISHERS LTD.

British Library Cataloguing in Publication Data

Knight, Bernard.
   According to the evidence.
   1. Forensic pathologists–Fiction. 2. Wye, River, Valley
   (Wales and England)–Social conditions–20th century–
   Fiction. 3. Detective and mystery stories.
   I. Title
   823.9'14–dc22

ISBN-13: 978-0-7278-6986-9   (cased)
ISBN-13: 978-1-84751-317-5   (trade paper)

All Severn House titles are printed on acid-free paper.

Severn House Publishers support The Forest Stewardship Council [FSC],
the leading international forest certification organisation. All our titles that
are printed on Greenpeace-approved FSC-certified paper carry the FSC logo.

MIX
Paper from
responsible sources
FSC
www.fsc.org   FSC® C018575

Typeset by Palimpsest Book Production Ltd.,
Falkirk, Stirlingshire, Scotland.
Printed and bound in Great Britain by
MPG Books Ltd., Bodmin, Cornwall.

PROLOGUE

May 1955

B renda Paxman stopped her grey Morris Minor outside the chemist's shop in the High Street, ignoring the nearby 'No Parking' sign. A few miles from Stow-on-the-Wold, Eastbury was a sleepy haven of peace, well off the main roads. No one was likely to object, as the small Gloucestershire town had no traffic problem – and even if it did, who was going to complain about the local District Nurse?

Short and dumpy in her navy-blue uniform, Nurse Paxman went into the shop clutching her large medical bag and advanced on the assistant with a list of items she needed replenishing.

'Get these together for me, please, Molly.' She brandished an order form at the skinny girl behind the counter, just visible in a gap between a pyramid of baby food and a pile of assorted cough medicines.

'Can you have them ready first thing in the morning, dear? I can't stop now, I've only just finished at the Parkers.'

At this, there was a rapid clicking of heels from the dispensary at the back of the shop and an older woman appeared alongside the girl. She had sharp features and a narrow mouth, with greying hair pulled back severely into a bun at the back of her head. A long white coat and a glass measuring-cylinder in her hand marked her out as the pharmacist. In fact, Sheila Lupin, MPS, owned the business, being the only chemist in the town.

'How is she now, Brenda?' she demanded abruptly.

The plump middle-aged nurse shook her head sadly.

'Not much different from usual, Miss Lupin. She should be in hospital, just for nursing care, but she won't hear of it.'

'The other nurse will be in this afternoon, I hope?' snapped the pharmacist.

Brenda nodded. 'I'm doing mornings this week; Audrey will go in again about three o'clock.' As she turned for the door, Sheila Lupin called after her. 'Is he there now?'

'Arrived back from a call just as I was leaving,' she answered as she left the shop. The nurse walked to her car and sat in it for a moment, a frown on her face. It was such a pity that Sheila was so antagonistic to her brother-in-law Samuel. It was common knowledge that she had been dead against her sister Mary marrying the local veterinary surgeon fifteen years ago. Brenda, being in the same age group as the sisters, knew that they had not been all that attached to each other, each going away to different boarding schools at an early age. Sheila was always the plain one and Mary the prettier of the pair, which she felt was the root cause of Sheila's antipathy to Samuel Parker. Never having married, the pharmacist seemed to have devoted her life to disliking the 'vet', and now that Mary was terminally ill she never missed an opportunity to disparage the long-suffering husband. With a sigh, the nurse started her car and drove off to visit her next patient.

A few minutes after the Morris left, Sheila Lupin hurried out of the shop. She had changed her white coat for a mackintosh, as a few spots of drizzle were falling. Walking rapidly, she crossed the road in front of the parish church and continued down the pavement for a few hundred yards until she turned into the drive of a substantial Victorian house set well back from the road. A wide expanse of gravel lay before it, on which was parked a maroon Lanchester car. The house had a central porch with bays each side and a red gabled roof surmounting a row of upstairs windows. Built on to the further side was a large extension, with a muddy Land Rover standing outside. This was Samuel Parker's animal surgery and waiting room. It had its own entrance, but Sheila went straight to the front door, which she opened with a key.

Entering the rather gloomy hall, she took off her raincoat and hung it on the hallstand. She could faintly hear distant noises of pots and pans, but the kitchen was down a long corridor leading past the stairs, where the cook-housekeeper, Mrs Cropley, was no doubt making lunch.

The first door on the left, which had been the lounge, was now her sister's sickroom, as for some months she had been incapable of climbing the stairs. In fact, for several weeks she had been unable to leave her bed, except to be helped on to a commode by the nurses or members of the family.

Sheila turned the knob and walked in, familiar with the dim

light penetrating the partly closed blinds. A hospital bed was against one wall, with a locker on one side and the commode on the other. She walked across the room, her heels clicking on the parquet floor.

'How are you today, dear?' she asked gently, but was not surprised to get no reply from the still shape in the bed. Mary was now on twice-daily doses of morphine to alleviate the pain in her bones from secondary tumours, and much of the time she was either asleep or in a state of near stupor from the drug.

When she reached the side of the bed, Sheila stood looking down at her sister. Though not a woman given to emotion or dispensing much of the milk of human kindness, her eyes blurred with sadness and compassion, for this was her sister. Though they had never been all that close, mainly due to Sheila's rather flinty nature, Mary was all the family she had left, and to see her fading away in this pathetic fashion wrenched even her lukewarm heart.

She whispered her name again, not wanting to wake her if she was sound asleep, but again there was no response. Sheila gently laid her fingers on Mary's hand, which was lying palm up on the coverlet. It was then that she noticed that there was a bead of blood in the crook of her elbow. Both arms had a number of needle marks, as painkillers had been given frequently for the past few weeks, but this one looked very recent. There was a kidney dish on the locker containing some lint swabs, and the fastidious pharmacist took one and gently wiped away the dribble of blood.

'That's better, Mary,' she said softly, but then looked more closely at her sister's face as she lay on the pillow. Her eyes were half open but they were fixed and sightless. Sheila was not a nurse or a doctor, but she had worked in the dispensary of a London hospital during the wartime Blitz and knew death when she saw it.

At first almost rigid with shock, she rapidly recovered and felt for a pulse in the wrist and then the neck to confirm that life had ebbed away. Though she was quite sure that her sister was dead, she realized that a doctor should be called immediately and hurried out of the room. Back in the hall, she brushed away a haze of tears with the back of her hand and turned down a passage that went across to an internal door into the veterinary annexe. As soon as she went through it, she was in the waiting room, lined with a collection of hard chairs, now empty as the next surgery was not until the late afternoon. Another door led into Samuel Parker's examination room, and as she burst in she urgently called out his name. He was not there, but she could hear the sounds of a dog barking and water running. Yet another doorway led to several more rooms containing animal cages, an operating table and all the paraphernalia of a vet's practice.

'Samuel, quickly!' she cried out urgently. 'Where are you?'

'Coming, just washing my hands. What is it?'

He appeared in the doorway, rubbing his hands on a towel. A tall, stooping man, Samuel Parker was in his late forties, his dark hair forming a prominent widow's peak on his forehead.

'Mary! It's Mary. I've just been in there and I think she's dead!'

His long face, normally ruddy from working outdoors, instantly blanched. Without a word to her, he rushed from the room, the doors crashing open as he ran towards his wife's bedroom. Sheila suddenly felt dizzy, overpowered by the suddenness of events, and she leaned on the zinc-topped examination table where clients presented their cats and dogs. In spite of the urgency of the situation, as the room stopped spinning her eyes focused on some objects near her supporting hand. There was a used syringe, an open box of glass vials and a bottle half full of a colourless liquid.

An experienced pharmacist, she automatically glanced at the labels and a moment later was tottering after her brother-in-law, screaming at the top of her voice.

'Samuel, you bastard! What have you done, damn you?'

ONE

Breconshire, September 1955

T he burly youth pedalled his way along the lane, its high hedges still green, with just a few signs of approaching autumn. The Raleigh was old and clumsy and he made heavy weather of the slope up towards the barn. The bike was his father's cast-off and, though Shane had tried to modernize it with a pair of drop handlebars, it still remained an old bone-shaker. If his employers weren't so tight-fisted, he grumbled to himself, he could have got in a bit of overtime to afford the down payment on a new machine.

It was just seven o'clock when he dismounted at the gate and leaned his cycle against a post. Hauling a pair of keys from the pocket of his stained dungarees, he undid the padlock and pushed the metal gate wide open with a squeal of protest from the rusty hinges. He was always first here in the mornings, as Jeff and Aubrey were milking down at the main buildings, almost a quarter of a mile away. That lazy bugger Tom Littleman never got here before eight – or even later if he'd been hitting the beer the previous night.

Shane wheeled his bike into the large yard, the ground sticky with yesterday's rain mixed with years of old oil from the vehicles scattered around like an elephant's graveyard. Land Rovers, tractors, a couple of small trucks, muck spreaders, reapers and even an ancient threshing machine littered the area, laced with old tyres and unidentifiable pieces of rusty metal. Some of the debris had been there so long that grass, nettles and even briars were growing through it.

The young labourer propped the Raleigh against the wall of the barn, a huge structure with a corrugated-iron roof. The walls were of concrete block up to head height, from which rose vertical slatted timbers. A large corrugated-iron door gave access for vehicles, but the youth went to a small door alongside it and again unlocked another large padlock.

Whistling tunelessly between his teeth, he went into the gloom within the barn and pulled back the two metal bars that locked the main door and, with a heave, pushed it open. He kept walking until the door was flat against the outside wall, where he secured it by a rusty chain to a staple. In high winds, it was a beast to push open, but today the air was warm and still.

With the full light streaming into the barn, he could now see the usual collection of farm machinery under repair, a couple of tractors with their radiators and fuel tanks removed and a Land Rover minus its engine.

It was a moment before his eyes, used to the familiar scene, realized that something was not right. He was looking directly at the soles of a pair of boots which were projecting towards him from under a large blue tractor. They were attached to a pair of legs and, as he slowly moved forward, his uncomprehending mind was forced to accept that not only was the top end of the body directly under the huge back wheel of the Fordson but that the dark stain that had spread beneath it was certainly not motor oil.

After gaping at the body for long enough to recognize the clothing as that of their mechanic, Tom Littleman, the apprentice grabbed his bicycle and pedalled like fury back along the road to Ty Croes Farm, four fields away.

In the countryside, dealing with a death can be a slow process.

It was forty minutes before the first policeman arrived on his little Velocette 'Noddybike' from the police house in Sennybridge and almost another hour before the coroner's officer appeared from Brecon.

The constable had been phoned by the owner of the farm, Aubrey Evans, who had left the milking shed as soon as Shane Williams had arrived to gabble his news. He had immediately raced back to the barn in his old Bedford pickup truck, the boy bouncing up and down on the seat beside him.

When they reached the yard, the farmer had jumped out and run to the threshold of the big door. After a single glance, Aubrey had dropped to one knee alongside the still form and grabbed the nearest outstretched hand. A dour, practical man, he felt the deathly cold of the skin and knew that his mechanic was beyond any help.

'Bloody fool!' he muttered uncharitably to Shane as he looked at the massive treads of the tyre crushing the victim's neck. The pile of large wooden blocks that had been propping up the back axle of the Fordson were scattered under the vehicle. 'I told him to get this job finished, but not when he was half pissed!'

With a muttered command to his shaken apprentice to get the big door closed again and to stand guard, he jumped back into the pickup and clattered off to use their only phone, which was back in the farmhouse.

By nine o'clock the group outside the barn door had grown appreciably and soon the arrival of a black Wolseley 6/90 brought two more, a detective inspector and a plain-clothes sergeant.

The DI was a tall, thin man of an age approaching retirement. He wore a long fawn raincoat and a permanently miserable expression, perhaps because of his name. After almost thirty years in the police, Arthur Crippen had heard every variation of the joke and it had long been worn thin. He advanced on the group and fixed his mournful eyes on the coroner's officer, PC William Brown.

'Right, Billy, what's going on and who are these people?' he demanded.

Brown was a thickset fellow with a pronounced limp, caused by a shell splinter in the Italian campaign. His Monte Cassino disability had gained him the job of coroner's officer when he returned to the police force.

'Like I said on the phone, sir, we've got an apparent accidental death from a chap squashed by a tractor.' He jerked a thumb back at the barn, where the main door was open again and the body covered with a tattered canvas sheet. 'But it's a bit unusual, so I thought it better to be on the safe side and ask you to have a look before we move him.'

Crippen's eyes peered out from under the wide brim of his brown trilby, scanning the other men standing around him.

Billy Brown pointed them out, one at a time.

'This is Aubrey Evans. He runs the farm down the road in partnership with his cousin here, Jeff Morton.'

The two men nodded in acknowledgement. Aubrey Evans was a typical Mid-Wales farmer, impassive in nature but with shrewd eyes beneath the flat cap that he wore at a rakish angle. About forty years old, his big muscular body was clad in a brown warehouse coat, held closed by a length of binder twine tied around his waist.

Jeffrey Morton had a family resemblance to his slightly older cousin, but he was slightly shorter, though still sturdy. He had a fuller, more open face, marred by a large purple birthmark on his left temple. Like Aubrey, he wore a crumpled tweed cap, but it was perched on the back of his head, revealing slightly gingerish hair. Being as much involved in their mechanical repair business as working the farm, he wore faded blue dungarees, oil stained at the front.

'And this gentleman?' demanded Crippen, staring at an older man standing behind the two cousins.

'I'm Mostyn Evans, owner of the farm,' came a deep voice as he stepped forward. 'At least I own the land and used to work it until I passed the business on to these two here. Aubrey's my son and Jeff is my nephew.'

He was in his seventies, the DI estimated, but still a strong man both in physique and temperament. Wiry grey hair covered a big head, his craggy face lined with a lifetime's exposure to the elements. A baggy brown suit, with an old-fashioned waistcoat, covered a collarless flannel shirt fastened at the neck with a brass stud.

'What about this young fellow?' growled Crippen, staring at the youth, who lurked at the edge of the group.

'That's Shane Williams,' said the coroner's officer. 'Sort of an apprentice mechanic. He was the first to find the body.'

The lad shuffled uneasily. 'I'm not a proper apprentice,' he mumbled. 'Just working here, while I'm waiting to be called up for National Service.'

For the next five minutes the detective inspector dragged what little information he could from the four men about their scanty knowledge of 'the occurrence', before going towards the barn to look at the scene. Billy Brown and his sergeant walked each side of him as they went up to the big Fordson, where the coroner's officer carefully removed the tarpaulin and put it to one side.

'They shouldn't really have put this on,' he said. 'But I suppose they didn't want to leave him exposed until we came.'

Arthur Crippen stood for a long moment looking at the scene.

The tractor was on an almost even keel, its offside back wheel resting squarely on the neck of the corpse, the head hidden by the massive tyre. A few spanners lay scattered around, amid the rough wooden blocks, which appeared to be sections sawn from a railway sleeper.

'Why shouldn't it be an obvious accident, guv?' murmured Sergeant Nichols.

'Bloody daft thing to do if you're a proper mechanic, putting your head under a jacked-up wheel!' objected Billy Brown, who felt obliged to justify his calling out the CID.

Crippen continued to stare at the inert body lying on the stained concrete floor. He slowly rubbed his face, pushing his sallow cheeks into even deeper wrinkles as he tried to make up his mind.

'Shall I get the tractor jacked up again, so that we can get the poor sod out?' asked John Nichols. The sergeant was quite young, a slim, fair man with a narrow Clark Gable moustache.

Crippen came to a decision and slowly shook his head from side to side. 'I don't think we will, John,' he grunted. 'Like Billy here, I feel we need to be cautious about this one.'

Aubrey Evans broke away from the group still standing in the yard and came up to the policemen. 'Are you going to leave him there much longer? It doesn't seem very respectful.'

The senior detective didn't answer him directly but countered with another question. 'What was he doing, to be under there like that?'

'I'm not sure. It's Jeff who mostly looks after the repair side – I do the farming.' He turned and called across to his cousin, who ambled over to join them.

'What was Tom doing with this Major?' he demanded.

'Fitting new brake shoes,' replied Jeff Morton. 'He should have finished them yesterday morning, but the idle bugger didn't turn up until midday.'

Crippen ignored the lack of respect for the dead but filed the comment away for later enquiry. 'So he had to have the tractor jacked up for that?' he asked.

'Yes, one side at a time. Get the wheels off, then open the drums to change the shoes.'

'But the wheels are on now?' objected Crippen.

'Yes, but the shoe clearance would have to be set by using a spanner on the adjusters behind the drums. Each side would have to be jacked up again for that.'

'Is putting a pile of wooden blocks under the axle a safe way of doing that?' demanded the sergeant.

Morton shrugged. 'We've always done it – and so does every other farm repairer. Never had trouble before.'

'Can't you use a proper trolley jack?' asked the coroner's officer.

'We do, to get it off the ground. Then we stick the blocks underneath and take the jack away. It's always being needed for other jobs.' He swept his hand around the barn, where half a dozen other vehicles were in various states of disorder, some up on their own blocks.

Crippen returned to staring at the man lying dead at his feet.

'Would any sensible mechanic trust his head underneath more than a ton of tractor?' he asked.

'Tom Littleman wasn't what you'd call sensible, officer,' said a deeper voice, as Mostyn Evans had walked up to stand behind them. 'He was a lousy mechanic, if the truth be told. I told the lads that when they employed him – and I was dead against them taking him into partnership with the repair business.'

'What was wrong with him?'

'He was far too fond of the booze, for one thing,' growled the older man. 'Lost a lot of working time, and when he was here he was often half-cut. I'm not all that surprised that the stupid sod ended up like this.'

Aubrey murmured something to his father in Welsh, but Mostyn Evans shook his head. 'No, it's got to be said, son! Tom was a liability and a disaster waiting to happen. Now it *has* happened.'

The detective inspector seemed to have made up his mind. He turned to Billy Brown. 'Has a doctor been here to look at him?' he asked.

The coroner's officer shook his head. 'I left a message with Dr Prosser, the local police surgeon. He was out on his rounds, but I left a message for him to come here as soon as he gets back for his morning surgery. I doubt he'll do more than certify death,' he added rather caustically.

Crippen did some more face-rubbing, which seemed to aid his decision-making. 'I want a pathologist to have a look at this, before we write it off. Any chance of getting one up here this side of Christmas? I suppose we'll have to go through the forensic lab in Cardiff.'

His sergeant shook his head. 'There was a circular from

headquarters last week. The Cardiff man is away, so a new Home Office chap from the Wye Valley is standing in for him.'

Crippen shrugged. 'I don't care if he's from Timbuktu as long as he clears this up for us. Get hold of him, then shut that barn door and leave the PC here on watch.'

He loped back to the waiting police car and ordered the driver to take him back to Brecon. 'I'll come back when the pathologist is due,' he called through the window.

TWO

When the call came through, Dr Richard Glanville Pryor was drinking a mug of Nescafé in the staffroom of Garth House. This was an Edwardian villa perched above the road that meandered through the Wye Valley, one of Wales's prime beauty spots along the border with England. 'Staffroom' was rather a pretentious title, as there were only three other people in the house and the room was his late uncle's old study, situated between the kitchen at the back and his partner's office at the front.

He sat in an armchair with sagging springs, part of the furniture left in his aunt's house when he had inherited it almost a year earlier. Opposite, his secretary-cum-cook, Moira Davison, shared a more modern settee with Siân Lloyd, a lively little blonde who was their laboratory technician. On his right, Dr Angela Bray, his partner – solely in the professional sense – occupied a new Parker-Knoll easy chair, as she had declared that if she had to spend most of her life perched on a laboratory stool, at least she intended to be comfortable at other times.

When the phone rang in the corridor outside, they were talking about the news on the wireless that the first independent television channel was to open later that week, but as they had no television set the discussion was rather academic.

'I'll get it, I've got to go to the kitchen anyway,' offered Moira, taking her empty cup and saucer with her. A moment later she put her head around the door and beckoned to her boss.

'It's the police in Brecon, doctor. Sounds as if they're calling you out.'

'Your fame is spreading quickly, Richard!' chaffed Angela.

It was only a few weeks since Pryor had been put on the Home Office list of forensic pathologists, primarily to stand in for other areas when the designated doctor was not available.

He uncoiled his lean body from the deep chair and went out into the passage, which ran from the front hall to the kitchen at the back. Though Post Office Telephones had recently installed extensions in their office opposite, as well as in Richard's room, the original instrument was still on a small table in the passage, an old Bakelite model with a tarnished dial.

Moira had vanished into the kitchen with her cup and saucer and left the receiver on the table. Picking it up, he soon found that a detective sergeant from Brecon was asking him to turn out to visit a scene.

'Probably an accident, doctor, or possibly even a suicide. But my DI wants to make sure that there's nothing fishy about the death.'

Something in Nichols' tone suggested to Richard Pryor that he felt that there might well be something fishy, but he did not want to pursue it on the telephone. Taking directions to Ty Croes Farm, which was between Brecon and Sennybridge in the next county, he promised to be there within a couple of hours.

As he put the phone down, Angela Bray and Siân came out of the staffroom.

'Do you want a trip out into the jungle, Angela?' he asked flippantly. 'There's a body lying under a tractor about forty miles away.'

'Doesn't sound very forensic to me,' said Siân in a disappointed tone. She marched off to the laboratory, where she had several alcohol analyses waiting. Angela grinned at Richard.

'She wants every call to be a serial murder, poor girl!' she said. 'Do you really want me to come with you?'

'I thought it might be a change for you. You've been stuck here for days with those paternity tests. And you never know, the keen eye of a forensic scientist might be vital!'

The handsome biologist smiled at him. 'It would be nice to have a ride in the country on such a nice day. You're off straight away, I suppose?'

She went off to her room at the front of the house to get a coat and the 'murder bag', a leather case which contained their tools of the trade. Ten minutes later they were rolling down the steep drive in his black Humber Hawk, turning left on to the main road and setting off up the valley towards Monmouth. As she had said, it was a nice autumn day, with the dense woods on the steep sides of the gorge beginning to glow with a spectrum of colours, from green through gold to orange. The River Wye meandered down below them, its meadows bright green on either side.

'We're lucky to work in such a lovely place,' said Angela. 'This beats Scotland Yard, even if I could just see the Thames if I leaned out of the window!'

Five months ago Angela, a scientist with a PhD in genetics, had given up her job in London's Metropolitan Police Laboratory and joined Richard Pryor in this risky venture in South Wales.

Though the Met Lab was a prestigious place, she had become disenchanted with a repetitive workload and the poor chance of further promotion. That, together with a traumatic broken engagement, had persuaded her to join Richard when he proposed setting up a private consultancy after returning from years in the Far East. He had been given a generous 'golden handshake' from his university appointment in Singapore, where he had been Professor of Forensic Medicine. This coincided with his aunt's bequest of Garth House, and he had decided to take the plunge and go private, persuading Angela to become his partner. He had met her months earlier at a forensic congress and they had hatched this plot to go it alone.

As they drove, he related what little the sergeant had told him about the death they were attending. Angela wondered what could be so odd that the CID wanted a Home Office pathologist at the scene of what sounded like an industrial accident.

'Ours not to wonder why, just prepared to do or die!' sang Richard. Angela smiled to herself at his happy mood, brought on by this first call in his new role for the police. He was a nice chap, she thought to herself, never snappy or unpleasant. He had these moods of elation but was sometimes anxious at the gamble they had taken at giving up salaried jobs for the uncertain nature of private practice. After months of living in the same house, their relationship was still strictly professional, but she liked him a lot.

The black Humber, which he had bought second-hand on returning to Britain, was a spacious, comfortable car, and the forty miles through Abergavenny and Brecon passed quickly. Richard had a set of Ordnance Survey maps for all the counties along the Welsh Marches, and with Angela as pilot they easily found the secondary road off the A40 that led to Cwmcamlais, the nearest hamlet to the farm that the detective sergeant had described.

Beyond the empty rolling farmland, the profile of the Brecon Beacons lay on the skyline, and to the west the high ridges of Carmarthen Van and the Black Mountain could be seen from the higher points of the road. A little further on, a police constable was waiting at a small junction and, after the pathologist had identified himself, the officer climbed into the back of the car and directed them down the side lane.

'Past the farmhouse, sir, then on for a bit and you'll see the yard and buildings on your left.'

A few moments later the Humber pulled in to the cluttered yard, where a police Wolseley, a blue Vauxhall and a small white Morris van were parked. A small group of men were standing smoking near the van but came across as soon as they arrived. Introductions were made all around before Arthur Crippen launched into an account of the incident.

'Behind that big door, doctor, there's a fellow lying dead with his neck under the back wheel of a tractor.' He jabbed a finger towards the barn. 'No doubt about who he is – it's the mechanic who does most of the repair work. In fact, he's a partner of the other two men.'

'This is not just a farm, then?' asked Richard Pryor.

The DI shook his head. 'They've got this business repairing agricultural machinery and implements. I suspect it's paying better than actual farming these days, though they've got a fair-sized dairy herd.'

He returned to his main story. 'This chap, Thomas Littleman, was a bit of a boozer, it seems. Not the best of workers and, from what I gather, the other two from the farm, who are cousins, were not too keen on continuing the partnership. Anyway, last evening Aubrey Evans had a bit of a barney with him, as he was well behind in finishing a job on a tractor that had been promised for yesterday.'

'Who exactly is Aubrey Evans?' asked Angela.

'He's the senior partner; lives in the house and does most of the farm work,' explained the sergeant. 'The other one is his cousin, Jeff Morton, who lives in a cottage at Ty Croes and does some of the mechanical work as well.'

Crippen picked up the thread of his tale once again.

'Aubrey told Littleman that he had to finish the job last evening and that's the last anyone saw him alive. They have a young chap as a sort of apprentice, who opens up the barn every morning. That's him over there, name of Shane Williams.' He jerked a head towards the youth, who was sitting on the tailboard of a Land Rover at the other side of the yard, aimlessly swinging his legs.

'He opened up at seven today and found the body under the tractor. He raced up to the farm and raised the alarm. Bit of a shock for him, no doubt.' Crippen's long face looked even more mournful, and Richard sensed that he was sorry for the boy.

They began walking across to the big corrugated door, which a constable began to push wide open for them.

'Why are you concerned that it might be anything other than an accident?' asked Richard Pryor.

The detective shrugged. 'Just covering all the options, doctor. It's bloody odd that an experienced mechanic would stick his head under a jacked-up vehicle, unless it's a weird sort of suicide.'

With the door wide open and hooked back against the barn wall, full daylight now illuminated the scene. Richard and Angela stood a few yards away and looked at the inert body sticking out from under the big blue tractor.

'We've taken photos, but if there are any others you want, just tell Jim.' Crippen indicated one of the detective constables from the van, who had a large camera slung from his neck.

Angela stood back, holding their case-bag while Richard Pryor crouched down alongside the corpse.

'It's safe enough. The tractor can't drop any further,' said DS Nichols, reassuringly.

'When you're ready, we'll jack it up and get him out,' added Crippen as the pathologist began feeling the dead man's arms and legs for warmth and rigor mortis.

'Has the police surgeon been?' asked Richard.

'Yes, he certified death. Said he was stiff then, so he must have died some time ago.'

Pryor examined the hands, then pushed up one of the loose trouser legs of the mechanic's stained dungarees to look at his shin. This seemed to interest him, and he did the same on the other leg, taking a few minutes to repeatedly press his thumb into the purpled skin. Then he stood up and looked at the expectant faces of the small group gathered around.

'I can't do any more until we get him out, Mr Crippen. Are you ready to do that now?'

The detective inspector nodded. 'I've sent the cousins back to the farm. Best not to have them around if they're possible witnesses for the coroner. Our chaps here can pull him out.'

With a coroner's officer, three detective constables acting as photographer, exhibits officer and a dogsbody, as well as a uniformed PC, there was no lack of muscle power. Within minutes one DC had dragged a trolley jack from the back of the barn and, pushing several of the fallen blocks out of the way, set it under the right-hand side of the back axle.

'This will lift three tons, so no problem with an E27N like this,' promised the DC, who was something of a tractor enthusiast.

He pumped away at the long handle, and the hydraulic jack smoothly lifted the back end of the Fordson.

'That'll do it!' shouted Crippen from the doorway once the big tyre had risen about nine inches from the floor. 'Pull him well clear, lads. We don't want any more accidents.'

Richard gave Angela a look that, combined with the raising of his eyebrows, suggested to her that something was not quite right. However, he did not elaborate and watched as the policemen carefully lifted the body by its arms and legs and laid it gently on the tarpaulin a few yards from the tractor. Beneath the wheel where the head had been lying, the concrete floor was stained with blood, but there was not sufficient to leave a pool.

The senior detective became aware that Shane Williams was still across the yard, staring fixedly at what the police were doing. He motioned to the only officer in uniform.

'Best send that kid back up to the farmhouse, Davies. We

don't want him having nightmares, but I may want to speak to him later.'

With the corpse now clear of the tractor, both Richard and Angela crouched alongside the head. She had been in the forensic service for many years and had attended scores of scenes of death, so, although she did not relish blood and gore at such close quarters, she was not particularly distressed by this one.

As she pulled a pair of rubber gloves from their murder bag, she gave him a quizzical look. 'What's bothering you, Richard?' she asked in a low voice.

'I want to see his feet and legs as well as his neck,' he muttered cryptically, before turning his attention to the top end of the body. The tyre had been almost a foot wide and had crushed everything from the upper chest to the lower jaw. With over a ton weight above pressing against the concrete below, the tissues and bones had been converted into a bloody pulp, the skin torn and grossly discoloured. Pryor lifted the head up, feeling it wobble obscenely because of the shattered neck vertebrae.

'I'm trying to see the back of the neck. The skin there hasn't suffered so badly,' he murmured to his partner. But without turning the whole body over on to its face, there was no way he could get a satisfactory view, so he laid it down again and went to the legs. This time, he pulled down the woollen socks, as well as dragging up the trouser legs as high as they would go.

'That's just post-mortem lividity, surely?' asked Angela, pointing at the purplish staining that covered all the exposed skin.

'That's just the problem,' he said quietly, then looked across at the police officers, who were keeping at a respectful distance.

'I'd like to get him to a mortuary as soon as we can, Mr Crippen,' he said. 'I can't examine him properly out here, though I'll have to take his temperature or it'll be too late, given that he almost certainly died last night.'

Like Angela, Arthur Crippen picked up a note of concern in the pathologist's voice. 'D'you think there's a problem, doc?' he asked.

Richard declined to be drawn too far. 'Let's just say I'll be happier after I've had a good look at him on the slab,' he said.

'Meanwhile, I'd suggest you preserve the scene until we know what we've got. And perhaps it would be wise to get a few more pictures of him, now that he's out in the open.'

The detective inspector, with years of experience behind him, recognized a hint when he heard one and rapidly began organizing his troops.

THREE

t was now a little late to have lunch, but the two scientists found a small cafe in the twisty little streets of Brecon that could offer them bacon, egg and chips with their bread, butter and tea.

They had tried a pub on the way from Cwmcamlais, but after threading their way past sheepdogs and local farmers drinking Buckley's Bitter, all that was on offer at the bar were crisps, desiccated pork pies or Scotch eggs.

'So what's all this mystery, Richard?' demanded Angela as they sat over a second cup of Brooke Bond in the bay window of the little shop. He had refused to be drawn during the short journey from Cwmcamlais, promising to explain it after he had had more time to think.

'Those legs,' he said, stirring sugar into his tea. 'Why is there all that lividity in them, especially on the front of the shins? The fellow had been on his back for hours.'

Though she was a biologist, not a medical doctor, Angela immediately realized what he was implying. 'But that seems impossible! He was found lying under a tractor with his neck squashed.'

'The whole thing is bloody odd! No wonder Hawley Harvey Crippen wanted me to have a look at it.'

She ignored his facetious renaming of the DI and demanded to know what he was going to do about it.

'Depends on what else we find when I can go over every inch of that body.' He looked at his wristwatch. 'They should be at the hospital by now, so let's get on with it.'

It was a small hospital and a small mortuary, little more than a brick shed near the boiler house. There was no mortuary attendant, but Pryor was used to fending for himself. With the help of Billy Brown, the coroner's officer, he was able to deal with the examination after two undertakers had carried the corpse in from their van and laid it on the solitary slate slab in the small, dingy room.

Arthur Crippen and one of the detective constables

crowded in behind, while the photographer took more pictures of the clothed body. Richard and Billy began removing the heavy boots, socks and then the crumpled dungarees and flannel shirt. As soon as the body was bare, Pryor again took great interest in studying the legs, then moved to the hands. Pulling off the underpants, he took the long thermometer which Angela handed him from their bag and slid it into the corpse's back passage. Standing back, he waited for the mercury to settle and used the moments to speak to the detective inspector.

'There's something not right here, Mr Crippen. I'm not sure yet, but I suspect you've either got a concealed suicide here – or possibly even a murder.'

The DI remained impassive, his features retaining his usual gloomy frown. 'It didn't ring true to me either, doc. But what makes you think that?'

Richard turned to put on a long red rubber apron that the coroner's officer took from a hook on the wall. After he had looped the chain over his neck and tied the tapes at the back, he put on the rubber gloves that Angela produced from their bag, then explained his suspicions.

'A lot for me to do yet, but it's those legs and hands that worry me. Look, from the knees right down into the feet, the skin is reddish-purple, even on the front of the shins. And both hands are the same colour.'

This time Crippen's face allowed itself to crease into an expression of incomprehension. 'And that tells you what?' he demanded.

'That this poor chap didn't die where he was found on the floor. At least, he hasn't been lying there ever since he died. He must have been upright for some hours. And about the only way corpses can stay vertical is when they are hanging!'

The four police officers stared at him incredulously.

It was Crippen who reacted first. 'You're saying that someone put him under the tractor after he was dead?'

Richard nodded. 'The blood has drained down after death into the lowermost parts, the legs, feet and hands. Sure, it can move again afterwards, but often it becomes fixed within a few hours.'

He moved to the body again and pulled out the thermometer.

Glancing at it, he called out 'eighty-one degrees', which Angela wrote down on a clipboard. Then he helped the coroner's officer to roll the body over on to its face.

'See, very little lividity on the back, where it usually settles. Most of it went down into the legs.'

Arthur Crippen, by no means an unintelligent man, struggled to adjust his mind to this new set of circumstances.

'Doc, are you telling me that this fellow was hanged first, then stuck under that tractor?'

Even Angela looked at her partner a little dubiously. She didn't want him making an ass of himself on his very first Home Office call-out. However, Pryor's quietly confident manner seemed to reassure her as he explained further.

'The logical reason is that someone wanted to conceal the true cause of death by faking an apparent accident. Whether or not it's a hanging remains to be seen, which is what I'm going to do next.'

Taking a block of wood that stood on the foot of the autopsy table, he slipped it under the corpse's chest as the coroner's officer lifted the upper part of the body. This allowed the head to drop down on its mangled neck, so that the pathologist could get a good look at the skin between the hairline and the upper shoulders. It was wrinkled and bloodstained, with a few tears from the crushing weight of the great tyre, but Richard studied it with minute care.

'I don't want to wash it yet in case there's trace evidence,' he said, more to himself than the others. This prodded Angela into voicing her concern.

'If this turns out to be criminal, what about forensic evidence?' she asked crisply. 'I've got no official standing here, so I can't become involved, even though I've been doing the job for years!'

Richard looked quizzically at the detective inspector. 'That's a point, Mr Crippen. What are we going to do?'

The DI looked at his watch. 'It's mid-afternoon already. I don't feel like hauling a chap up from the laboratory in Cardiff; it would put us back until after dark.'

He looked across at the photographer and the other detective constable. 'We can get all the pictures we need and Amos here can act as Exhibits Officer. As Dr Bray is your colleague, already helping you with the post-mortem, I don't see why she can't collect any trace evidence you find and hand it over to Amos. That'll keep the chain of continuity intact.'

It was always vital, if there was any chance of a case ending up in court, for any specimens to be accounted for every inch of the way, to be able to counter any defence accusation that samples had become mixed up.

Angela gave a little shrug, though she was secretly pleased to be more directly involved, even if it was only as a go-between.

'Fine, but I'm only acting as a collector of any traces. I don't want to get my knuckles rapped by the director of the Cardiff lab for sticking my nose in!'

Richard was busy peering at the back of the corpse's neck. There were wide smears of dried blood all over it, obscuring the view.

'Considering the damage to the neck, which is virtually squashed, there wasn't all that much blood on the floor,' he observed, turning his face up towards the DI. 'Tends to confirm that he was dead before that wheel landed on him.'

He continued to study the neck, twisting the head a little each way to get a view of the sides. Then he straightened up and beckoned to the photographer. 'Best get some pictures as close up as you can before I start cleaning it up,' he suggested.

He stood back as the DC took his photos, a slow process as he had to change the one-shot flashbulbs between each exposure. When he had finished, Pryor asked Angela to come around his side of the table and have a close look at the neck.

'Is there something there to pick off or is it my imagination?' he asked her, pointing at the side and back of the neck with a gloved finger.

The biologist stared for a moment, then put on her own rubber gloves. She took a small lens and a pair of forceps from their case and bent back for another look.

'There are a few fibres stuck in the dried blood,' she murmured, delicately picking something off, though they were invisible to the watching policemen. She carefully placed whatever she had recovered in a small screw-top vial from the case and handed it to Amos, the detective constable whom Crippen had nominated as the Exhibits Officer.

'What about taping the neck?' asked her partner.

Angela nodded. 'Better do it, though we'll get a lot of dried blood as well.'

Another dip into the apparently bottomless murder bag produced a roll of Sellotape and some glass microscope slides. Cutting lengths off the tape, she pressed the sticky side against the skin of the neck, dabbing the whole area to pick up any tiny threads and fibres that might be there. Then she placed the tapes firmly on to the slides and again handed them to the DC, who placed them in brown exhibit envelopes which he had brought from his van and began to fill in the labels.

'Better keep all the clothing, especially the shirt,' she advised. 'The lab may want to look for more fibres on them.'

What had started as an accident or possibly a suicide had escalated into a suspected homicide, so all the usual forensic precautions had to be taken.

Richard Pryor went back to his labours. 'I'll have to wipe it down now, if there's nothing wanted,' he announced.

Billy Brown brought over a sponge and an enamel pan of water from the sink so that the pathologist could clean away the blood from the neck. As soon as he had done so, he gave a grunt of satisfaction.

'I was right, thank God! I was afraid that I might have been making a fool of myself!'

The detectives crowded closer as Richard's finger pointed at a brownish line on each side of the neck, rising at the back towards the hairline between the ears but vanishing in the centre.

'Typical hanging mark! Strung up with a rope or some sort of line, with the knot at the back.'

As the photographer got busy again, he explained to Arthur Crippen. 'The rope cuts into the front of the neck, then the mark comes around the sides and rises because of the down-drag of the body. As the head falls forward the suspension point is moved away from the skin, unless it's a slip knot, causing a gap in the mark right at the back.'

'So he died by hanging?' growled the DI.

'That's jumping ahead a bit, but it's certainly the favourite at the moment,' replied Richard, moving back to the mortuary slab. Again with the help of the coroner's officer, he turned the body on to its back again. After more photographs, Angela came with her sticky tape and did her best to cover the wreckage of torn skin that had mangled the whole of the front of the neck and chin.

Then Pryor sponged it down as well as he could, holding the ripped segments of skin one at a time. Then he tried to reassemble them to cover the jagged wound made by the tyre treads. The half-inch brown-red mark was now seen to run across the throat below the jaw, but there were other marks as well, apart from the tyre crushing.

'Ho ho, the plot thickens!' He looked across at Arthur Crippen again. 'Just as well I didn't plump for a hanging just now. I think this chap had been strangled first!'

As the DI and his sergeant pushed nearer, Richard pointed out a series of blue bruises the size of a fingertip each side of the rope mark and some more up under angles of the jaw on each side. In addition, there were several crescent-shaped scratches among the larger abrasions from the tractor tyre.

'No doubt that he's been squeezed around the neck while he's still alive. But that rope mark and the grazes from the wheel are post-mortem.' He turned back the flaps of skin and showed that the only blood in the tissue under them was where the tears went across the blue bruises.

His next examination was of the eyes, which were well above the destruction of the neck and lower jaw. In the outer lids he found some fine blood spots in the skin and on opening the eyes with his fingers there were several more small haemorrhages in the whites.

'They could be either from hanging or strangulation,' he admitted. 'But if the hanging was done after death, then they're down to throttling.'

Arthur Crippen digested these rapid changes in the nature of the case. 'Why the hell would anyone want to go through all this rigmarole, doc?'

Pryor shrugged. It wasn't his job to be a detective, but he allowed himself an opinion. 'Whoever did this started off by strangling the fellow, then thought he'd cover it up by hanging the body. Later he saw that the neck bruises gave the show away, so he devised a way he thought would destroy the evidence on the neck by crushing it.'

'You say "he", doctor,' interposed Sergeant Nichols. 'So we needn't be looking for a woman?'

Richard grinned. 'A good forensic motto is never say never, never say always, but I doubt if you need to *cherchez la femme* this time. In fact, manual strangulation is uncommon in men;

it's usually inflicted on women and children. But there are
plenty of exceptions, of which this seems one.'

Crippen looked at his watch. 'Four o'clock now. Any idea
when you'll finish up here, doctor? I'd like you and Dr Bray to
come back to the scene afterwards, to have a look at a possible
hanging site.' He moved towards the door, sighing deeply.

'Meanwhile, I'd better go and phone the good news to my
chief inspector. It'll make his day, I don't think!'

It was almost three hours later before they got back to the
barn.

After finishing the post-mortem and closing the body, they
were taken into the hospital dining room and given tea and
sandwiches. Billy Brown, being coroner's officer, knew all
the staff and had no problem in arranging some refreshment,
the ghoulish activities of the past few hours having had no
effect on their appetites.

When they returned to Ty Croes Farm, they found the same
police team, but reinforced with two more uniformed constables, as the scene was to be guarded all night. It was now
early evening and, although there was still full daylight, another
van had brought a floodlight powered by a gas cylinder and
some large torches, in case they were needed.

Arthur Crippen was waiting for them at the gate, where a
PC stood to repel any spectators, not that this was likely in
such a remote spot.

'I've spent the time since I left you in questioning all the
folks at the farm,' he said mournfully. 'But no one admits to
hearing a damned thing last night. The farmhouse where
Aubrey Evans and his family lives, as well as his cousin's
cottage nearby, are a good quarter of a mile away and no one
had any reason to come down here until this morning.'

They walked over to the barn, where the big door was still
open. Richard and Angela stood on the threshold and looked
at the cavernous space, half filled with vehicles. The blue
Fordson was still propped up on the jack, a few spanners scattered under the back end.

'We didn't put those blocks back under the axle,' explained
the detective sergeant. 'They might have to be fingerprinted,
though probably a dozen people will have handled them, like
everything else in this jumble sale!'

doing her technical work, so it was a godsend when they found an efficient lady almost on their doorstep who could not only do some cooking and cleaning but keep on top of the office work.

Moira put her pie on a cork mat on the big table, another legacy from Richard's aunt. Together with local carrots and peas, the two scientists tucked in hungrily, washing the food down with cider from a large flagon.

'Aren't you joining us, Moira?' asked Angela, eyeing the apple tart that she was taking from the warming oven.

'No, I had something at home earlier. But I'll make some coffee and have one with you, so that you can tell me what you've been up to today.

'By the way,' she added. 'There were a couple of messages today, nothing urgent. I've left a list on your desk, doctor. The only one that sounded interesting was a call from a firm of solicitors in Stow-on-the-Wold, who wanted to talk to you about giving them a medical opinion in a criminal case.'

'Did they say what it was about?' asked Angela.

'No, but they left their number, and I promised that we would get back to them tomorrow. Perhaps it's another murder!'

Like their technician Siân, Moira was very enthusiastic and partisan when it came to the work of the Garth House consultancy. They took a pride in being part of it and wanted to be involved as much as possible. The cases were often highly confidential, often being sub judice until cases came to court, but both employees had shown in the past months that they could be trusted to keep their mouths shut. Moira had been a secretary to a local solicitor and Siân had worked in a hospital laboratory, both jobs requiring strict attention to confidentiality.

Between the pie and the apple tart and then over coffee, the partners gave Moira the details of the unusual case in Breconshire that had occupied them for most of the day.

'How extraordinary! A good start for your first Home Office call-out,' she exclaimed. 'Who on earth could have done such a thing?'

'Our friend Dr Crippen seems set on blaming one of those up at the farm,' said Richard, making Moira giggle over the poor detective's name. 'I suppose he's right, as there are very few others to suspect in that lonely place.'

'I spoke to the liaison officer in the Cardiff lab,' added Crippen. 'He's coming up in the morning with a scientist. We'll keep the place battened down until then, but I just wanted you to point out any spot where the hanging could have taken place.'

The pair from the Wye Valley stood and looked around them. The barn had a high-pitched roof of galvanized sheets laid on wooden rafters supported by a number of thick metal cross-beams held up by rusty steel pillars. At one place on their right, a chain was slung over a beam, the two free ends holding a large pulley-block. From this dangled a continuous loop of thin chain, the lower end of which was at shoulder height. Hanging below the drum was a sturdy metal hook, and a length of heavier chain dangled down to floor level.

'That chain hoist looks a likely candidate,' said Richard, pointing at the device.

Crippen nodded his agreement. 'I thought that, too. How's it work?'

The DC with the passion for tractors enlightened him. 'You keep pulling on that loop of chain, which lowers the hook down. To lift it up, you just reverse the direction of pull. It's geared so you can lift a hell of a weight, though it's slow.'

'What's it for?' asked Angela.

'Lifting anything heavy – here it would be for hoisting an engine out of its chassis, things like that.'

The DI contemplated the device hanging up in the air. 'It's the obvious place, but that was a rope mark around the neck, not a chain.'

'The surface of the hook should be taped for fibres,' said Angela. 'If there are any, they might match those I took from the victim's neck.'

'Better leave that for the lab chap tomorrow,' growled Crippen. 'We'll get all the fingerprints first, just in case. Not that that rusty chain will be much use for prints.'

'Where's this rope, I wonder,' asked Richard, peering around the barn, which apart from the tractors, a couple of Land Rovers and an old car, had all sorts of junk lying around. There were parts of engines, oil drums, dismantled farm machinery and numerous shapeless pieces of rusty metal. Among all this there were several lengths of rope of various lengths and sizes.

'Those fibres were coarse and looked like hemp or sisal,' said Angela. 'And the mark on the skin suggests it was about half an inch wide.'

'Some of that coil over there would fit the bill,' said John Nichols, pointing at a hank thrown over a drum of Duckhams lubricating oil standing alongside a grey Ferguson tractor.

'All the rope will have to be packed up and taken back to Cardiff tomorrow,' said the biologist. 'Those fibres from the neck will have to be matched against them.'

Richard Pryor was staring up at the chain hoist hanging innocently above their heads. 'Apart from the other evidence, it certainly rules out a suicide,' he commented.

'How d'you mean, doc?' asked Crippen.

'Well, he would hardly sling a rope over the hook, put the noose around his neck and then start hauling himself up by pulling hand over hand on the chain. He'd pass out before he got his feet off the ground!'

The detective inspector agreed. 'No doubt someone did it for him, after strangling him. Then he must have spotted those fingermarks on the neck and realized that they gave the game away. So he decided to have him down again and squash him under the Fordson.'

Richard rubbed his chin, now bristly after a long day. 'He must have been left hanging for some time, otherwise that lividity wouldn't have had a chance to settle in his legs.'

'How long, doctor?' queried the sergeant. 'The killer must have either hung about here all that time or come back later.'

'Can't put an exact time on it; it's very variable,' said Pryor. 'But I suspect it must have been at least a couple of hours to get that intense.'

Crippen mulled this over. 'So unless he waited here for a hell of a long time, he must have come back to the barn. Sounds like a local job, not just some passing thug.'

His sergeant snorted. 'One of those buggers up at the farm, sir! Got to be. Who else would want to croak a boozy mechanic?'

Richard Pryor decided that he didn't want to get involved in any police business, so he prepared to leave them to it.

'Dr Bray and I will get back home, if we can't do any more for you. It's been a long day.'

The DI was sincere in his gratitude when he walked them to the Humber.

'You've done a damned good job for us – and you, ma'am!' he added. 'I'll keep you informed of what's going on here. Perhaps you could have a word tomorrow on the phone with the forensic people in Cardiff, to tell them what specimens you took and that sort of thing.'

Angela promised to liaise with her old colleagues, as she knew all the case officers in Cardiff. 'We've collected blood and urine samples for alcohol, especially as he's got this history of drinking. Maybe that's at the bottom of all this?'

As Crippen opened the car door for Angela, he gave a grim promise.

'You may be right. Tomorrow, I'll be squeezing all I can from those folk up at the farm.'

It was dark before they got back to Tintern Parva, the village nearest to Garth House at the lower end of the Wye Valley.

As Richard was putting the car away in the coach house at the back, Angela was surprised to see a light in the kitchen window. She had expected Moira Davison, the young widow who looked after them, to have left something cold for their supper in the old fridge, maybe sliced ham and salad. But when she opened the back door and went into the kitchen, she found Moira there, pulling something out of the Aga stove.

'I thought you could do with a hot meal after such a long day,' she announced, her gloved hands placing a large cottage pie on top of the big cooker.

'Moira, you're a wonder!' Richard sniffed the aroma appreciatively as he came into the room.

'You've not been waiting here for us all evening, have you?' asked Angela, pulling off her coat and dropping thankfully into one of the chairs at the table, which was already set with two places.

'No, but I've been back and forth, keeping an eye on the oven,' said the trim, attractive woman. Slim and petite, she had an oval face framed by jet-black hair cut in a bob, straight fringe across her forehead. Moira lived a few hundred yards away down the main road to the village. When the partners had started up the forensic consultancy six months earlier they were virtually camping out in the dusty old house, living out of packets and tins. Also, their laboratory technician, Sian Lloyd, couldn't keep up with the typing of reports as well

By the time they had helped their housekeeper to clear up the kitchen, it was getting late. Richard saw her to the bottom of the steep drive and watched her go down the road with her torch, keeping well into the hedge as there was no verge or pavement.

When he got back inside, Angela declared that she was going up to her room to listen to the wireless and read for a bit, before going to bed.

Accommodation had been something of a dilemma when they had first come to Garth House. Though there were plenty of rooms, there was only one bathroom. At first, Angela had stayed in a bed and breakfast in Tintern, but soon rebelled at the cost when there was a large house available. It belonged equally to both of them – or more accurately to the legal partnership that they had set up. When she left London, Angela had sold her flat and put the money into the firm, Richard contributing Garth House itself, a substantial Victorian dwelling with four acres of land. His aunt had died in a retirement home twelve months ago, her husband having passed away years before. She left her estate to her only nephew Richard, who used to stay with her when a boy and even when a medical student in Cardiff. This legacy coincided with the offer of a 'golden handshake' from his university post in Singapore. As he had been divorced not long before, there seemed nothing to keep him in the Far East, so he took the plunge and came home to Wales to set up in private practice with Angela.

The problem with the house was that even in these enlightened 1950s, it was a little daring for two unmarried people to live together in the same house. However, after a few nights in the B&B, Angela had declared that she had had enough and moved in with Richard.

It was a purely platonic relationship – she had a sitting room and a bedroom upstairs and he took another bedroom on the other side of the house. Downstairs was devoted to the business, each having a study, the other rooms being an office, a laboratory and staffroom, as well as the kitchen. The original problem was the single, old-fashioned bathroom, as his aunt had done nothing to improve the house for thirty years. However, in the intervening months a local jobbing builder had divided the cavernous bathroom in half, with two separate doors. This

his-and-hers arrangement now worked very well, with a new modern bath in place of the cast-iron monstrosity in Angela's half. Richard was content with a shower cabinet, so their problem was solved and they were happy to ignore any scandalized gossip in the village.

After seeing Moira off, Richard took the samples of blood and urine he had collected in Brecon and put them in the new refrigerator in the laboratory, for Siân to deal with the next day. Then he went back into his own office on the ground floor, opposite the staffroom. Here he had a desk, a work-bench and a microscope, as well as shelves with all his medical textbooks and journals.

Next door was Moira's office, the main features being a filing cabinet and a typewriter. A new communicating door went into the laboratory, a large front room with a wide bay window looking out on to the valley below. The house had two such windows, one each side of the central front door. The one on the other side was Angela's study, with the same superb view of the woods and cliffs opposite.

Sitting at his desk, he drew a yellow legal pad towards him and began to write a draft report of his visit to Ty Croes Farm and the subsequent post-mortem in Brecon. In the morning, Moira would type it up for him, with a couple of carbon copies, so that he could send one to the Brecon coroner and the other to DI Crippen.

As he sat writing under his table lamp, Moira was sitting alone in her own house down the road. Her comfortable armchair was pulled up near the hearth, where a small fire was burning, as October evenings were becoming cool. Her Yorkshire terrier was asleep at her feet and a small glass of sherry stood on a table alongside her. An open copy of a Georgette Heyer novel lay on her lap, but she was not reading it, just staring at the flames flickering between the coals in the fire.

The thirty-year-old was thinking once again of the profound changes in her life that had taken place over the past couple of years. Happily married, three years earlier she had suddenly become a widow when her husband, an industrial chemist, had been killed in a factory accident in Lydney. Generous compensation and a modest pension had allowed her to live on comfortably in their house, but she found herself somehow aimless and lacking direction in her life.

Moira had not contemplated marrying again, though she was certainly attractive enough, as no one she knew remotely interested her. Then six months ago, a postcard advertisement in the village post office had spurred her to apply for a job as a part-time housekeeper with the new people who had just moved in to Garth House, virtually next door. It was the best move she could have made, as it jolted her out of her rut and she soon found the position fascinating. She had rapidly become an indispensable part of the 'forensic family'.

Staring into the flames of her fire, she wondered yet again about the relationship of Richard Pryor and Angela Bray. Though they slept in the big house every night, she had never seen any sign of intimacy or affection between them, just a pleasant friendship. She knew the story of their meeting at a forensic conference eighteen months ago and their eventual decision to set up in partnership. Her main source of information had been Siân Lloyd, who seemed to know every bit of gossip. She and Siân had often discussed the nature of the relationship between their two employers, but they came to no conclusion. Siân, young romantic that she was, was inclined to think that they were secret lovers, but Moira felt that though the situation could one day go that way, at present Richard and Angela appeared to be in a purely professional relationship.

She sighed and took a sip of her sherry. A rather prim woman, it would be brash to suggest that she 'fancied' Richard Pryor, but certainly he was often in her thoughts. She had enjoyed marriage and missed all aspects of her former wedded state. Maybe it was time that she began to look around, she thought – taking this stimulating job had started to nudge her out of her previous apathy.

Her book forgotten, she stared into the fire and visualized Richard's lean face and wiry body. He was quite tall, with abundant brown hair and appealing hazel eyes. Siân, who was an ardent film fan, claimed he was very like Stewart Granger or Michael Rennie, an image that was reinforced by the way he dressed. Richard was fond of light suits with a belted jacket and button-down pockets, strengthening the Granger image of a big-game hunter. As he had lived in the Far East for the past fourteen years, it was natural that he had these Singapore-made suits, but the women in the house had recently ganged up on him and sent him off to get clothes better suited to the British climate and appearing in local courts.

Though she always thought of him as 'Richard', Moira never failed to address him as 'doctor', as did Siân. Apart from being their employer, they had a genuine respect for him that discouraged overfamiliarity, even though he was the son of a Merthyr general practitioner, a valleys boy still with a slight Welsh accent even after all his years abroad.

He was certainly an attractive man, she thought once more. In his early forties, he was more than a decade older than her, but these days that was no bar to a romance – or so she fantasized.

This led her to think of the age of another woman – Angela Bray, who was only slightly younger than Richard. Here was competition indeed – a tall, handsome woman with a similar academic background to the doctor, coming from an affluent family in the Home Counties. Siân Lloyd, that fount of all gossip, had soon discovered that Angela's parents ran racing stables and a stud farm in Berkshire and that she had gone to a select boarding school in Cheltenham. A London University degree in biology, followed by a PhD, had led her to fifteen years in the Metropolitan Police Laboratory, where she had risen to a responsible position but then stuck halfway up the promotion ladder.

Moira sighed when contemplating the challenge Angela posed in her daydreams of a romance with her boss. The scientist was elegant, poised and extremely well dressed – and, most of all, she was living in the same house as Richard Pryor!

Almost angrily, Moria pulled herself together, mentally chiding herself for being such an adolescent fool. Drinking down the rest of her sherry, she opened her Georgette Heyer and determinedly began to read.

FOUR

Next morning the people from the Home Office Forensic Science Laboratory in Cardiff were due at Ty Croes Farm at ten o'clock, so DI Crippen used the waiting time to interview the residents more thoroughly than the previous day had allowed.

Milking was finished, and by eight o'clock he sat with his sergeant in the parlour of the farmhouse, a musty little-used room. A bobble-edged velvet cloth covered a round table, and there was even an ancient aspidistra on the window sill. On the wall above Crippen's head was a framed sampler dated 1864, the faded threads displaying in Welsh a gloomy extract from the Psalms.

The householder, Aubrey Evans, was the first one they spoke to. He came into the room and sat at the table between the inspector and John Nichols, who had a notebook at the ready. Aubrey wore a thick check shirt buttoned at the neck, his brown corduroy trousers held up by wide red braces.

'Let's start again at the beginning, Mr Evans,' began Arthur in a mild voice. 'You run the farm, but it actually belongs to your father?'

'He's kept the freehold of the land, but he's given me a lifetime lease on this house, just as he has to Jeff in regard to the cottage next door.'

'What happens when he dies?'

'It's all arranged with the lawyer. He's leaving the land to me, as he doesn't want it split up. It's been in the family since Noah's Ark was afloat. He's giving the freehold of the cottage to Jeff.'

'And what about the business?' queried Crippen.

'My cousin and I split the farming two ways, then we've got a partnership that runs the agricultural repair business. Jeff and I have got a third each, the other thirty-odd per cent is Tom Littleman's.'

He stopped as if a new thought had just struck him. 'No, we've got half each now, with him gone.'

'His family will surely inherit his share?' suggested Nichols.

The farmer shrugged. 'He hasn't got any family. Lived alone, not married and I've never heard of any other relatives. He came from up in England somewhere after the war.'

Crippen's lined face developed a few more furrows. 'He's the dead man here, so I've got to know everything about him. How come he became one of your partners?'

Aubrey stretched out his legs, his feet encased in thick socks. Even at this fraught time, he couldn't come into the parlour in his work boots.

'Worst thing we ever did, taking him on! When we began building up the repair business six years ago, we needed a real mechanic for the engine work. Jeff's cousin had been in the army through the war, in the REME, mending trucks and tanks. Tom Littleman was a pal of his, and when we wanted someone he suggested him.'

'So he's been here about six years?' asked the sergeant.

Aubrey nodded. 'He worked for us as an employee for a couple of years and was fine before he really took up the booze. Later, when my father gave us the farm and we set up a partnership, we took him on as a partner rather than pay him wages.'

He sucked on a hollow tooth. 'And regretted it ever since!'

'Was he that unreliable, then?' asked the sergeant, who was making notes as Aubrey spoke.

'Unpredictable, he was! Sometimes as good as gold, for he certainly knew his stuff with machinery. But he'd been getting slacker and slacker – coming late, sometimes not turning up at all.'

'Just because of drink?'

'I suppose so, no reason otherwise. But he'd show up drunk some mornings, then get ratty when we told him off. He gave that poor kid Shane a hard time.'

Aubrey leaned back in his chair and scratched his head. 'My dad was always sounding off about him, said we should never have taken him on. He warned us that he was going to be trouble. We've kept trying to buy out his share, but he wasn't having any.'

'So, really, it's quite handy that he's gone?' said Crippen with an air of false innocence.

The implication was not lost on the farmer, and he scowled at the detective. 'We didn't want the bugger killed, if that's what you mean,' he said sullenly.

Arthur Crippen changed tack. 'Let's go through what happened yesterday and the previous evening,' he said placidly. 'When did you last see Littleman?'

'About five o'clock that evening. I drove down to the barn to pick up Jeff, as we were going to an NFU meeting in Brecon. Shane was just knocking off, and I wanted to check that the brakes had been finished on that Major. The owner had been getting shirty because we'd promised to have it ready for him the previous day.'

'And it wasn't finished?'

'No way. Tom hadn't turned up at all on Monday and he was even late coming that day. I tore him off a strip, as the owner had been bawling down the phone at me, threatening to take his work elsewhere.'

'You had a quarrel, then?' suggested the sergeant.

'We were always having shouting matches, either me or Jeff. But Tom always had some excuse – or he just shrugged it off. Drove us bloody mad, it did!'

John Nichols wrote rapidly in his notebook as the DI continued.

'When you left, Littleman was still working on the tractor? How far had he got, d'you know? Was it jacked up then?'

Aubrey shrugged. 'I didn't really notice, to be honest. See, I do the farming and Jeff splits his time between that and seeing to the machinery side, especially since Tom became so unreliable.'

The questions went on for a few more minutes, but there was little else that they could get out of the man, apart from how Shane had rushed up to fetch him and how he had rung the police in Sennybridge the previous morning. As he got up to leave, Crippen had one last question.

'You said that you and your cousin went into Brecon for a National Farmers' Union meeting the night before. What time did you get back here?'

'The meeting finished about half eight. We went for a couple of pints in the Boar's Head and got home about ten, I suppose.'

When he reached the door, the inspector asked him if he would send his wife in for a word.

Aubrey stared at him. 'What d'you need her for? Betsan never went near the damned barn!'

'Just routine, Mr Evans. She might have noticed something about Littleman, you never know.'

The farmer grunted something and left the room. A few moments later his wife appeared, and the two police officers stood while she sat down. Betsan Evans was in her mid-thirties and was still a good-looking woman, slim and straight-backed, with a long face framed with dark hair. Though a hard-working farmer's wife, she had an innate elegance that could be envied by many women living a softer city life. She wore a blue wrap-around pinafore dress above lisle stockings and house slippers.

Betsan sat calmly with her hands in her lap and waited for the inspector to speak.

'We won't keep you long, Mrs Evans,' he said. 'Just a few points to try to clear up this nasty business.'

'Is it definite that someone killed Tom?' she asked in a flat voice. 'I can't believe it.'

'I'm afraid it looks that way. How long have you known him?'

Betsan looked up sharply at this, a movement that was not lost on the two detectives. 'Known him? Well, since he came here, about six years back. Out of the army, he was. Good with machines, that's why Aubrey and Jeff wanted him here.'

'We've heard he was a heavy drinker. Is that right?'

She nodded. 'He got worse these past two years. He was fine when he first came.'

'Any idea why?' asked the sergeant.

She shook her head vigorously. 'He never said much about himself, and we never got under his skin, as they say. Don't even know if he had any family, he never mentioned them.'

'Not married, then? Did he have any lady friends?'

Betsan shrugged, just as her husband had. 'Not that we knew about. He lived eight miles away in Brecon. Used to come on a motorbike every day, so we didn't know what he got up to when he wasn't here.'

'Never see any strangers hanging about, maybe talking to him?' hazarded Nichols, running out of things to ask this quiet woman. 'Didn't gamble on the horses or perhaps had debts to someone?'

Again she twitched her shoulders. 'I wouldn't know, would I? I didn't see much of him. He didn't come up here to have his dinner; he used to bring his food with him – often in a bottle!' she added with a touch of bitterness.

'But as far as you knew, he was a good mechanic?' persisted Crippen.

She nodded. 'Never had any complaints about his work – it was getting him to do it was the problem. Aubrey and Jeff always had to nag him to get things done, he lost so much time lately with the drink.'

She was silent for a moment. 'It was a mistake having him here in the first place!' she burst out vehemently. 'My father-in-law was against it from the first. We should have listened to him. This would never have happened then.'

Though she was nowhere near tears, she seemed to be building up a head of emotion, so Crippen decided to let her go. When the door had closed behind her, he looked at his sergeant.

'Something's going on there that she's not letting on about,' he murmured.

'Maybe they had a fling together at some time,' said Nichols.

He got up and went out into the passage of the old house, which, though it had been modernized, was a typical centuries-old Welsh longhouse. Originally, the family would have lived at one end and the animals at the other, but a series of sheds and outbuildings had now separated the humans from the live-stock. All the family, including the cousin and his wife, were sitting eating breakfast in the huge kitchen. Crippen and the sergeant had been given tea when they arrived, declining the offer of a fried breakfast.

Now Nichols asked Jeff Morton to come in, and soon he was sitting between them at the parlour table. He was slightly shorter than his cousin, but still had the powerful build of a countryman, toughened by hefting bales of hay and all the other physical tasks of farm labour. He had an amiable face, but Crippen's eyes could not avoid being drawn to the livid birthmark on the side of his head.

'Bad business, this!' he began before the DI could say anything. 'I wasn't keen on the fellow, but I wouldn't wish that on him.'

'I gather he wasn't popular around here?' observed Crippen.

'Lately he was a pain in the arse. He was alright when he

first came and for a fair bit afterwards,' said Morton, echoing
Mrs Evans. 'You could never get close to him; he always had
a tight mouth. But the drink ruined him.'

'When did you last see him?' asked the sergeant and got a
recital of the facts that Aubrey Evans had given them about
going to Brecon.

'I understand you worked with him more than your cousin
did?' queried Crippen. 'You must have talked to him a lot,
being with him every day?'

Jeff shook his head. 'Never got much out of him, only what
he did when he was in the army and stuff about football.
Crazy about the pools, he was. God knows what he spent a
week on them. But he never opened up at all about personal
things. He'd shy off them if you brought the subject up.'

'How did the drink affect him? Was he drunk on duty, so
to speak?'

Again Morton shook his head. 'He wasn't falling about or
anything,' he replied. 'Slowed down, but he could still do the
job. It was just that often the bloody man didn't show up at
all or came hopelessly late when we had a job to finish.'

'And that was the situation on the last day, with that blue
tractor?' said Nichols.

'Yes. I nagged him all day – at least all afternoon, as he
didn't show up until dinner time. Then Aubrey had a go at
him and there was a row about not getting that Fordson ready.'

'Did it get nasty, that row?' asked the inspector. 'Violent,
I mean?'

'No, it was Aubrey and me that used to do the shouting.
Tom would just get sullen and turn away. He wouldn't even
reply half the time.'

They went through the same questions again, but Jeff Morton
was adamant that, as far as he knew, Littleman had no debts
or enemies that came pestering him. No one had ever come
asking for him at the farm, and once he rode away on his
BSA motorbike he was an unknown quantity as far as his life
was concerned.

As he got up to leave, Crippen asked him if his wife was
in the house. 'I'd just like a word with her, same as with Mrs
Evans, to see if there might be anything useful she might have
heard or seen.'

The cousin looked surprised. 'Rhian wouldn't have a clue,

sir. She hardly ever spoke to Tom. He was always down at
the barn, a few fields away.'

'Just the same, I'll have to speak to her, just for the record.
Same as we'll have to take fingerprints from everyone, just
to eliminate any we find in the barn.'

Morton gave a wry smile. 'You'll find prints from half the
people in Breconshire down there! Most of the farmers around
here come in and handle the stuff they bring in.'

Arthur Crippen thought he was probably right, but it would
still have to be done. Just as Jeff Morton was leaving the
room, one of the uniformed constables put his head around
the door to say that the forensic people had arrived.

The DI got up to follow him out. 'I'll have to go down to
see them. We'll leave talking to Mrs Morton and the father
until afterwards,' he said to his sergeant.

'And the lad, this Shane Williams,' said Nichols. 'He was
the one who found the body, after all.'

In the next county, Angela Bray and Siân Lloyd were working in
the laboratory of Garth House, trying not to be distracted too
much by the striking view through the wide bay window.

The technician had one side of the room for her chemical
equipment, a long bench covered with glassware and some
optical instruments. It was divided in the centre by a fume
cupboard, a glass-sided cabinet with an exhaust fan that vented
out through the side wall of the house.

The scientist reigned on the opposite side, where Angela
handled the biological investigations, ranks of small tubes for
blood-grouping tests being lined up on the white Formica top.
Two box-like incubators were held at body heat and against
the third wall, next to the door into Moira's office, was a large
white refrigerator.

Siân was working through the specimens that Richard Pryor
had brought in from recent post-mortems at Chepstow and
Monmouth – a carbon monoxide analysis from an industrial
coal-gas poisoning and a barbiturate identification from a
suicide. Before coming to Garth House, she had been a medical
laboratory technician in a large Newport hospital and was
currently studying for an external qualification in biochemistry.

Angela was dealing with a batch of paternity tests, one of
the mainstays of their practice. In the six months since they

had started, she had worked up quite a reputation among solicitors far and wide for helping them in cases where mothers were claiming that a certain man was the father of their child and should be paying maintenance. She checked the complex pattern of blood groups of the mother, child and putative father to see if he could be excluded, though the tests could never positively prove his paternity.

As they worked, they chatted sporadically. Angela had told Siân about their experiences the previous day in the depths of Breconshire, as the girl was always avid for details of their forensic cases.

'From what you say, whoever killed that man must be someone on the farm,' she declared with her usual forthrightness. Siân always saw everything in black and white, rather than acknowledging shades of grey.

'It seems most likely, as there's hardly anyone else within walking distance,' agreed Angela. 'But we mustn't jump to conclusions in this game. Proof has to be according to the evidence.'

There was a silence as Siân put one eye to the Hartridge reversion spectroscope sitting on her bench. She adjusted a knob to line up the spectra of a solution of blood from the victim of the factory accident, which would give her a percentage saturation with the deadly gas carbon monoxide. She noted down the reading, then picked up the conversation where they had left it.

'But who else could have done it? You say the place is way out in the sticks?'

'No doubt that's what the police are doing today, knocking themselves out to see if there's any possibility of someone else being involved. Maybe there's somebody in this chap Littleman's past that's relevant. He was a heavy drinker. Maybe he gambled as well and owed a lot of money.'

Siân thought that strangling the fellow wasn't a very good way of collecting the arrears, but she contented herself with remarking that she would be doing the alcohol estimations on his samples that afternoon.

Moira came in from the office at that point with the typed copies of the short statement that Angela had dictated earlier about her involvement. 'What about these fibres you collected?' she asked. 'You haven't examined them yourself?'

'No, it's an odd situation. I could have dealt with them – it's just up my street – but I can't get involved any further than just handing them over to the police as exhibits. I've got no official standing in the case, unlike Richard. It's the forensic lab in Cardiff who will have to do the business.'

'Couldn't the cops have employed you to do it, instead of them?' persisted Siân.

Angela shook her head. 'Then they'd have to pay us, but they get the forensic lab for free, as it's part of the Home Office system. Anyway, Cardiff will probably have to examine other stuff from there, like the clothes that people were wearing, so it would be pointless having two lots of scientists involved, especially if eventually we had to go to court about it.'

Moira went back to her office and Angela swung back on her rotating stool to get on with adding sera to her racks of tubes, while Siân began a duplicate run on the carbon monoxide test. All was quiet for a while, until the sound of a car was heard, hauling itself up the steep drive outside.

'He's back. I wonder if he's brought me more work?' observed Siân. She was not complaining, as every aspect of the job intrigued her, even after six month's familiarity. Richard Pryor had been doing his routine post-mortems for the coroner at the shabby public mortuaries in Chepstow and Monmouth, which, like Angela's blood tests, were his main contribution to the finances of the partnership. He had been fortunate in that an old classmate of his, when they were medical students in Cardiff before the war, was now a general practitioner in Monmouth and also the part-time coroner for the area. He had given the post-mortem work to Richard, and this, together with a similar function in several hospitals as a stand-in when the regular men were away, brought in a steady income to the Garth House business.

When he came in through the back door and dumped his bag in his room, Moira declared a tea break and went off to the kitchen to put the kettle on the Aga. As she passed him in the passage, she reminded him about returning yesterday's phone call from the lawyer in Stow-on-the-Wold. When they assembled in the staffroom ten minutes later, Richard told them about the brief telephone conversation.

'It was a chap called Lovesey, a solicitor in Stow. He was a bit guarded about the details, but he wants an expert medical opinion on behalf of the defence of a veterinary surgeon who's been charged with murdering his wife.'

Siân and Moira leaned forward eagerly, wanting to hear more, though Angela's interest was mainly concerned with the possible fee that this might bring to the partnership.

'How did he do it?' asked Siân, with morbid curiosity. 'Did he shoot her or strangle her?'

'The juicy details don't normally get discussed over the phone. He wants an urgent conference, as the case goes to trial at Gloucester Assizes in a few weeks.'

'Bit late to think of a defence, isn't it?' asked Angela critically.

'Apparently, they've had one already, but it didn't help them. Now they've got a new defence counsel, some hotshot QC from London, and he's demanding another opinion.'

Moira's brow wrinkled in puzzlement. 'I don't understand this defence business. If they get a first post-mortem in a murder, then that doctor's opinion is accepted, surely?'

Richard Pryor put his mug of tea on the table, ready to lecture.

'Don't you believe it! There are almost as many different opinions as there are pathologists. Some of them have very strange ideas and some are just plain inexperienced in forensic work, being basically clinical pathologists in hospitals.'

'Few forensic pathologists are free from strange ideas,' commented Angela drily. 'Present company excepted, of course!' she added mischievously.

He made a face at her and carried on with his explanation.

'In most murders, either the defence gets an opinion from another independent pathologist who has read the first chap's report or who has done another examination of the body himself, as I did a few months ago in that Swansea case.'

'They had three PMs on that poor woman,' observed Siân, critically.

Now Moira entered the discussion. 'In this Stow case, you said the defence already had a second opinion and they didn't like it. Presumably, they're hoping you will come up with a different view?'

'That's obviously the idea – but I may also agree completely with the first pathologist,' replied Pryor. 'It often happens that way, but at least it means that the accused has had a fair crack of the whip. Doesn't always happen abroad; they have a different system on the Continent.'

'So what have you arranged?' asked the ever-practical Angela.

'I'm going to see the solicitor tomorrow afternoon. Perhaps you'd like to come, Angela? There may be some forensic science angle to it.'

The handsome brunette nodded. 'I've never been to Stow-on-the-Wold. Here's a chance for me, even if it is a homicidal visit, so to speak!'

FIVE

When Arthur Crippen and Sergeant Nichols drove down to the vehicle barn, they found two men talking to the constable left there on guard duty. They had met both of them before, as one was the liaison officer and the other a forensic scientist from the Cardiff laboratory.

The first was Larry McCoughlin, a detective inspector seconded from the Carmarthenshire Constabulary who acted as a go-between when any police force needed technical help.

The scientific officer was a short, rotund man named Philip Rees. 'I hear Dr Bray was up here yesterday,' he said. 'She's a well-known name in our business. We were all surprised when she resigned from the Met Lab.'

Crippen explained that she had come up with the pathologist. 'She was a bit embarrassed at being involved, but we were afraid of losing evidence if we delayed,' he said.

'No harm done. Your motorcyclist brought the samples down last night,' said McCoughlin. He looked across at the barn, where the big door was now closed. 'We'd better have a look around, I suppose.'

As they went to the small side door, Arthur Crippen explained the circumstances and what the pathologist had found on the body. 'Dr Bray suggested that the fibres she found on the neck may have come from a hemp or sisal rope. We sent the lengths that were knocking around the barn down to you last evening.'

As the new arrivals surveyed the inside of the building, Dr Rees asked the detectives if they had all they wanted from the place.

'Yes, we've got all the photographs we need, and the fingerprint boys were here earlier,' said John Nichols. 'We've bagged up all the clothes the four men were wearing that day, ready for you to take.'

'That's probably a waste of time, but I suppose you'll have to look for some bloodstains and try to match those fibres,' observed Crippen. 'Though as those ropes have been knocking about here for years, I doubt they're of much evidential value. Anyway, the place is all yours now.' He waved a hand at the barn.

The two men from the laboratory unpacked their kit and started on the scene, concentrating on the chain hoist and the area around the Fordson tractor. After watching for a few moments, Arthur Crippen decided that he and his sergeant would be better employed back at the farmhouse and left them to carry on.

Seated once again at the parlour table, they called in Mostyn, the elder of the Evans family. He was a large man, but Crippen felt that he must have lost weight lately, as his wrinkled neck seemed too narrow for the collar of his flannel shirt. A thick thatch of iron-grey hair surmounted a big, craggy face, from which a pair of watery blue eyes looked out with disconcerting directness.

'You farmed Ty Croes for many years, I understand?' asked the DI, rather deferentially in the presence of this chief of the clan.

'I was born in the room above this one and worked on the land here since I was about four years old, feeding fowls and herding sheep,' he said proudly in a voice that would have earned him a place in the bass section of any choir.

'And then you handed it on to your son and your brother's lad?'

Mostyn nodded, folding his large, veined hands placidly in his lap. 'I lost interest when my wife died five years ago. The boys will get it all when I die, and they can work it until then. I still lend a hand when necessary, but after seventy-six years I reckon I deserve a bit of a rest.'

Crippen gave an almost imperceptible nod to his sergeant, and Nichols took up the questioning. 'I gather you weren't all that keen on Tom Littleman becoming a partner in the machinery business?'

Mostyn shook his leonine head. 'It was alright for him to come here as a mechanic on a wage. I grant you, he knew his stuff where engines were concerned, but he started going downhill as a worker. The boys were daft to cut him into a share of the business. I warned them against him, but they would have their way.'

'Why were you so against him, Mr Evans?'

The old farmer considered this slowly. He rubbed his hands together and then stroked his bristly chin. 'There was something about him from the first. He was an outsider, see, from up in England somewhere. Never fitted in here, always seemed to hold himself apart from us.'

'I don't quite follow you, Mr Evans,' said Crippen. 'Did he cause any trouble?'

Again there was a pause, but shorter this time.

'Only when his boozing started to interfere with his work. By then, it was none of my business – I'd given the place over to Aubrey and Jeff – but I warned them! We lost some customers over it, and we've got plenty of competitors. Not delivering on time is a serious business. These days since the horses went, a farmer without a tractor is worse than losing the use of his legs!'

John Nichols was busy writing in his notebook, though more formal statements would have to be taken from everyone later.

The detective inspector brought the questioning around to more immediate matters. 'You know, of course, that Littleman was strangled and then an attempt made to cover it up?'

The older man nodded. 'Must have been somebody from his past – or his present! God knows what he was up to in Brecon after he left here every day.'

'And you've no idea what that might have been? Did he ever let drop anything to you about his private life?'

'Naw, did he hell!' exclaimed Mostyn contemptuously. 'Tight-mouthed bugger, he was!'

The rest of the interview was barren of anything useful, and soon the father went back to the kitchen for another cup of tea and to discuss his interrogation with Aubrey and the others.

Arthur Crippen stared out of the small parlour window across the muddy yard to the large milking parlour and the cow pen alongside it.

'Like the woman, I reckon our Mostyn could tell us a bit more if he had a mind to,' he said ruminatively.

Nichols nodded. 'I got the same impression. Think this Littleman was making a nuisance of himself with the two wives?'

His superior shrugged. 'It bears keeping in mind. We'll be

having another go at them later on. Now where's that damned kid Shane. He's the last one, until we start visiting the neighbours, wherever they are.'

As if in answer to his question, he saw a red David Brown Cropmaster drive into the yard, pulling a filthy muck spreader. The tractor itself was not much better, caked in mud and manure. It stopped near the cattle pen and the driver vaulted off, a lanky youth in soiled dungarees with a woollen bobcap on his head.

'Here he is. Better late than never,' grunted Crippen.

There was a short delay, obviously caused by Betsan forbidding the boy to enter the parlour in such a state. When he put his head around the door and hesitantly entered, he was in a check shirt and brown trousers, with only socks on his feet, his muddy boots having been confiscated.

He sat nervously on the chair between the two police officers, his narrow, wary face regarding them suspiciously. He had an untidy shock of mousy hair hanging over his ears and neck. John Nichols, a former military policeman, grinned to himself when he thought of the National Service haircut that Shane would soon have to endure.

'You're waiting for your call-up papers, I hear?' he said easily.

The young man shook his head. 'I've had me papers already. Got to go to Brecon Barracks at the end of the month.'

This was where the regimental headquarters of the South Wales Borderers was situated.

'Now then, lad, you were the one who found Tom's body?'

The DI made it more of a question than a statement of fact.

Shane scowled. He had seen plenty of police films where the finder was always the main suspect.

'That don't mean I had anything to do with it,' he muttered.

'Not saying it was, Shane. I just want to get things straight for the record. Now the body was just as we saw it when we came later, was it? You didn't touch anything?'

'No bloody fear! I took one look and ran like hell to me bike!'

'You worked with him every day,' said the sergeant. 'How did you get on with him?'

Shane Williams suddenly became animated. 'He was a bastard! I hated his guts!' he snarled.

Nichols raised an eyebrow at his inspector, but Crippen seemed unmoved.

'Why do you say that, Shane?' he asked softly.

'He was always at me, complaining and shouting. Sometimes he pushed me around, when he'd had a few too many.'

'Drunk, you mean? Was he incapable, sometimes?'

'Not incapable enough not to clout me across the earhole if I didn't fetch him something quick enough!' whined the youth.

'You were a sort of apprentice. Didn't he teach you anything?'

'Only how to keep out of his reach whenever I could,' answered the boy cynically. 'I learned bugger all about machinery from him. All I was was a gofer – go for this, go for that!'

'What about when Jeff Morton was there? He did a lot of the mechanical work, didn't he?'

The young man sneered. 'Tom was clever. He never had a go at me when Jeff was there. He could cover up his boozing, too, when either Aubrey or Jeff was around. They don't know the half of it.'

'Why did you stick it, then? Didn't you complain to the others?'

Shane seemed to pull himself more upright from his usual slouch. 'Nah, I'm not a sneak! Anyway, I'm leaving the bloody place in a few weeks.' He suddenly realized the changed circumstances. 'That's if I've still got a job here now – and that sod's gone anyway.'

Crippen fixed him with a steely eye. 'Are you glad he's dead, Shane?' he demanded.

The lad slumped again. 'I hated his guts, but I never wanted him croaked,' he mumbled.

Sergeant Nichols changed direction once again.

'You were with Littleman every day. Did you ever learn anything about his life away from the farm? Anything that might have a bearing on his death?'

Shane stared suspiciously at the detective. 'What d'you mean?'

'Do you know what interests he had outside work, apart from drinking? Did he mention women, or gambling or anything like that?'

An almost lecherous grin appeared on the youth's face. 'He was fond of the dames, I reckon. I saw him eyeing Betsan and Rhian when they happened to come down to the barn. That wasn't often, but sometimes they were in the pickup or Land Rover with Aubrey or Jeff.'

'Is that all? Just looking at them?' snapped Crippen, but Shane just shrugged. Then he added another snippet.

'I saw him in Brecon a few times, on the weekend, like. I used to go for a few pints with my pals sometimes and I saw him twice in one of the pubs, with women.'

'Anything odd about that, then?' asked Nichols.

'It was a different girl each time, half his age and pretty tarty, both of them.'

'What about gambling?' asked the inspector, not too concerned with accounts of sitting in pubs with loose women.

'He was mad on the pools, spent an hour every week filling them in. And he was always reading the racing news in the paper and marking things with a pencil, so I suppose he was having a flutter on the gee-gees or the dogs.'

As they had with the other witnesses, the two officers got virtually nothing more out of him and Shane slouched off to his muck-spreading, as there was no work in the barn until the forensic team and the police had finished with the place.

After yet another cup of tea and a slice of fruit cake supplied by Betsan Evans, the two detectives thanked the family for their hospitality but warned them that they would have to have their statements taken down and signed later that day.

Back in their black Wolseley, Nichols drove down to the barn in time to see the two from the forensic laboratory before they left for Cardiff.

'Not a lot to find, Mr Crippen,' admitted the liaison officer. 'We've taped all the parts that might be involved and found a few fibres on the hook of that hoist.'

Dr Rees looked up from signing exhibit labels on the brown envelopes containing their samples and waved a hand at the interior of the barn, now exposed through the open door. 'There's so much junk in here, we can't possibly cover everything. I suspect you'll have a similar problem with your fingerprints. Probably everyone for miles around has left their dabs here.'

When the laboratory men had packed up and left, Arthur

Crippen sat with his sergeant in the car in the yard outside the barn, each having a quiet smoke.

'Not much further forward, are we?' complained John Nichols.

'It's got to be one of these on the farm,' muttered the DI. 'They're not telling us everything – yet.' He emphasized the last word in a menacing way.

'So what do we do next?' asked Nichols. 'I can't see the lab telling us anything we don't know already.'

Crippen flicked his cigarette end out through the window to join the others that were already squashed into the mud.

'You'd better organize a house-to-house, I suppose. More like a farm-to-farm out here. Get a couple of DCs on to it, ask about any strangers knocking about, the usual routine – though I suspect it will be a waste of time.'

The sergeant started the car and they began making their way back to Brecon.

'I have to go and bring the DCI up to date,' grunted Crippen. 'Then have a look at Littleman's lodgings.'

'We sent DC Lewis around there last night. The address was in the dead man's wallet and a key was in his pocket. He rented two rooms above that chip shop near the market.'

The inspector sighed as he looked at the green countryside passing the windows. 'This is a bugger of a case! It should be so simple, but I bet it'll be hell to sort out.'

'We've only got the pathologist's word that it *is* a murder,' observed Nichols. 'I hope we're barking up the right tree, so to speak!'

'Pryor seems to know what he's talking about,' replied Crippen. 'What else could it be? The guy couldn't have strangled himself, then failed with a hanging, so then he laid down under a tractor and kicked the blocks away!'

Grudgingly, the sergeant had to agree.

SIX

Stow-on-the-Wold was an ancient town in the north-east corner of Gloucestershire. Filled with old buildings of Cotswold stone, it was redolent with history. Its churches, hostelries and public buildings owed their existence to its position at the junction of ancient roads and the prosperity brought by the wool trade, the backbone of English commerce through the Middle Ages. It claimed to have the oldest pub in England, going back to the tenth century.

None of this was in Richard Pryor's mind as he parked his Humber in Market Square. It was about sixty miles from Tintern, taking almost two hours to drive through Gloucester and Cheltenham, and he could kill for a cup of tea.

'Time for refreshment, Angela,' he announced, looking at his watch. 'We've got half an hour before we see this chap.'

They walked through the picturesque streets, between the old buildings of yellow-brown stone, and found a cafe of the 'olde tea shoppe' variety. He held the door open for his partner, who today was looking even more elegant than usual in a tailored grey suit with a narrow waist and a long pencil skirt. High heels and a small jaunty hat completed the picture, and he wondered if the solicitor would believe that she was a senior scientist of considerable experience.

Angela saw him looking at her and correctly guessed what he was thinking. 'Too dressy for the occasion, Richard?' she said sweetly. 'A girl's got to put on the style now and then, after sitting for weeks at a bench squirting sera into tubes!'

He grinned and, as they found a table in the window, pulled out a chair for her. 'You look bloody gorgeous, partner!'

Richard knew she was very keen on fashion and spent a lot of money when she had a shopping spree in Bath or London. He suspected that her well-off parents subsidized this, as certainly the income from Garth House in their first six months wouldn't run to the outfit she had on today.

'You don't look too bad yourself,' she countered, looking at the double-breasted charcoal suit that he used to attend court. 'Since we ladies took you in hand and weaned you out of those awful safari suits you're so fond of!'

A pot of tea and a selection of cream cakes were demolished, and as he paid the waitress Richard asked for directions to Digbeth Street, which was the address given to him over the telephone.

It turned out to be directly off the square, and in a couple of minutes they were being shown into George Lovesey's room in a house probably built before Cromwell was born. It had long been the offices of Lovesey, Sayers and Greene, the present senior partner being a great-grandson of the founder. He was a portly man with double chins and silver hair circling a wide bald patch. Richard thought his general appearance was Churchillian, though he was not sporting a large cigar.

After the hand-shaking, introductions and seating rituals had been completed – and the offer of tea declined – George Lovesey settled behind his large mahogany desk and got straight to the point.

'A client of mine is in deep trouble and faces what might be a capital charge,' he began solemnly. 'He has been indicted for murdering his wife and has been committed by the magistrates' court to stand trial at Gloucester Assizes in the coming session. We have already obtained an expert medical opinion, which I am afraid does nothing but concur with the prosecution.'

'May I ask how you came to seek my advice?' asked Pryor.

'A fellow solicitor in Lydney, with whom I did some business recently, highly recommended you after you had assisted him with one of his cases.'

That would be old Edward Lethbridge, thought Richard – the legal grapevine was the best form of advertising.

Lovesey opened a thick file on his desk. 'The circumstances are unusual, to say the least. The accused is a respected veterinary surgeon, Samuel Parker. He has a practice in the small town of Eastbury, a few miles from here. Mr Parker is forty-eight years of age and was married for fifteen years to Mary, four years his senior.'

'And how did she die?' asked the pathologist, keen to get to the heart of the problem.

'The prosecution allege that he injected her with potassium chloride,' replied the lawyer heavily.

Pryor's eyebrows rose, and he looked across at Angela with

a look of astonishment. 'That's very unusual! I've read about a few cases, but never encountered one myself. What were the circumstances?'

'His wife was bedridden – dying in fact, from cancer of the pancreas. She had discharged herself from hospital some weeks before and refused to be readmitted. She was being looked after by the District Nurses, as well as by her husband, housekeeper and her sister, who is the local pharmacist and lives nearby.'

'So is your client claiming it was a mercy killing?' asked Angela.

George Lovesey shook his head. 'Indeed no. He robustly claims he had no part in her death whatsoever! Furthermore, he emphatically denies that she could have died of potassium poisoning, as there was no way in which it could have been administered.'

He slid the file over to the pair sitting opposite.

'I think it better if you took this copy of all the depositions and counsel's advice and studied it yourselves, rather than have me go through the whole story now.'

Richard took the big lever-arch file and laid it on his lap.

'Obviously, the first medical opinion you obtained will be in here?'

Lovesey nodded. 'Everything's in there. I fear that asking you to become involved is a last-ditch effort, but our new leading counsel, Nathan Prideaux, insisted on it. There's not much time, I'm afraid, so if you could let me have even a preliminary opinion in the next few days, it would be much appreciated.'

A few minutes were taken up with important matters such as an expert medical fee, which was difficult to assess, as the amount of work involved was unknown at this stage, so an hourly rate was agreed.

The business completed, they left the solicitor's office and made their way back to the car, the vital file clutched under Pryor's arm. When they were driving out of Stow, he jerked a thumb towards the back seat, where he had laid the documents that Lovesey had given them.

'We're not going to look at those until we get back,' he declared. 'Let's enjoy the rest of the day. I told Moira we'd be late and not to leave anything for us for supper.'

Angela gave him a stern look. 'So I have to go to bed hungry, do I?'

Richard grinned. 'No, let's anticipate that nice expert fee we're going to get. We'll stop at the Victoria Hotel in Newnham on the way back and have dinner – no expense spared!'

After a leisurely dinner at the old coaching inn, it was indeed fairly late by the time they got back to Tintern, but Angela and Richard could not resist staying up even later to go through the file from Stow.

They took a couple of gin and tonics to the staffroom, where Richard started on the papers. As he digested them, he handed them over one by one to Angela, curled up on a settee opposite.

There was silence for over half an hour, then Angela placed the last sheet on the coffee table and looked at her partner.

'Well, what about that? Can you do anything for them?'

Richard sighed. 'Doesn't look good, does it? Finding that high concentration of potassium in the eye fluid seems to be the main plank of the prosecution's medical evidence.'

'So you feel that he must be guilty?'

He shrugged. 'I know virtually nothing about these biochemical markers. Perhaps Siân has heard of them on this degree course she's doing?'

Their technician was going every week on day release to Cardiff to do the practical work for her external bachelor's degree.

Angela uncoiled herself from the settee and announced that she was making for her bed. 'You can ask Siân in the morning – I'll bet she and Moira will be agog to hear the details of this one.'

Richard was sitting with a frown on his face, staring at the file on the table.

'There's a niggle in the back of my mind about potassium in the vitreous humour,' he said. 'Something I must have heard in one of the forensic meetings. It'll come to me eventually, but I think I'll go over to Bristol tomorrow afternoon and have a root through the medical school library. That solicitor needs some quick action, if the case is going to trial very soon.'

When they left the room, Richard headed for his study at the back to dump the file and look at a couple of textbooks, in case there was something useful in them. At the foot of the stairs, Angela stopped and laid a hand on his arm.

'Thanks for a nice day – and a lovely dinner, Richard!'

She leaned forward and gave him a swift kiss on the cheek, then mounted the stairs without looking back. He stared after her until she vanished into her bedroom, then continued on his way to his office, touching his cheek almost experimentally.

'Well, well, it has been an interesting day!' he murmured.

Just as Angela had predicted, the other two women in the house soon wanted to hear all about the new case. Pryor had to go up to Monmouth by eight thirty, to carry out two routine coroner's post-mortems at the seedy public mortuary in the council yard. He was back by coffee time and he and Angela had to tell them all about Samuel Parker, the allegedly homicidal vet.

'His wife was dying of cancer, but she was being nursed at home until the end,' he began. 'No one is denying that he was totally solicitous towards her, as well as arranging for two District Nurses to come in twice a day – and having help from their housekeeper.'

'Don't forget the sister, the local pharmacist,' Angela reminded him.

'Yes, Sheila Lupin, the one who started the allegations in the first place. She was a spinster who owned the village's chemist's shop.'

'So is this going to be one of those mercy killings?' asked Moira.

Richard explained that the prosecution wanted to establish that a 'mercy' motive was a smokescreen for Parker's deliberate desire to get rid of his wife, but that the accused himself denied there was any killing at all and that Mary had died of her cancer.

Siân almost intuitively anticipated her boss. 'Another woman involved, I'll bet!' she exclaimed.

'That's what the sister claimed,' said Angela. 'Though she sounds a nasty bit of work. According to the statement of one of the nurses, who has known the family since they were children, this Sheila Lupin always had a down on Samuel since he married her sister.'

'So what exactly happened?' asked Moira, leaning forward in her chair, eager to hear the details.

'The nurse had just left, having settled the patient and given her the first of her two daily morphine injections,' continued Pryor. 'Samuel Parker came back to the house as she was leaving, having been out to a farm on a call. The veterinary clinic is an annexe to the house, so he didn't have to go near his wife's downstairs sickroom.'

Quoting from the depositions in the file, Richard went on to describe how Sheila Lupin had come across from the shop on one of her many daily visits and found her sister dead in bed.

There was an injection mark on her arm, still oozing blood.

'She dashes around to the surgery to fetch the husband, who races into the house to see his wife. The pharmacist notices a couple of used syringes on the surgery table, together with a box of Pentothal ampoules and a bottle labelled "potassium chloride". Recalling the recent needle puncture on her sister's arm, she literally starts shouting "murder" and a nasty scene takes place.'

'Sounds a bit fishy, I must admit,' commented Siân.

'But not so suspicious when Samuel explained what had happened,' interposed Angela. 'The call he had just returned from was to put down a badly injured goat that had been kicked by a horse on a farm. Intravenous Pentothal and potassium chloride are used by some vets to destroy animals painlessly.'

'So why didn't everyone believe him?' asked Moira.

'Depends on what the post-mortem showed,' suggested Siân, displaying her more scientific attitude.

'Exactly, but there was also a lot of emotional pressure as well. The sister was hysterical, screaming at the husband and calling him a murderer. He immediately called the doctor, but their regular GP was on holiday and a self-important young locum turned up instead, anxious to make a name for himself.'

Richard scowled at the thought of some people he had known in the past, who seemed keen to find suspicion on the flimsiest of evidence.

'Whereas their usual medical attendant, knowing of the severity of the wife's terminal illness, would probably have signed a death certificate for natural causes, this locum listened to Sheila Lupin's accusations and ran off to report the death to the coroner, telling him of the allegations. The coroner had little option but to inform the police, through his coroner's officer, and next morning a couple of CID men were knocking on the vet's door.'

Angela finished the rest of her coffee. 'Reading between the lines, it sounds as if neither the coroner nor the detectives were very enthusiastic about pursuing the matter, but they took some statements and seized the syringes and bottles just in case.'

'What about "the other woman" angle?' asked Moira.

'Unfortunately for Samuel Parker, it turned out to be true,' said Pryor. 'The sister gleefully named the lady, an attractive widow living about ten miles away at Lower Slaughter, perhaps an unfortunate name in the circumstances. Then, more reluctantly, others confirmed this, including the lady herself.'

'Men are rotten swine!' muttered Angela obscurely and walked out to take her coffee cup to the kitchen.

Their housekeeper and technician were not yet satisfied with the details, and Richard told them of the main plank of the prosecution's case.

'There was a post-mortem next day by the usual pathologist at the hospital, and he found nothing except the extensive cancer, which had spread widely to many other organs. He said that normally he would have been satisfied to give the lung cancer as the cause of death, but given the allegations and the lack of any immediate cause of death, such as coronary thrombosis or a pulmonary embolism, he felt someone else should examine the body.'

'And presumably this second chap did find something?' concluded Moira.

'Well, they got Angus Smythe up from Oxford. He's at the Radcliffe Infirmary and covers that area for the Home Office. Knowing of the potassium allegation, he took a number of samples of blood and even the fluid from the eyeball for analysis.'

'Vitreous humour? That's what they call it, don't they?' asked Siân, who had obviously been reading widely since taking this forensic job.

'Yes, that's it – and his laboratory found a very high concentration of potassium in the fluid. In fact, it's that which led the Director of Public Prosecutions to charge Parker with murder, as the police were not very impressed with the strength of the circumstantial evidence.'

Moira Davison gave Pryor a look, which though it fell short of adoration was filled with pride. 'And now they've called you in to save him!' she said.

Richard grinned. 'I'm not exactly a knight in shining armour, Moira! But I'll do my best to make sure that there are no loopholes in the prosecution case – that's what defence experts are for.'

'They've had one opinion already, so Angela said,' objected Siân. 'But he couldn't help, so what can you do?'

'Perhaps nothing at all; I might agree with him totally. But there may be a different interpretation I can find.'

'So a lawyer can shop around cherry-picking expert opinions until he finds one that suits him?' demanded Siân. She was always ready to crusade for the correct approach. Her father was a shop steward in a local foundry and the whole family were staunchly socialist in outlook.

Richard nodded. 'That happens, and it's quite legal. Though there has been talk of making the defence admit they've done that and to disclose what the unfavourable opinions were. But so far it hasn't become law.'

Angela had come back into the room and heard the last exchange. 'It's even much more common in America,' she said. 'But of course there they even spend weeks picking a jury, to get the ones they think might be most sympathetic to their client!'

Siân muttered something about 'And they call it justice!' as she went back to her bench to start work again.

'Do you think you'll find anything useful in the literature?' Angela asked her partner.

'I'll have a good look in the Bristol university library,' he replied. Richard had a contract to give twenty lectures a year to medical students there, which gave him access to the library. 'I've got this niggling memory of seeing something about potassium after death. I think it was from Germany.'

'Do they have all the forensic journals in Bristol?'

'I'm not sure – if not, I'll go down to Cardiff and look in the Home Office lab; they should have some. And then try the medical school library there. I'm an old student, so they should let me in.'

As he went back to his room, Angela decided she admired his tenacity and strength of purpose. She hoped he hadn't read

Arthur nodded, albeit reluctantly. 'He's a strong lad, admit-
lly. And the deceased was a scrawny sort of fellow. It's just
at I can't see this boy having enough brains to think out a
mplicated scheme like that.'

Claude Morris ruffled the pages of the report on his desk.
'It's a bloody funny way to commit a murder,' he grum-
led. 'Are we absolutely sure that it's not some bizarre kind
of accident or suicide? We'd look right fools if we start a
homicide investigation and then discover there wasn't one.'

'The pathologist was quite definite about it – and I saw the
injuries he was relying on with my own eyes.'

The DCS still looked dubious. 'This Dr Pryor – I'd never
heard of him. He's not the regular Home Office fellow, is he?'

Joe Paget, who always read all the bumf that was sent around
by headquarters, answered this time. 'There was a circular
from the Home Office some time ago. He was put on their list
a few months back, with a sort of roving commission to fill
in wherever he was needed. Seems he was a pathologist in the
army and in Singapore – had a lot of experience.'

'And the forensic lab did their stuff, I see. What came out
of that?'

Crippen again took up the baton. 'The doctor found some
fibres on his neck which the lab said corresponded with
some that were stuck on the hook of an engine hoist – and
they matched some rope that was lying around the barn, so
the hanging part has to be accepted.'

'But that was a cover-up for a previous throttling?'

'So it has to be a murder, sir,' confirmed Paget. 'No other
way he could end up under a tractor wheel. The doctor said
he must have been hanging for some hours before that, by
the settling of blood in his legs.'

'He was a heavy drinker, so you say. Was he pissed when
all this happened?'

'Not all that much. He had the equivalent of a few pints in
him, though again the doctor says it depends on when he last
had a drink and at what time he died,' said Crippen.

'Anything in his background at all?'

Joe Paget shook his head. His only contribution to the investigation so far had been in snooping around Brecon. 'He was
a Londoner originally. We traced his family through army
records. Parents long dead, no other relatives found. He lived

too much into the little peck she gave him o₁
previous evening, but he had been such goo₁
dinner. She found that she was glad she had him ₁
and friend.

Next day, while Richard Pryor was sitting in his
Beachley–Aust ferry, crossing the Severn Estuary ₁
to Bristol, Arthur Crippen was in a meeting with
riors.

The Mid-Wales Constabulary had been formed o₁
years earlier by amalgamating three county forces, ₁
its headquarters were in Newtown, right in the middle o₁

He had travelled up from Brecon with his DCI Joe F
discuss the Ty Croes case with Detective Chief Superint₁
Claude Morris, the head of the CID.

'We're getting nowhere at all so far, sir,' announced F
Crippen thought the 'we' was a bit rich, as the chief inspe
had had virtually nothing to do with the matter and knew c
what Arthur had told him about it.

The DCS slumped behind his desk, tapping on his blot₁
with the end of a pencil. He was a fat man, nearing retir₁
ment, like Crippen, and was keen on having a quiet life fo₁
the next couple of years.

'So you think it has to be an inside job?' he grunted.

Paget deferred to his DI for an answer, and Crippen leaned
forward over his cup of tasteless canteen coffee.

'I can't see it being anything else, sir. It's not a casual
assault by some chancer trying to steal something. There's no
one else around there apart from those who live or work on
the farm.'

The portly DCS considered this for a moment, still tapping
his pencil. 'So we've got two farmers, their wives and a
father?'

'And there's this young chap you told me about, Arthur,'
chipped in Paget, just to show that he was on the ball.

The DI shrugged. 'Can't see him involved, though he
admitted he hated the dead man's guts.'

'I wouldn't write him off,' advised Morris. He had been a
good detective before he was kicked upstairs to his armchair
job, and his opinion was still worth listening to. 'Is this Shane
boy big enough to have done it?'

in a couple of scruffy rented rooms in Brecon. Plenty of empty bottles, betting slips and a few girlie magazines, that's all.'

'No known associates? Any hard men he owes money to?'

Paget turned up his hands appealingly. 'Damn all, sir. We'll keep on looking, but I think Arthur's right. It has to be someone at Ty Croes.'

Morris threw his pencil down on the desk. 'So what do we do now? Are we going to call in the Yard? If so, we've got to get a move on.'

For many years, small police forces had been able to call on Scotland Yard for assistance, who would send a detective superintendent down to offer their expert help. This had to be done within a week, otherwise financial charges would be imposed. Most provincial police forces, especially the larger ones, made it a point of honour not to call in the Yard, feeling it was a slur on their own abilities. DI Crippen was certainly in this category.

'Oh, not the bloody Yard, sir! We don't want them throwing their weight about down here. There's nothing they can do that we can't.'

His chief nodded gravely, his double chin bobbing. 'I'm not keen myself, but it's up to the Chief Constable, as he'll have the press and the Watch Committee on his back before long. Thankfully, few people seem to have got wind of this yet, but it can't stay under wraps forever.'

They kicked the problem around for a further half-hour without coming to much of a conclusion. Arthur Crippen's last contribution seemed the only way forward for the moment.

'It's got to be someone at that damned farm. I'll go back there and worry the life out of them until something breaks, sir!'

SEVEN

B y the time Richard Pryor returned to Tintern from Bristol, both Moira and Siân had left for the day. He drove his Humber up into the yard at the back of Garth House and parked it in the coach house, alongside Angela's little white Renault 4CV.

He took his old briefcase from the back of the car and began walking towards the back door, but he was accosted by a figure coming down from the garden behind. It was Jimmy Jenkins, their gardener and odd-job man, who sometimes added being their driver to his accomplishments. Jimmy had been inherited with the house, as he had been employed by Aunt Gladys for years and when Richard took over he seemed to have continued in his job by default.

A well-known character in the area, Jimmy was about fifty, with a weather-beaten face decorated by a broken nose and a set of crooked, tobacco-stained teeth. He always seemed to have half a Woodbine stuck to his lower lip, and Richard could never remember seeing him smoking a whole cigarette. His bristly grey hair was surmounted by a greasy cap perched over one eye – Jimmy habitually wore thick flannel shirts, over which were the braces that held up his corduroy trousers.

'I've run the cultivator over your patch again, doctor,' he announced in an accent from the Forest of Dean, which lay just across the river. 'Needs doing once more before you puts in them fancy plants. Best do it soon, before the cold weather comes.'

The 'patch' that he rather sarcastically referred to was a quarter of an acre of the four acres of land that rose up the hill behind Garth House – and the 'fancy plants' were vines that Richard had ordered from a distant nursery. He had ambitions to start a small vineyard on the south-facing slope, as the climate of the sheltered Wye Valley was mild. Jimmy was contemptuous of the idea, trying to persuade his boss to grow strawberries instead, but Richard was adamant, even though he knew virtually nothing about horticulture.

They spoke about his pet project for a few minutes before Richard could escape. 'I've got to go to Cardiff in the morning, so could you give the car a wash tonight?'

He declined Jimmy's offer to drive him there, and as the man went off to fix up the hosepipe he went into the house.

Angela was still at her bench, finishing off a batch of paternity tests. Richard put his head around the laboratory door to let her know that he was back.

'Did you find anything useful in Bristol?' she asked, looking up with a pipette hovering over a rack of small tubes.

He hefted his document case to show her, a battered crocodile-skin bag that he had bought years ago in Ceylon.

'I think so, but I'd like your opinion on it this evening. I'm going down to the library in Cardiff tomorrow to see if I can dig out anything else.'

She nodded as she pulled another rack towards her.

'Fine. We'll talk about it after supper.'

He went off to his room down the passage and spent half an hour reading the mail and checking some reports that Moira had typed that day on post-mortems he had done at Chepstow and Monmouth. Then he pulled down a couple of textbooks from his shelves and began pursuing some of the matters that he had discovered in the medical school library in Bristol.

Eventually, his partner banged on his door and called out 'Supper!' to call him into the kitchen. Here Moira had laid out two places on the big table and left a casserole for them in the warming oven of the Aga. Originally, she had been employed to do basic housekeeping, some cooking and a little typing, but as the business had increased, Moira had become overburdened. Now a buxom woman from the village came in for two hours each day to clean and make beds, while Moira made lunch and left them something each evening for supper. It was great improvement on the early days, when Richard and Angela virtually camped out in the old house, eating out of tins.

Only the two partners took meals, as figure-conscious Siân always brought sandwiches, an apple and a bottle of Tizer, while Moira herself went home at midday to feed her dog. As Pryor sat down in anticipation of one of Moira's casseroles, for she was an excellent cook, Angela opened a tin of Heinz oxtail soup and warmed it for their first course. When she first came to Garth House, she was adamant that she was not going to be involved in any domesticity, but her resolve had slipped a little and now she was prepared to do a few things, but she drew the line at proper cooking and cleaning.

They finished up with a fruit salad and local cream, which Moira had left for them in the old Kelvin refrigerator, then Richard made coffee, his contribution to the domestic scene. He took this into the staffroom next door, and the pair settled down on each side of the low table.

'So what have you got from your ferreting around in Bristol?' she asked.

He delved into his briefcase and brought out some loose papers and a foolscap legal pad, several pages of which were covered with his handwriting.

'I wish they had one of those new copying machines in their library,' he complained. 'I had to write everything out longhand.'

He slid the papers across the table and settled back with his coffee to wait for her to digest the contents. When Angela had looked through the first couple of pages, she looked up at him.

'Can you prove this beyond reasonable doubt?' she asked soberly, using the standard for evidence that applied in criminal cases. In civil matters, only the 'balance of probabilities' was needed, but they both knew that this would not be sufficient in a murder trial.

Richard shrugged. 'All I can do is offer the conclusions of this chap who did the research. The other stuff you have there is watertight, as it's been accepted fact for years.'

He watched her intently as she went back to her reading. Angela was a very intelligent woman whose opinion he valued highly. With an honours degree and a doctorate in a biological science, and years of experience in its forensic applications, she would be able to appreciate the significance of the material at least as well as he could with his medical training.

Her coffee neglected, her head was bent over the papers, a swathe of dark brown hair falling over her face. Richard experienced a wave of respect tinged with affection for her. Though there had been no repetition or even reference to the momentary episode on the stairs the other evening, he felt that their relationship had somehow warmed and that they felt more comfortable with each other. When he first met her and, indeed, even when she came to take up residence in Garth House, he found her manner rather cool, showing him a purely professional face. Now she felt more like a sister or an attractive cousin, and he briefly wondered if it would ever go further. His daydreaming was interrupted when she dropped the papers back on to the table and took up her now lukewarm coffee.

'If you can harden all this up into solid fact, you may well be on to a usable defence,' she said crisply. 'This first proposition is very new. You say you found only one published paper?'

'Yes, it appeared this year, though the research must have been going for some time for him to get all that data.'

'And the other contention is established fact, accepted by the scientific establishment?'

'That's what the books say, so I doubt it can be challenged. There must be plenty of physiologists who could be dragged along to confirm it.'

She finished her coffee and put the cup back on its saucer. 'So what's the next move?'

'Tomorrow I want to go through the medical library in Cardiff and visit the physiology department there, to see if I can find anything else and confirm what I've already got.'

He had qualified in the Welsh National School of Medicine in 1938, then did two years' pathology there before being called up in 1940. He had spent the war years in various military hospitals, mostly in Ceylon, ending up in Singapore as soon as the Japanese were thrown out. Now he trusted that his old Alma Mater in Cardiff would not begrudge him the use of their library.

'When will you tell the lawyers what you've found?' asked Angela.

'I'll ring the solicitor on Friday and arrange to go and see him early next week. I'll get Moira to type up a draft submission as soon as I've satisfied myself that there's nothing else to find.'

While Richard Pryor was on his way to Cardiff the next morning, Arthur Crippen and his sergeant were arriving at Ty Croes Farm once again. The DI had considered hauling all the residents to the police station in Brecon for more interviews, but he had lived long enough in a rural area to realize the disruption that would cause to the daily routine of a farm. However, he felt that their parlour was not the place to conduct what might turn out to be a more rigorous interrogation, so he had arranged for a police caravan to be towed out from Brecon and parked in the farmyard. It was normally used as a mobile police station at agricultural shows or at scenes of accidents, but with a small table and a few chairs it would serve his purpose as an interview room.

The constable who had dragged it there with a Land Rover was sent down to the barn to fetch Shane Williams. The repair work was back in operation and the irate farmer who had been waiting for his Fordson had been placated, as Jeff Morton had worked with Shane the previous day to get the brakes finished. What the owner felt about his machine having been involved in a murder was unknown, but getting his fields ploughed took precedence over any sentiment.

Shane duly appeared and slumped down in a folding chair on the other side of the table to Crippen. Sergeant Nichols sat at one end with a pile of blank statement forms as the inspector opened the questioning. Crippen had decided to play it tougher from the start, as the only hope of squeezing something useful from these taciturn folk.

'Now then, Shane, we'll have a bit of sense from you today! You know more than you told me last time about what goes on in this farm, so let's have it!'

The lad protested that he'd told Crippen everything, but there was a shiftiness about him that the experienced detective recognized.

'We'll start from the beginning again, right!'

Crippen went through every minute of the morning when Shane said he had discovered the body, but nothing new appeared.

'You say you discovered Tom Littleman lying under the tractor – but how do I know that you didn't put him there yourself, eh?'

The apprentice squeaked in horrified denial. 'I never did! Why should I?'

'You told me the other day that you hated his guts, boy,' thundered Crippen. 'No one else has admitted that, so you're my best suspect.'

'Suspect? You must be off your head, mister! I left the barn at five the night before and didn't get back until seven that morning. When could I have done those awful things?'

The DI was implacable in his accusations.

'You could have come back later that evening. You knew Littleman had to stay on to finish those brakes. You had a key – you could have locked up after you when he was dead.'

Crippen didn't believe a word of what he was saying, but he wanted to soften the youth up to winkle other matters from him.

He let Shane gabble his protestations of innocence for a while, then abruptly changed the direction of his questions.

'If you want me to believe that you had nothing to do with it, we'll have to find the real villain, won't we? Now tell me something more about Littleman's relations with the people up here at the farm. Did he come up here much?'

Relieved at the pressure being taken off him, Shane was ready to open up a little more.

'No, he hardly ever did, not that I know of. Jeff was down here every day, working with us when he'd done his bit with the cows, so there wasn't much call to go up to the house or the cottage. Jeff used to talk to him about the machinery business, and Aubrey called in every day to see how things were going.'

'What about their wives, Rhian and Betsan?' put in John Nichols. Shane's eyes swivelled between the two policemen.

'What about them?' he mumbled.

'Come on, boy, spit it out!' snapped Crippen. 'You know something, don't you?'

Shane's head was bent down, staring at the cap that he twirled between his knees. 'I saw them together a couple of times, that's all,' he muttered.

'Together? Littleman and which one, Betsan or Rhian?'

The lad raised his head and stared at Crippen almost defiantly. 'Both of them,' he replied.

The DI looked across at his sergeant with raised eyebrows. 'Where and when was this?' snapped the inspector.

'I saw Betsan going into the cinema in Brecon with him, one Saturday afternoon a couple of months ago. And I saw Rhian with him one evening back in the summer, when I was cycling home after working late.'

'What d'you mean "saw her with him"? What were they doing?'

'Lying in a field about three miles from here, snogging under the hedge,' was the surprising reply.

'How could you see them from your bike, then?' demanded Nichols.

'His motorbike was standing in a gateway. I thought it might have been pinched or something, so I stopped and looked over the gate. As soon as I saw them, I pushed off quick, like.'

Another fifteen minutes of hard questioning could not drag any more from the youth and, after getting him to sign the statement the sergeant had written out, Shane was dismissed with dire warnings not to reveal anything of the interview to anyone else, especially those in the farm.

When he had gone, Crippen and Nichols discussed the significance of what they had heard.

'Puts a different shine on the situation, doesn't it?' said Arthur. 'We still can't eliminate the lad, though I don't fancy him for it.'

John Nichols was puzzled by this. 'Why should he still be in the frame for it, sir?'

'What if Littleman saw Shane ogling him when he was with either of the women? He might have gone for him, threatening him if he didn't keep his mouth shut. If it got physical, maybe Shane croaked him! He's a strong enough lad, even though he's as thick as two short planks.'

The sergeant was unimpressed. 'That's the point, isn't it? He might have the muscle, but has he got the brains to think up a complicated scenario like this?'

Crippen made a face, indicating doubtful resignation. 'Maybe not, but we have to keep all options open for now. So who are we going to grill next?'

The decision was made for them, as they saw Betsan Evans through the caravan window. She was coming across the yard with three mugs of tea on a tray.

'This is going to get more and more bloody awkward as we go on, John,' muttered Crippen. 'I hate these domestic affairs; it's just embarrassment all round.'

His sergeant thought it odd for an experienced detective to feel embarrassed, but this was certainly an unusual situation. Nichols went to the door to take the tray from the farmer's wife.

'Thanks, Mrs Evans. I'm afraid we need to talk to everyone again. Can you come over in a few minutes, please?'

She nodded, albeit reluctantly. 'If you want to speak to my husband as well, I'm afraid he's gone over to Llandovery with his father and Jeff. They took the trailer to fetch some calves and won't be back until dinner time.'

She walked back to the house, and the two police officers handed a mug of tea to the PC outside before settling back to drink their own and discuss the new twist that had cropped up.

'This Tom Littleman seems quite a ladies' man, even though he was a boozer,' observed Nichols.

'Some women seem to fall for these naughty fellows,' said Crippen gloomily. 'Puts a bit of spice in their life, perhaps, after being stuck out here with a couple of husbands who smell of manure and talk only about the price of sheep.'

'How serious was it, I wonder? Being seen going into the pictures in Brecon is hardly grounds for divorce.'

'Depends on what their husbands thought about it, if they found out.'

The sergeant looked at Crippen. 'Do you fancy either of the women for it, then?'

'They're big and strong enough, tough country women. But no, not really. I've never heard of a woman throttling a man. It's always the other way around.'

'So your money's on one of the men – or even both of them together?'

The DI shrugged. 'Let's not jump our fences until we come to them, John. Drink your tea, then we'll hear what she's got to say.'

EIGHT

In the staffroom of Garth House others were also drinking tea when the telephone rang in the passage outside. Moira, as their nominal secretary, felt obliged to be the one who answered it.

A moment later she came back in again, an excited expression on her face. 'I think you'd better talk to them, doctor,' she said in a stage whisper, though the phone was outside.

'Who is it, Moira?' asked Angela, getting out of her chair.

'The War Office!' she replied in hushed tones. 'They wanted to speak to Dr Pryor, but I said he wasn't here.'

After a puzzled Angela hurried out of the room, Moira and Siân were consumed with curiosity, once again showing their intense interest in all the doings of the Garth House Consultancy.

'What on earth would the War Office want with Richard?' asked Siân. Though he was 'doctor' when they were with him, in private they spoke of both him and Angela by name.

'He was an army officer all through the war,' pointed out Moira. 'Let's hope they don't want to call him up again!'

Siân, who was surprisingly abreast of world events, thought this not beyond the bounds of possibility. 'There's so much trouble in the world these days – Russia has just formed the Warsaw Pact, Germany joining NATO, our rail and newspaper strikes! I'd not rule out them calling up reservists.'

But when Angela came back, she was able to reassure them that Richard Pryor was not being hauled off to Aldershot next day.

'It's another case for us, hopefully,' she announced. 'That was a lawyer from the War Office. I think he said it was something to do with the Adjutant-General's Branch. I'm not well up with these military outfits.'

'What sort of case could that be?' asked Siân, mystified as to why the army should want her hero.

'It seems there's some controversy about a compensation case following a shooting death. They need a second medical opinion.'

'Dr Pryor will be pleased at that,' said Moira confidently. 'I know he was quite proud of his army service. He said once that perhaps he should have stayed in the RAMC instead of taking that civilian job in Singapore.'

'Yes, I heard him say that, too,' chipped in Siân. 'He reckoned if he'd stayed, he'd probably be a brigadier by now.'

Angela smiled at their enthusiasm for her partner. 'Well, he'd better get his medals out and clean them up, because I arranged for this lawyer to come down to see us next week!'

Betsan Evans was not tearful or hysterical, just defiant.

When Arthur Crippen suggested to her that she had been economical with the truth over her relationship with Tom Littleman, the farmer's wife made no attempt to deny it.

'It was an awful mistake, but there it is,' she said. 'He was a good-looking chap, and in spite of the fact that I knew he was a bad lot there was something about him that I couldn't resist.'

'It was more than just a visit to the pictures, was it?'

Betsan looked down at her hands, which were rough compared with the smoothness of her face.

'We went back to that flat of his once or twice,' she murmured. 'It was partly that grubby place that made me end it so soon. It made me see how sordid the whole affair was.'

The sergeant looked up from writing on his statement forms. 'When did it finish, Mrs Evans?'

She sighed and ran a hand through her dark hair. 'A few weeks ago. He didn't seem all that bothered, damn the man! Shows how little it meant to him.'

'Does your husband know about it?'

The question certainly jerked the woman out of her state of dull apathy. 'No, of course not! For God's sake, don't tell him, will you?'

As he spoke again, the inspector felt as if he was walking on eggshells. He was a kindly man, but this was a murder investigation and he couldn't see how he was going to avoid hurting a few people.

'I'm afraid I can't guarantee anything, Betsan. It depends on how the investigation goes.'

'Aubrey mustn't know,' she said desperately. 'It would kill him – or he'd kill me!'

She realized what she was saying and her face took on a sudden ghastly pallor. For a moment Crippen thought she might be sick.

'What about Rhian? Does she know about your affair?'

Now on slightly less frightening ground, Betsan shook her head vehemently. 'God, no! She's so strait-laced. She wouldn't understand how I was tempted.'

Crippen looked at her gravely. 'I think she might, Mrs Evans. You're not the only one we've had information about.'

The implication of what he had said took a moment to register with Betsan. Her eyes widened, and the paleness of her cheeks flushed pink.

'You don't mean . . . I can't believe it! That bloody man! I thought he loved me – for a couple of weeks, anyway.'

'Are you sure you never told her about him – or that she told you a similar story?'

Tears now appeared in her eyes for the first time. Arthur felt that Littleman's infidelity troubled her more than her own. She shook her head and wiped her eyes angrily with her fingers.

'We aren't that close, not as if we were sisters – or even sisters-in-law,' she sniffed. 'Rhian lives over in the cottage, and although we see each other most days there isn't a lot to talk about, apart from the farm. It's not even as if either of us has kids.'

Crippen detected an underlying hint of loneliness and longing in her voice. 'So you wouldn't know if her husband knew about it? Nothing in a change of his manner or anything like that?'

Again she shook her head and found a crumpled hand-kerchief in the pocket of her apron, blowing her nose hard. 'Rhian doesn't know about me and Tom, does she?' she asked haltingly.

'I don't know. I haven't talked to her since this came to light. You see the different complexion it puts on Littleman's death, don't you?'

She shook her head fearfully. 'I don't know what you mean,' she whispered.

'Your husband or Rhian's husband – or even both of them – might have wanted to pay him back, or perhaps get rid of him altogether.'

She stared at him open-mouthed.

'That can't be true! Neither of them would do that. It must
have been someone from outside.'

John Nichols thought he would add fuel to the fire to see
if anything spat out. 'Or maybe it was you or Mrs Morton
who wanted him out of the way. He wasn't a big chap and
you are both strong farmers' wives.'

'Or perhaps you also did it together?' suggested Crippen
provocatively. 'That would have made it easier still.'

Betsan's eyes were like saucers at this, and she remained
speechless. It was only a few months since Ruth Ellis had
been hanged for murder. Though public and political opinion
probably made her the last woman ever to be executed, the
prospect of being accused of murder was shocking.

'Have you anything else that you want to tell us, Mrs
Evans?' asked Crippen, feeling instinctively that he had had
all he was going to get for the moment.

Betsan seemed to pull herself together, sitting up straight
and making a last dab at her nose and eyes with the handkerchief. 'I think I've said more than enough. Thank God
Aubrey is out of the house, so that I can settle myself before
he comes home.'

Crippen stood up and opened the caravan door for her.
'We'll need you to come over and sign a statement after it's
finished,' he said. 'And we'll need to speak to your husband
and his cousin, as well as his wife later.'

When she had walked slowly back to the farmhouse, the
DI sat down again and watched his sergeant finishing the tran-
script of the interview.

'Shane was right, then,' he said reflectively. 'We'd have
been right up the creek if he'd been having us on.'

'Let's hope Dr Pryor wasn't having us on, too,' replied
Nichols. 'You said the chief super was concerned that maybe
the pathologist was wrong about a murder.'

Arthur Crippen sighed. 'He's got to be right – and the lab
found those fibres. But maybe I should have a word with him
over the phone, just to see if he's still cast iron with his
conclusions.'

After finishing their smoke, the constable was sent over to
the cottage to fetch Mrs Morton to the caravan for another
interview. Their session with her turned out to be broadly
similar to that with Betsan Evans.

Confronted with the bald statement that the police knew of her affair with Tom Littleman, she capitulated straight away, but unlike Betsan she shed no tears and remained sullenly obstinate.

'I don't see that my private life is anything to do with the police,' she said coldly. 'It can't have anything to do with this business, especially as it was all over months ago.'

'That's for us to judge, Mrs Morton,' snapped Crippen, nettled by her attitude. 'And I'd point out that you are already guilty of withholding information from us. We asked you about him when we spoke to you first and you more or less said you knew nothing about him!'

'I didn't consider it relevant, that's why,' she answered.

Crippen decided to see how she reacted to a couple more awkward questions. 'Did your husband know about your affair with this man?'

Rhian flushed and looked down at the table. 'Of course not! I know I was a fool, but Tom could be very persuasive and there was something about him that appealed to me, even though I knew he was no good.'

'So you didn't know that he was also carrying on with Betsan Evans?'

Her head jerked up as if it was being pulled by a string. 'What? Are you trying to trick me into something?'

'Ask her yourself, if you like. She was equally surprised to hear that you had been unfaithful as well.'

She glowered at the detective. 'Unfaithful! It was that swine Tom who was unfaithful, blast him.'

John Nichols, as he sat busily writing, thought how similar the reactions of the two wives were to Littleman's deceit.

As if to confirm his thoughts, Rhian snapped out a question. 'So are you going to tell my Jeff?'

Crippen looked steadily at her, thinking that this was a much harder woman that Betsan Evans. Could she have been a killer, he wondered? But if she genuinely hadn't known that Littleman had been having it off with Betsan as well as with her, where was a motive?

'This is a murder investigation, Mrs Morton. Nothing that's relevant can be concealed. I think you'd better be frank with your husband before we talk to him again – though it's none of my business what you do.'

They watched her march off across the yard towards her own large cottage, which was a field away in the opposite direction from the distant barn.

'We're none the better off after all that, John,' said Crippen morosely. 'I could just about accept her screwing that fellow's neck, but I don't see a motive.'

In the absence of anyone else to interview for the time being, the two detectives sat in the caravan and had a smoke.

'We'll see the two husbands again this afternoon,' said Crippen. 'And the old man, I suppose. After all this, if we get no further towards charging someone, I'm afraid the chief will call in the Yard.'

However, the interviews at Ty Croes Farm were not going according to plan that day. Though the DI and his sergeant had managed to interview Betsan and Rhian, by noon there was no sign of the men returning from Llandovery – and half an hour later the radio in the police car recalled them urgently to Brecon to deal with an attempted hold-up at a building society.

Richard returned from Cardiff at the end of that afternoon in time for Moira to give him various messages.

'A few phone calls, doctor,' she announced. 'The lawyers in Stow rang to see if you were able to tell them anything yet. I said you'd been working on it for the last two days and would get back to them.'

She looked at her notepad. 'And Detective Inspector Crippen rang from Brecon. He'd like to talk to you. The coroner's officer in Monmouth said there'll be two post-mortems there tomorrow and one in Chepstow. Hereford County Hospital phoned to ask if you could do a fortnight's locum for their pathologist next month.'

She kept the juiciest message until last. 'And I think Dr Bray will want to tell you about a call she had this morning from the War Office.'

Like Siân, for a moment Richard thought that he was being 'called back to the flag', as they used to say, but Angela put his mind at rest when he hurried into the laboratory to see her.

'It was someone from the army legal branch or whatever they call it now,' she explained. 'It's a civil claim for death, though there's some possibility of a manslaughter charge. Apart from the fact that it's a shooting, he didn't give any details, but they want a pathology opinion. I told them they can come down to see you next Tuesday afternoon – that'll give you time to do any local post-mortems in the morning.'

He grinned at her, pleased at the growth of their venture.

'It's all happening, Angela! At this rate, in another year we'll be able to get some better equipment for you and Siân.' He waved a hand expansively around the laboratory.

'I'll have a UV spectrophotometer!' called Siân from across the room.

'In the queue, girl. I need some new golf clubs first,' chaffed Richard, feeling euphoric with the prospects of expansion of the Garth House partnership.

The phone rang in the office and Moira called out for Pryor. 'It's Brecon again, doctor,' she said, handing the receiver to him when he came through the connecting door.

'This is Arthur Crippen, doctor. I thought I'd keep you up to date with what's going on here.' This was hardly true, as the DI really wanted reassurance once again that he was undoubtedly dealing with a murder.

'Any progress, inspector? It's a very odd case.'

'You can say that again,' said Crippen. 'To be honest, we still haven't a clue who did it, though it has to be someone at the farm.'

He paused. 'Er, doc, any more confirmation from your end about what happened?'

Richard knew very well what he was getting at and had himself had a few worrying hours, concerned that he was right about Littleman's death.

'There's not really anything more we can do from the pathology side,' he admitted. 'I've looked at those neck marks under the microscope and there's no doubt at all that they are very recent bruises. The hanging mark showed no vital signs, so it was made after death.'

Crippen was at least reassured that nothing had been found to throw any doubt on the original findings and, after telling Richard what they had gleaned so far from the family, he rang off.

'Anything new from deepest Breconshire?' asked Angela as he came back into the lab.

'Dirty work behind the cowsheds, it seems,' he replied. 'That Tom Littleman might have been an unsavoury drunkard, but he seems to have had a way with women.'

He repeated what the DI had told him about both wives now admitting that they had had affairs with the victim. Moira, who tended to be a little strait-laced, was primly disapproving.

'I can't understand how decent women get taken in by these rogues,' she said. 'But what could that have to do with his death?'

'They have jungle law up in those parts of Wales!' said Angela, whose very English origins surfaced occasionally. 'Cuckolded husbands might have organized a lynching.'

Richard took this more seriously. 'The guy wasn't lynched, but you might be near the truth otherwise.'

'You think the murderer must be one of the family?' asked Siân, revelling in the drama.

'The police certainly think so, mainly from lack of anyone else to suspect.'

As he moved off to take his papers to his room, Angela asked him if he had found anything useful in the libraries in Cardiff.

'Nothing new, but confirmation of what I found in Bristol. I think I may have to make some enquiries in Germany next week.'

Siân's eyes opened wide in surprise. 'You're going to Germany, doctor? Can I come with you to carry your bag?'

Richard grinned at her enthusiasm. 'Not much point. I can't speak a word of the language. But maybe some telephoning through an interpreter might help. We'll see what the lawyers have to say about it.'

He remembered promising to ask if Siân knew anything about potassium in body fluids, so he did so now.

'I know how to estimate the levels in plasma,' she replied, pleased to be consulted by the great man. 'I used to do a lot at the hospital, but you need a flame photometer for that. I was never asked to test an eye fluid sample – it would be hardly likely on a live patient!'

'You never did any samples from the post-mortem room?'

She shook her head, and it reassured him that he had not missed out on some new technique that had been developed while he was away in the Far East for so long.

After a ham and salad supper, followed by one of Moira's cream sponges, Richard talked to Angela over coffee, going again over the ideas he had gleaned from his library researches.

Then he left her to go up to her room upstairs and listen to her radio, while he put together a draft report for George Lovesey, the solicitor in Stow-on-the-Wold.

NINE

Next morning, a rather damp Friday, he went off early to deal with the post-mortems at Monmouth and Chepstow, each a few miles away at either end of the Wye Valley. All were straightforward natural deaths, but because of their sudden nature the family doctors were unable to sign a death certificate and they had to be referred to the coroner. Richard was back at Garth House by late morning and decided to phone George Lovesey to arrange a meeting, as time seemed pressing.

'I'm glad you rang, doctor,' said the lawyer. 'I was going to contact you to see if you could attend a pretrial conference with our counsel tomorrow morning. I know it's a Saturday, but Nathan Prideaux is at the Old Bailey every weekday.'

On the principle that the customer is always right, Richard Pryor readily agreed, especially as he discovered that the meeting would be in Gloucester, much nearer than Stow.

'Our junior counsel has his chambers in Gloucester, so it would be a convenient place to meet,' went on Lovesey. 'We had to change our QC only a few weeks ago, as the original one will be tied up in another trial in Winchester. Nathan Prideaux is very well spoken of as a defence counsel, so I hope we can find him some ammunition to use.'

Richard had been going to see his parents on Saturday morning, but it was only an hour's drive to Merthyr Tydfil, so he could go later in the day. His father was a retired family doctor in that historical industrial town and it was where Richard had been born and went to school. He liked to spend a weekend there fairly often, to be fed by his mother's massive meals and to make up for the long years during the war and afterwards in Singapore, when he had hardly seen them at all.

Angela was also going off that afternoon to see her family in rural Berkshire, where she could relax in what Siân covertly called her 'hunting, shooting and fishing' lifestyle.

Richard decided that in the morning, he would leave a

message and his father's telephone number with the forensic laboratory in Cardiff in case there was a call-out. To the best of his knowledge, none of the other pathologists on the Home Office list were away, so he thought it unlikely that he would be needed anywhere over the weekend.

Such thoughts are only a temptation for fate to confound them.

That same morning Detective Inspector Crippen and his sergeant were back in the caravan at Ty Croes. The hold-up at the building society the previous day had been solved within an hour, when a Brecon constable had grabbed the youth as he came out of a nearby betting shop after placing his stolen thirty pounds on a no-hoper horse.

Now they got back to their interviews, and Aubrey Evans was the first to be called. One look at his face told Crippen that his wife had made her confession. His first words made this abundantly clear.

'I wish to God that bloody man had never set foot in this place!' he growled bitterly. 'He's brought nothing but trouble on us.'

'I gather that your wife has told you what happened, Mr Evans,' said Arthur, quite softly. 'You must realize that it puts a different complexion on this death, with a possible motive now on the cards.'

Like Rhian the day before, Evans was truculent rather than apprehensive. 'Listen, inspector, my main concern is what happened between Betsan and that bastard. I don't really care about your motives, though I can't see what our personal problems have to do with anything.'

'I've only your word that you didn't know about it before this,' retorted Crippen. 'You might have revenged yourself on him and got rid of a drunken partner at the same time.'

'Nonsense! Prove it, that's what I say. You can't, because it didn't happen like that.'

'Then how did it happen, Mr Evans?' asked John Nichols.

Aubrey rounded on him. 'You're the detectives – that's up to you to find out. I don't give a bugger what you do or say. I've got too many troubles of my own, thanks to you for meddling in my family affairs.'

'I think it was Tom Littleman who did the meddling, Mr

Evans,' snapped Crippen. 'Now let's go through the whole matter again.'

Minutely, but uselessly, he was grilled as to his movements on the relevant day and the following night and morning, but the farmer admitted nothing and stuck to the story he had given days earlier. At the end of it, Crippen told him he could go but that he would probably be interviewed again, next time at the police station in Brecon.

'I'll not say another word without my solicitor being present – nor will my wife,' growled Aubrey. 'You've got it all wrong, Inspector. Yes, I hate that man's guts now a hundred times more than I disliked him before, but that's as far as it goes!'

He stomped out and left the two CID men time for another Player's Navy Cut while their constable went to find Jeff Morton.

'Do you fancy him for it, John?' asked Crippen ruminatively.

The sergeant shrugged. 'He makes no bones about his dislike of Littleman, even before this revelation about his wife. I think he's a hard man. He could have attacked the victim in a temper, maybe after a flaming row, then thought up this elaborate scheme to conceal it.'

'But that surely would happen only after he'd found out that Littleman was having it off with his wife – and he denies that pretty strongly, as does Betsan.'

Nichols grimaced. 'They could both be lying. It's not something anyone wants to own up to.'

Crippen stubbed out his cigarette in the tin lid that served as an ashtray. 'Here's the other one coming. Let's see what he's got to say about it.'

Sitting in the chair opposite Crippen, Jeff Morton presented a very different picture from the cousin who had just left. He was subdued and frightened, the pallor of his face making the livid birthmark on his face all the more prominent in contrast.

'I need a smoke!' were the first words he uttered. His trembling hands pulled out a small tin box, from which he rolled his own cigarette. The inspector waited patiently until the man had lit it with a brass lighter, then started his questions.

'Do I gather that you have had a certain discussion with your wife over a personal matter?'

Morton looked at the police officer as if Arthur was a

poisonous snake about to strike. 'Yes, and I can't really believe it,' he muttered.

'Are you sure you didn't know before this? Or even suspect it?'

The man hunched down even further into his stained mechanic's overall. 'Of course I didn't. I still can't believe this is happening.'

'Have you spoken to your cousin about what's happened?'

The inspector put the question in that way, as he wasn't quite sure if telling a man that his cousin's wife had been unfaithful might be some breach of confidence, murder investigation or not. However, Jeff's reaction removed any possible problem.

'I can't believe that, either. Betsan, of all people!' Then he seemed to realize that his own wife was even further beyond his belief.

'Perhaps you discussed it with him a long time ago!' cut in John Nichols, performing his bad cop role. 'Perhaps you both knew and decided to settle scores with Tom Littleman?'

This accusation seemed to restore some mettle into Morton's backbone. He sat up and agitatedly crushed his wrinkled cigarette into the tin lid.

'What are you trying to say?' he said in a strangled voice. 'For Christ's sake, you can't think that Aubrey or I had anything to do with it!'

'You had good motives, both of you,' accused Crippen. 'The man seduces your wives, you already disliked him for being a drunk and an unreliable worker – and you wanted to get rid of him as a partner, which he refused. People have been murdered for far less than that!'

'And two of you would make this elaborate killing a lot easier,' added the sergeant remorselessly. 'Though I suppose at a pinch either of you could have done it alone. He wasn't much of a match for strong fellows like you.'

Morton stared at the two officers as if they had suddenly taken leave of their senses. 'This is madness! Of course we didn't kill the bastard, much as I'd have liked to more than once.'

Then he again rallied and, as if he had been coached by his more resolute wife, he repeated his cousin's declaration that he refused to answer any more questions unless his solicitor was present.

The DI ignored this, and in a more matter-of-fact tone went

on to rehearse with him all the details of Morton's movements on that fateful day and night.

The answers were the same as before, and with some frustration Arthur Crippen let him go after a further quarter of an hour's fruitless interrogation.

As Morton stumbled out of the caravan, they saw Aubrey Evans and his father waiting for him across the yard at the door of the farm. Aubrey put an arm around Jeff's shoulder to lead him inside, but the sergeant called across to the older man.

'Mr Evans! Mr Mostyn Evans, could we have a word with you now, please?'

The older man looked across. As his son and nephew vanished into the house, he began to walk slowly across to the caravan. Crippen watched him coming through the window and saw that in spite of his big frame he looked much more gaunt than when he was interviewed a few days earlier. When he came in and sat down, Arthur saw sadness and despair on his face.

'This is a terrible business – terrible!' were his first words. 'I can hardly credit what's happened to Ty Croes. Seventy-six years I've lived here and this is the saddest day of my life.'

The lids below his blue eyes had a red rim, and his cheeks seemed more sunken than before. He blew his nose on a large red handkerchief and sighed. 'So what d'you want with me, officer?' he asked resignedly.

'I assume you've been talking to your son and nephew about certain personal matters?' said Crippen.

'If you mean hearing that that evil little swine Littleman had been having his way with Betsan and Rhian, yes, I've heard about it,' he said with sudden savagery.

'Are you sure you had no inkling of this before they told you?' persisted the inspector.

'Of course not! If I had, I'd have kicked the sod's arse all around the farm before throwing him out into the road – partner or no partner!'

'You never approved of him, I gather?' asked the sergeant.

'At first, I had no reason to think one way or the other. He seemed to know his stuff with vehicles and machinery. It was a great mistake later to let him have part of the business, but we didn't realize then that he was fast becoming a drunken sot. And how could we know that he was going to turn into a seducer?'

'You never saw him with either of the wives?'

Mostyn Evans shook his head. 'He must have been damned careful, the bastard! Only played away when the girls were well off the farm.'

He shook his head as if to fling off images in his mind. 'They had a day off now and then, to go to Brecon or even down to Swansea. There was the car, the Land Rover or the pickup they could use. That's when it must have happened.'

'You live with your son and daughter-in-law in the farmhouse?' asked Nichols.

'Yes. I was born there and will probably die there. I don't get under their feet, I've got a couple of rooms upstairs at the back.'

'You didn't see much of Littleman, then?' asked Crippen.

Mostyn shook his head, wiping his face again with the red handkerchief. 'No occasion to, thank God. He knew I didn't like him, and the feeling was likewise. I help out a bit at the farming, mostly driving our new Fergie T-20, an old man's privilege. But I rarely had cause to go down to that damned barn where Littleman was.'

There was a silence while the sergeant caught up with his writing and Arthur Crippen gathered his thoughts.

'You realize that this was a murder, Mr Evans,' he said at last. 'The most serious of offences, one, as the law stands now, with a capital penalty at the end of it?'

The old man stared at the detective as if he failed to understand his meaning.

'We are almost convinced that it was committed by someone living at Ty Croes,' went on Crippen. 'If you have any reason to think it was an outsider, for your family's sake say so.'

John Nichols picked up the questioning. 'Did you ever see any strangers hanging around the farm – or even nearby on the roads? Anyone who came to talk to Littleman, for instance?'

Mostyn looked from one officer to the other. 'I told you, I hardly ever went down to the workshop, so I wouldn't know who talked to that bastard. As for strangers, I don't recall any, apart from some delivery men, though we know most of those. And, of course, our farming friends came, plenty of those – and customers having mechanical jobs done, they'd come up here to pay Aubrey or Jeff. Sure there were plenty of visitors, but we know almost all of them in a rural place like this!'

His shrewd eyes seemed to lose their former worried vagueness, and he fixed Arthur with a penetrating stare.

'You're trying to tell me that you think one of the boys did it, aren't you?' he growled. 'That either my son or my nephew is a murderer and that they might be arrested and might end up on the gallows! Is that it?'

Crippen held up his hands, palm up in an almost French gesture. 'A murder has been committed. Someone did it, and they will eventually be caught and arrested. I can tell you now that a decision will be made in the next day or two whether to call in Scotland Yard. If they come, then I can promise that this place will be turned upside down again and that the level of questioning will be a lot harder than ours.'

He stood up and looked down at the father figure of the farm.

'If you have any influence with the others here, please use it to suggest that if they have anything else they want to tell us, now is the time to do it. If there are any circumstances that might excuse what happened to Tom Littleman, this is the last chance.'

Mostyn Evans hauled himself to his feet and straightened his back, giving him an extra inch over Crippen.

'I'll do whatever I can, officer. You can depend on it.'

He went out into the yard and walked with a new determination across to his house.

TEN

After Angela left for Berkshire in the late afternoon, Richard found himself alone in Garth House. He spent a hour in his study, looking at some of the microscope sections that Siân had prepared for him from post-mortems during the past week, then went outside to 'walk his broad acres', as he liked to think of it. He had never owned any land before or even a house, having spent his life either in hospital accommodation, an officers' mess or, in Singapore, in a rented apartment. Though the house and four acres was technically the property of the partnership, he still had a proprietorial feeling towards it and enjoyed 'potching about' on the sloping ground behind the house. At the end of September, though the evenings were starting to draw in, there was still broad daylight for him to examine the two long rows that Jimmy Jenkins had prepared for those elusive vines, which still had not arrived from the nursery in Sussex.

Jimmy had hacked off the coarse turf with a spade, then turned the soil with a small motor cultivator, a gadget like a lawnmower with rotating blades on either side. As he walked the length of the two rows of churned soil, he heard the roar of a motorcycle coming up the steep drive. A few moments later Jimmy appeared lugging a sprayer which he kept in a shed alongside the coach house.

As usual, half a cigarette dangled from his lip as he approached.

'You're working late, Jimmy. What are you going to do?'

The gardener-handyman put down the yellow tank and started pumping the handle on top to raise the pressure.

'Got an hour before the darts match down at the Swan, doctor,' he informed Richard. 'Thought I'd give that patch a dose of weedkiller before you puts in them vine plants – if they ever come.'

They talked for a few minutes about the weeds and couch grass that were already appearing in the tilled soil. 'They'll choke your bleeding grapes unless you keep them down,' he warned.

Richard was pleased that Jimmy was at last reconciled to a vineyard and had given up his campaign for strawberries.

'Where did you learn that about vines?' he asked curiously.

The other man looked a little sheepish. 'I saw that book you had in the kitchen, when I was in having a cup of tea with Moira the other day. Quite a few good tips, there was!'

Pryor suspected that this was the first time Jimmy had ever read a word about horticulture of any sort, having learned all his lore from half a century as a countryman – but he was pleased that he was now taking an interest in Richard's pet project.

He watched as Jimmy slung the spray tank on his shoulder and began walking alongside the long ribbon of bare earth, spraying it from the nozzle on the end of the hose. He stopped at intervals to pump up the pressure, needing a couple of passes to cover the width, before taking the device back to the shed.

'There's a bottle of beer in the pantry, if you want to wet your whistle,' offered Richard. There was an old bench outside the back door, and the pair of them sat comfortably in the evening light to empty a flagon of Rhymney bitter between them.

'Must be a bit different here to Singapore,' said Jimmy.

'Damned sight cooler, though you get used to the heat,' replied the pathologist. 'I had three years in Ceylon and that was much the same, hot and damp.'

The gardener reached across to top up Richard's glass. 'In the army, was you? See any action out there?'

Pryor grinned. 'Not the military sort, no. I was in an army hospital there, and when we took back Singapore I was posted there to help get theirs up and running again. The Japs had played hell with it, including a massacre of patients and staff.'

He took a long satisfying drink. 'Were you ever in the forces, Jimmy?'

'Nah, protected occupation, me! Farming up the valley, I was. Damned hard graft it was then. Mind you, I had perforated eardrums and flat feet, so they wouldn't take me anyway, 'cause I tried to join.'

After a companionable silence, Jimmy began to probe again, with the insatiable curiosity of people in a small village.

'Was you ever married, doctor?'

'Yes, I was married all right! It didn't work out, I'm afraid. We were divorced last year.'

Jimmy downed the last of his ale and stood up.

'I reckon you'll soon be married again, doctor, living in there with three great-looking ladies!' He picked up Richard's empty glass and made for the kitchen to put them in the sink.

'Point is, doctor, which one of them will it be?'

He tapped the side of his nose knowingly and vanished through the back door.

A little later Richard decided he had better see what Moira had left for his supper but was surprised to find nothing obvious in the Aga or in the refrigerator. This was odd – though she knew that Angela would be away, she was also aware that he was staying that night.

He was just thinking of opening a tin of corned beef when there was a tap on the back door and Moira came in, bearing a tray covered with a cloth.

'You thought I'd forgotten you, no doubt,' she said apologetically. 'It took longer than I expected.'

She set the tray down and pulled off the cloth to reveal a large domed dish cover. Removing this with a flourish, she exposed a pie dish with a golden crust rising above it. Alongside was a Pyrex dish under whose lid could be seen potatoes, peas and carrots. An elegant trifle with a cherry on top sat alongside.

'I'll just put the dishes in the oven to keep warm and the trifle in the fridge, while I lay the table for you.'

The efficient woman busied herself with her culinary operations, and soon she had him seated at the table with a large plate carrying the steak pie and vegetables.

'It's not my birthday, Moira!' he protested. 'Why are you spoiling me tonight?'

She placed pepper and salt before him. 'I knew you would be on your own, so I thought I'd make something special for you. It's easier for me to cook things at home, as I've got all my gadgets to hand. It's no distance to carry it up.'

He looked down at the substantial pie, which gave off a mouth-watering aroma. 'Won't you sit down and help me eat this? It looks marvellous!'

She shook her head. 'I ate earlier, thanks. You just enjoy it, then I'll make coffee, clear up and leave you in peace.'

'Only if you stay and have a drink with me afterwards, then!' he demanded. 'There's a nice bottle of Mateus Rosé in the cupboard – or gin and tonic if you prefer it.'

'Would you like a glass of wine with your meal?' she asked and without waiting for a reply she jumped up and got the familiar round, flat bottle and two glasses. Pouring one for Richard, she half filled another and sat quietly on the other side of the table, watching him devour her cooking with satisfaction.

Between mouthfuls and sips of wine, he told her of the latest developments in the Brecon case. Then, as he finished the last morsels of pie, he toasted her with a raised glass.

'That was great, Moira. You're very kind to me!'

She blushed slightly. 'You've been so kind to me, you and Dr Bray. Taking me on has made such a difference to me. I feel alive again after losing my husband.'

She got up to fetch his trifle and then put the kettle on the Aga to make coffee. When she sat down again, he had refilled both their glasses with the pink wine.

'I don't drink much. I'll be giggling after this,' she said archly as they again raised their glasses to each other.

They talked about matters other than the business as they waited for the kettle to boil. Moira told him of the factory explosion that had taken her husband from her and the several years of numb despair that followed. Thankfully, her parents were still alive and living in Chepstow, where she was brought up.

'I don't think I could have survived without their support,' she said sadly. 'But I feel much more alive now that I have Garth House and you nice people to look after every day.'

As she went to make coffee, Richard wondered if one glass of wine was making her open up like this, as normally she was very reticent about her own affairs.

'Let's sit in comfort in the staffroom,' he suggested, picking up the glasses and half-empty bottle. 'The springs are gone in some of the chairs, but they're softer than these in the kitchen.'

Moira brought the coffee on a tray, and they sat in the twilight coming through the window that faced up the valley, until she switched on an old table lamp with a faded silk shade that Richard still remembered from the days when he stayed with Aunt Gladys.

Emboldened by a glass or two of wine, Moira cautiously probed into Angela's background, as even Siân's talents at worming out gossip had left some blanks.

'Dr Bray's gone home to her parents,' she said. 'I gather it's some sort of big farm?'

'Her father breeds horses and her mother breeds golden retrievers, as I understand. There's a younger sister as well, but I haven't heard that she breeds anything!' he added whimsically.

'Sounds a very grand family, real Home Counties stuff!'

Richard nodded as he finished his coffee. 'Her father was a top civil servant, I gather, until he retired at the end of the war and took to horses.'

He leaned across the low table between them and topped up her wine glass. 'May as well finish this, it won't keep,' he said. Moira looked a little apprehensive but made no protest. She was always a neat woman, petite and shapely, but this evening she seemed to have taken more trouble than usual with her appearance. Her glossy black hair shone in the lamp-light and she seemed to be more carefully made up. When she took off the white apron she wore for serving the food, Richard saw that she wore a smart blue linen dress, tightly cinched at the waist, with a flared skirt. He had always had an appreciative eye for an attractive woman and thought that Jimmy was quite right when he had commented on the trio in Garth House.

Moira ventured again to bring the conversation around to personalities. 'I'm surprised that Dr Bray isn't married, though Siân mentioned that she had been engaged.'

Richard didn't want to break any of Angela's confidences – not that he knew all that much himself, though he suspected that Siân knew as much, if not more, than he did.

'She was, until just before she moved here. Her fiancé was a senior detective in Scotland Yard, but it seems it didn't work out.' He smiled ruefully. 'Just as my own marriage didn't work out, I'm afraid.'

Moira's brown eyes widened. 'Oh, I'm sorry, doctor! I had heard that you had been married, but I didn't want to pry.' She added this with a pang of conscience at being mildly untruthful.

Richard grinned at her. 'There's no secret about it. It was

one of those impulsive wartime things. She was five years younger than me. I met her in the military hospital in Colombo, where she was a civilian-attached radiographer.'

'Did you get married in Ceylon?' asked Moira, seeing in her mind a romantic wedding under a tropical sun, with a handsome major in uniform and a bride with frangipani flowers in her hair.

'Yes, then the bloody Yanks dropped their atom bomb and I was posted to Malaya when the Japs surrendered. Miriam was left behind for a year, which was a bad start. Then she came to Singapore, but never really liked it.'

He forbore to explain that she had found solace in frequent affairs with a number of expatriates in the Colony, which led to a separation and eventually divorce. Moira couldn't think of anything useful to say, so she took refuge in sipping her wine, while she wondered if Miriam had been that much younger than Richard.

Thinking that he had better change the subject, he asked if she knew whether Siân had a boyfriend. 'I suppose I can still call it that at twenty-four,' he said. 'I always think it sounds a bit odd applied to mature people.'

Moira smiled, feeling a happiness that Richard sensed, fↄ he beamed back at her. Perhaps it was the Mateus Rosé, thought.

'Yes, I think there's a gap in the English language agreed. 'There needs to be something between boyfri↙ fiancé. Perhaps we can invent a word!' She giggled, ↗ thing that she normally did.

'So is Siân courting, as we used to call it?' he

'She did mention a boy in her biochemistry co↙ but I don't know if it's at all serious. She's s↗ in the world that I doubt she wants to settle

They talked on easily for another hour, f though Richard drank the lion's share. A↙ the window, Moira's sense of decorum her desire to stay in this lovely man's from her chair, feeling slightly unste

'I must go. Whatever would the knew I was sitting drinking wit↙ doctor?'

He got up and opened the door for ↖.

for quarter of a mile is you, Moira!' he said cheerfully. 'And frankly, I don't give a damn what they think.'

Promising to fetch her tray and dishes in the morning, she was about to say goodnight when Richard went to the hall-stand and took Angela's raincoat and draped it over Moira's shoulders.

'It's dark and chilly out there,' he said. 'I'm going to walk you home to see you safe.'

Going down the drive, he put her arm under his, partly because she was tottering a little on her high heels, but also because he wanted a little feminine contact. She kept it there for all the four hundred yards along the main road until they reached her gate, where she released him.

'Thanks for a lovely meal, Moira – and your company, it's made my evening,' he said.

'Thank you for everything, Dr Pryor, it was lovely. Even for getting me a little tipsy – I feel quite naughty!'

Before he could decide to say anything he might regret, she turned and clipped up the short path to her front door.

They called their goodnights and she vanished to the sound of a yapping welcome from her Yorkie. Richard turned to walk back home and sighed heavily. He enjoyed the company of women, especially such an attractive one as Moira.

'Perhaps I should have given her a goodnight kiss,' he murmured to himself. 'Though she is my cook and secretary. It would complicate matters, wouldn't it, Richard my lad?'

ELEVEN

The journey to Gloucester from Tintern was just under an hour, and on a fine morning it was a pleasant drive along the north bank of the River Severn. The tide was in and once again promising himself to come down to see the Severn Bore one of these days, Richard Pryor felt contented to be back in Britain after fourteen years in Asia.

The barrister's chambers were near the Shire Hall, in which the Assize Courts were situated. This impressive porticoed building was in Westgate Street, in the centre of the city. The huge cathedral loomed not far away, and after cruising around to find a parking space Richard Pryor walked back and was directed to the lawyer's hideout in a tall, narrow Victorian building.

The usual vertical list of resident barristers was discreetly displayed in the porch, and Mr Leonard Atkinson was fourth from the top in pecking order of seniority. This was the name that the solicitor had given him, and when he enquired in the clerk's office on the ground floor a ginger-headed girl led him upstairs to a spacious room replete with the usual fittings of a lawyer's domain. A large mahogany desk, heavy buttoned-leather chairs and several walls lined with legal books were the setting for the conference. The other four delegates were already present, and the man behind the desk rose to greet Richard.

'I'm Leonard Atkinson, doctor. I'm happy and relieved to meet you!'

He introduced the others, the first being a dark-haired girl, his pupil in chambers, whose main function seemed to be to sit and listen and hand out coffee from a tray on a side table.

'Mr Lovesey, our instructing solicitor, you've already met in Stow.' He turned to the remaining person with the air of a ringmaster introducing a new circus act.

'And this is our new leader, Mr Nathan Prideaux QC, from the Middle Temple.'

The leading counsel was a striking, almost eccentric figure.

Younger than Richard had anticipated, he was a large, almost overpowering figure, dressed in a black jacket and striped grey trousers. A white silk handkerchief flopped out of his breast pocket and a cravat-like grey tie hung around a stiff wing collar.

He had a craggy face with thick bushy eyebrows of a steel-grey colour similar to the cascade of hair that was swept back from his forehead to reach the back of his neck. Richard felt that he was a real showman, but no doubt this aspect of his character was matched by a considerable intellect. His coroner friend in Monmouth, whose brother was also a barrister, had informed him that Nathan Prideaux was one of the most sought-after defence advocates in London – and certainly one of the most expensive.

Prideaux rose to shake his hand across the desk.

'We are very relieved to hear that you may have something we can use, doctor,' he said in a sonorous voice that would have readily guaranteed him an alternative occupation as an archbishop.

Richard sat down and pulled his papers from his old case, which he laid against the leg of his chair. The group got down to business without delay, with Prideaux leading the discussion.

'Dr Pryor, we went through most of the non-medical aspects of this sad case before you arrived, so it's your contribution that we now need to explore.'

He put on a pair of gold-rimmed pince-nez, which Richard felt was another affectation in line with his flamboyant appearance. Sliding a large file across the desk, Prideaux opened it at a green tab.

'Perhaps I should briefly remind you of the relevant background of the alleged crime. Our client, Samuel Parker, is a respected veterinary surgeon who for some twenty years has practised in Eastbury. His wife Mary unfortunately developed a cancer of the pancreas early last year and, to put it bluntly, had been dying for the past few months.'

'Her regular medical attendant, Dr Rogers, has given a statement in which he says he did not expect her to live for more than another month,' offered the other barrister, Leonard Atkinson. 'He also said that he wouldn't have been surprised to hear of her death at any time.'

The solicitor joined in the discussion, with his more local knowledge.

'Dr Rogers has been their GP for many years and is a solid old-fashioned practitioner with plenty of common sense,' he said. 'Unfortunately, he was away at the material time and his locum, Austin Harrap-Johnson, came as a result of Parker's urgent telephone call. Having heard him at the magistrates' committal proceedings, I have to say that he sounds an officious and self-important young gentleman, out to make a name for himself.'

Nathan Prideaux peered at George Lovesey over his pince-nez and took up his résumé. 'Be that as it may, the sister of the dead woman immediately and stridently accused her brother-in-law of doing away with her sister and repeated this to Dr Harrap-Johnson, telling him of the recent injection mark on Mrs Parker's arm and the Pentothal and potassium chloride bottles in the animal surgery. Whereas perhaps Dr Rogers might have calmed her down and defused the situation, it seems that young Dr Harrap-Johnson seized on the accusation and promptly telephoned the coroner's officer, telling him that he was unwilling to sign a death certificate.'

Richard nodded and felt that he ought to say something. 'Once that had been done, it would have been very difficult to draw back. After the coroner is informed, it's virtually impossible to un-inform him!'

'Quite so,' agreed the Queen's Counsel. 'The coroner, a Mr Edwin Randall, had little option but to accept the case and ordered a post-mortem examination, ostensibly to allay any further suspicion. It was done next afternoon at the public mortuary in Stratford. The pathologist was a retired fellow, regularly employed by the coroner for routine cases.'

Richard nodded and shuffled among the papers that the solicitor had given him on his visit to Stow.

'I've read his report. He declined to give a cause of death until further investigations were carried out. Because she was on frequent doses of morphine, he wanted to have an analysis in case of some overdosage. That's fair enough. I would have done the same if I couldn't find any immediate cause of death.'

Prideaux's sharp blue eyes fixed on the pathologist. 'If the GP said she could have died at any time, would you need any immediate cause of death, doctor?'

Pryor considered this for a moment. 'Well, maybe the pathologist didn't know what the regular GP thought, as he was away and the statement you have from him was long after the event. Given that this locum doctor was so gung-ho about it and that the sister was yelling murder, he might well have been cautious. In really advanced cancer, of course people can die at any time, but often one can find a definite terminal event, like a pulmonary embolism or a haemorrhage.'

The QC nodded and continued his monologue. 'By this time, the sister, this pharmacist Sheila Lupin, was voicing her suspicions in the village, and she actually went to see Edwin Randall, the coroner, to demand a full investigation and inquest.'

George Lovesey was nodding his head like a mechanical doll. 'I know the coroner well; he's a solicitor in another practice in Stow. He felt a little pressurized by this, and to be on the safe side he had a quiet word with the local police superintendent and they agreed that the safest course would be to ask for a second post-mortem by a Home Office pathologist.'

Richard turned over another page in his own folder.

'That would be Angus Smythe, from the Radcliffe Infirmary in Oxford,' he said. 'I've seen him at forensic meetings. He must be nearing retirement by now.'

'He came up to Stratford two days after the first post-mortem and examined the body again, taking a number of samples. Again he declined to give a definitive cause of death until the results of various tests were available. However, while they were still in the mortuary there, he did say to the first pathologist in the presence of the coroner's officer that if nothing further materialized, he said he saw no reason why the cancer could not have been the cause of death.'

Leonard Atkinson, the 'junior' counsel, though he must have been at least fifty years of age, also felt he must contribute something to earn his conference fee. 'But a week later, when the results from the laboratory were available, Angus Smythe sent a report to the coroner and the police, saying that he was now of the opinion that the immediate cause of death was potassium poisoning.'

Nathan Prideaux gestured at his empty coffee cup and the silent young lady refilled it from the tall pot on her tray.

'From then on, it was all downhill!' he boomed. 'Samuel

Parker was interviewed several times by the police and two weeks later, after they had sought the advice of the Director of Public Prosecutions, he was arrested and charged with murder.'

'When it went before the magistrates, I tried to get bail,' said his solicitor. 'They refused, so he's been on remand in Gloucester Prison since last June. He was committed for trial two months ago, where we reserved our defence.'

The London barrister settled back with his cup of coffee.

'I've come late to this case, Dr Pryor, so perhaps you could summarize exactly what the prosecution medical evidence amounts to – and what we can do to counter it.'

Richard folded his hands on top of his papers, as he knew the facts by heart after hours of reading.

'Dr Smythe said that he could find no immediate cause of death, such as a coronary or a pulmonary embolus. The morphine levels were substantial, but not in a lethal range. No barbiturates were present, so Pentothal could not be implicated. He admitted that advanced pancreatic cancer with multiple secondary growths were present, but analysis of blood plasma, cerebrospinal fluid and the fluid from the vitreous of the eye showed high concentrations of potassium. He considered this last one quite abnormal and could see no other explanation but that a significant quantity of a potassium compound had been administered.'

'Why would Angus Smythe have taken samples from the spinal fluid and the eye fluid?' barked the QC. 'I can understand the use of blood samples – they are the obvious source of most analyses I've dealt with – but why these more exotic ones?'

Richard automatically slipped into lecturer mode.

'It's been known for many years that blood is rapidly contaminated and altered after death, so that many substances diffuse around and their concentration bears little comparison to their level during life – especially for small molecules like sodium, chloride and potassium. However, the eye and to a lesser extent the spinal fluid are in compartments relatively isolated from other tissues and may retain the living levels more accurately.'

The others digested this explanation in silence until Nathan Prideaux snapped another question. 'And what do you think of his findings, doctor?'

Richard considered this slowly, then made a careful reply. 'Until I was asked to look into this case, I would have agreed with him, as they have been the accepted wisdom for many years. But some very recent research, which is still ongoing and published only in preliminary report form at scientific meetings, casts doubt on his opinion.'

He paused before continuing even more carefully. 'In addition, there is another factor, known to physiologists but perhaps not to pathologists unless, like myself, they had specifically to seek it out.'

He then spent a quarter of an hour in laying out, in as non-medical language as he could manage for such a technical subject, why he thought Angus Smythe could be challenged.

After a number of supplementary questions by both barristers, the leading counsel again cut to the core of the matter.

'You say that one part of your hypothesis rests on very recent work, not yet published in the scientific journals. So how did you come across it, Dr Pryor?'

'I recall sitting through a paper presented at an International Forensic Congress in Brussels last year, when a German researcher gave a short account of his preliminary findings. That led me to delve in what little literature there was about vitreous humour, which is the jelly-like fluid inside the eyeball.'

The meeting in Belgium was one he had come from Singapore to attend, afterwards taking the opportunity to visit Britain to deal with his aunt's will and to finalize legal affairs concerning his divorce. It was also the meeting where he met Angela Bray and hatched their scheme to turn Garth House into a private consultancy.

Nathan Prideaux's leonine features became set in a scowl.

'So how are we to place your contradiction of Dr Smythe's opinion before the court in a form strong enough to convince a jury, if there is no published data to support it?'

Richard had anticipated this challenge and was ready with answers. 'The first proposition is no problem, as it can be supported by well-known authoritative textbooks – and if needs be, calling established experts in physiology. The other one, which is so new as not to have percolated into the forensic literature, will need direct contact with the pioneers of this technique.'

'And how do we do that, may I ask?' demanded the QC.

'With your agreement, I could contact the man I heard give the lecture in Brussels to confirm his findings and possibly to learn of others who may be following up the same line of research.'

'Where is this person, d'you know?' queried the junior counsel.

'Last night I looked up the old programme from that Belgian meeting and found his name and academic affiliation. He is a Professor Wolfgang Braun from the University of Cologne in Germany.'

'Presumably he speaks English, if he gave that lecture you heard,' growled Prideaux. 'Unless you are fluent in German, perhaps?'

Richard grinned. 'Not a word, I'm afraid. But Professor Braun was quite proficient in English.'

The two barristers looked questioningly at each other.

'Time is of the essence, doctor. We have only a fortnight before trial,' said Leonard Atkinson. 'If these foreign gentlemen have anything useful, we would have to arrange to get sworn statements made by lawyers in their home countries.'

'Or even get them over here in person to give evidence,' snapped Prideaux. 'I think that you are going to have a busy time for the next few days, Dr Pryor.'

The discussion went on for a time, but they all knew that they were dependent on the results of Richard's labours if this tenuous defence ploy was to be firmed up sufficiently to be used in court.

On the way out, Richard found himself talking to the solicitor, George Lovesey, as they went down the stairs.

'Keep in touch, doctor,' said the lawyer. 'Every day if necessary, as time is breathing down our neck. Spend what you like on phone calls overseas, as long as you get some results!'

As he went to his car and started the journey to Merthyr, Richard hoped that his optimism about contacting Professor Braun and getting something useful from him was justified.

It certainly looked like a busy week ahead.

TWELVE

He arrived at his parents' home in the early afternoon, to be faced with a huge cooked lunch that his mother had waiting for him. This was the usual routine for his weekend visits, Lily Pryor trying to make up for the two decades since he last lived at home. She was convinced that he had not been fed well enough through all these years, ignoring his normal wiry body, which he inherited from his equally stringy father.

After a couple of hours' relaxation, in which he was brought up to date with the local gossip, tea was served, with sandwiches and home-made cake. When he had recovered sufficiently to move, he was hawked off in the family Standard Vanguard to visit his widowed Aunt Emily and her spinster sister Bronwen, who lived in a terraced house in Cefn Coed a couple of miles away. Thankfully, he was only expected to have a glass of sherry and some Welsh cakes, while he was interrogated about his divorce and the prospect of getting married once again.

He took it all in good part, as he was fond of his family. It was just as well, as he had aunts, uncles and cousins scattered all over the nearby valleys and was dragged to visit them in rotation whenever he came home. Later that evening he went up to his father's golf club on a high plateau above the town and had a couple of pints with men he had known since he was a boy. Contentedly, he went to bed in his old room, with his pre-war books and toys still in cupboards and on shelves.

He slept well, though the task of pursuing the impending murder case revolved in his mind for a time before he fell asleep and was there again when he woke late in the morning.

A full Welsh breakfast was shaken down by a walk with his father around Cyfarthfa Park, where a Victorian castle belonging to one of the rich ironmasters was a visible reminder of the days of the industrial dominance of Merthyr Tydfil, as well as violent labour relations, squalid living conditions and epidemics of cholera and typhoid.

He planned to set off for Tintern Parva soon after the inevitable large Sunday lunch. When this was over, he was drinking his coffee when he heard the telephone ringing in the front hall.

As his mother went to answer it, his father smiled complacently.

'I wonder how many times your mother's done that for me?' he asked. 'That's the one thing I don't miss since giving up the practice – the damned phone dragging me out at night and weekends!'

As if to mock him, his wife's head came around the door. 'It's for you, Richard. It's the police. They want to call you out!'

'Sorry to drag you out on a Sunday, doc, but we felt we should get you to deal with this, as you are already involved.'

Arthur Crippen sounded genuinely apologetic as once again he stood with Richard Pryor outside the small door of the barn at Ty Croes Farm. Around them were the same team, Detective Sergeant John Nichols, the coroner's officer and one of the detective constables who had been here the previous week.

'I was already in Merthyr, so I was more than halfway here,' Richard said reassuringly.

The sergeant pulled the small door open and went in to release the bolts of the big door and push it back, letting the late-afternoon sunshine into the cavernous building.

The big blue Fordson Major had gone, but in its place on the floor sprawled a body. It lay on its back, the arms by its side. Richard hardly needed to look at the corpse to know the cause of death, as a shotgun lay on the concrete not far from the right hand. It also took only one step forward to discover the identity of the dead man.

'Mostyn Evans! Well, well! Has this cleared up your case, Mr Crippen?' In spite of the several thousand deaths that he had dealt with over the years, Richard always felt a little saddened at the loss of a life, whatever the circumstances.

'He left a note, doctor,' said the detective inspector. 'In fact, he left several notes. Will you have a look at him first?'

Richard went to crouch alongside the corpse, which was fully dressed in the same clothes as Mostyn had worn at his last interview. Under the chin was a narrow smear of soot around a central hole the size of a shilling piece. At one edge he saw a reddish-brown rim extending about halfway around the hole, where skin had been forced up against the muzzle by the expanding gas beneath. There was an ooze of blood and tissue from the wound, but for a shotgun blast the external damage was relatively slight.

'That gun is a four-ten, I assume?' he asked, looking up at the officers standing nearby.

Arthur Crippen nodded. 'Yes, with a single barrel. The typical farmer's rabbit and rat gun, but it seems to have done the job well enough.' The four-ten was the smaller of the two types of shotguns found on farms, the twelve-bore being its big brother.

Richard felt the forehead and hands of Mostyn Evans. They were cold, but the armpit still had some warmth. When he tentatively moved the elbow and knee joints, he could feel stiffness developing.

'Do we know when this happened?

John Nichols answered. 'Almost to the minute, doc. Jeff Morton heard a gunshot just after midday. That's why the body was found so quickly, as he came straight down to investigate. No one else would have been out shooting on the farm today.'

The pathologist still squatted, looking at the body. The face was quite peaceful, the eyes closed, though he knew well enough that it did not reflect the state of mind at death. Crime novelists' lurid descriptions of 'features contorted in fear' always exasperated him.

'Where did the gun come from?' he asked.

'It was his own, though there are several other shotguns locked up at the farm,' said the sergeant.

Richard got to his feet and faced the detectives. 'How much do you want to do about this? Are you treating it as suspicious, with the full works, like calling the Cardiff lab out?'

Crippen looked undecided. 'Given the gist of the suicide note, I can't see the point. I know there was another murder in exactly the same spot, but surely this clears it up. It's beyond belief that anyone else could be involved in both of them.'

'You'd like a post-mortem straight away, I expect? I've got a busy week ahead of me. I'd rather not have to come all the way back here tomorrow. Is it possible to use the mortuary in Brecon on a Sunday?'

'No reason why not, doctor,' said Billy Brown. 'I can get the key from the hospital lodge. There's no attendant anyway; the porters look after the place.'

Crippen turned to his sergeant. 'Just to be on the safe side, we'll take the gun for fingerprints and lock this place up until tomorrow.'

The detective constable who was acting as exhibits officer fetched a new brown-paper sack from his van and put on a pair of rubber gloves. He bent down to carefully lift the shotgun and for safety's sake opened the breech. He checked to make sure the cartridge inside had been fired by looking at the pin impression on the base.

'Stinks, sir. Not long since it was fired,' he reported.

Richard stepped nearer. 'Before you bag it, can someone measure the distance between the muzzle and the trigger?'

As Billy Brown went to the van to fetch a tape measure, Richard explained that it was best to check that Mostyn Evans' arm was long enough to fire the gun after it had been placed against his own neck.

'I've seen people use lengths of wood or even complicated bits of string to pull the trigger, when the barrel was too long, but there's nothing like that lying around here.'

The coroner's officer measured the distance Richard wanted, the DC recording it in his notebook. After the weapon had been safely packed, there was little to do except wait for the duty undertaker to come out from Brecon in response to a radio message from the police car.

Arthur Crippen and the sergeant retreated to the other side of the yard for their inevitable smoke, while the inspector explained to Richard Pryor what had been in the notes.

'He left three envelopes on the ground, a few feet away,' he explained. 'Two were addressed to his son and his nephew and were very personal, as well as talking about his will and the farm finances. The other one was for me and the coroner.'

'He seemed very well organized,' observed Richard. 'Makes a bit of nonsense about the usual suicide verdicts at inquest, when they say "while the balance of his mind was disturbed"!'

'I agree. He seemed very calm and calculating about the whole affair,' said the detective inspector. 'It was quite a detailed note, but the gist of it was that he didn't want any further suspicion to fall on anyone else.'

'I think your veiled threats about one of the family possibly

facing the gallows made up his mind to end the investigation,'
commented his sergeant. Arthur nodded, sending his half-
smoked cigarette spinning over the fence.

'He also told us that he was suffering from prostate cancer,
and his doctor had told him he wouldn't last another year.
The family didn't know, as he had refused any treatment.'

'So did he actually say that he'd killed Tom Littleman?'
asked Richard.

'He described it in some detail!' replied the DI. 'He found
out about the man's sexual adventures last week, when he
came across his daughter-in-law crying in the house one day.
She confessed to having allowed him to seduce her, though
he'd dumped her by then. She was dead scared that her husband
would find out.'

'So what did he do about it?'

'He wrote that he wanted to keep it from the others at the
farm, so he waited until he knew his son and nephew had
gone off to their NFU meeting, then went down to where
Littleman was putting in his overtime to finish that tractor.
He was in a rage to start with, but he says that the mechanic
told him to piss off and mind his own business.'

'Not the right thing to say to a big bloke like Mostyn,' said
John Nichols with a wry smile.

'No, especially when the silly bugger boasted that not only
had he been knocking off Betsan but Rhian as well,' growled
Crippen. 'Mostyn says in his letter that he was already in a
high temper and that made him lose it altogether. He grabbed
Littleman around the throat to give him a good shaking before
he "punched the lights out of him", as he described it. But
the fellow immediately went limp on him and dropped to the
ground, stone dead!'

'Is that possible, doctor?' asked the sergeant. 'I thought
they struggled for a time and went blue in the face and all
that!'

Richard shook his head. 'That's only if the air supply is cut
off first. It's well known that in some cases a sudden pressure
on the arteries at the side of the neck can stop the heart instantaneously. Squeezing the neck, even in fun, is a dangerous thing
to do.'

'So it could have been a manslaughter rather than a murder?'
suggested Crippen.

'Sure, the defence would certainly plead that, and I'd have to agree with them about the mechanism of death. It makes it less premeditated than squeezing for five minutes with the victim's eyes popping and the tongue sticking out!'

Crippen lit up another Player's Navy Cut, his preferred smoke.

'The rest of his story followed what we thought all along. When he saw the fellow lying dead, his temper evaporated, he says. He didn't want to bring down a murder hunt on the farm – and he didn't particularly want to go to jail or even the gallows himself. So he decided to fake a hanging and hoisted Littleman up on a length of rope. He locked up the barn and went home. He has his own entrance and even staircase to his room in the farmhouse, as it used to be divided into two cottages, so no one was ever sure of his comings and goings.'

'This must have been a long letter,' observed Richard. 'I suppose he wanted to clear up everything so that there would be no question of Aubrey or Jeff getting any blame.'

'There were quite a few pages of it, yes. He ended by telling us that he couldn't resist going down the barn well after midnight to check on the scene. Then he saw that the bruises on the man's neck were all too obvious under the rope and that he would have to do something different. So he hauled him down, put the rope away and laid the body under the tractor wheel, which was already jacked up. Then he hit the blocks away with a post and closed up again.'

'If it hadn't been for you, doc, he might have got away with it,' said Nichols.

'That's flattering, sarge, but it was pretty obvious what had happened,' said Richard deprecatingly. Even so, he felt gratified at the compliment. Pathologists rarely got thanks from their 'patients', not like his physician and surgeon colleagues, who were given bottles of whisky and chickens at Christmas!

Two hours later the penultimate act in the sad drama was played out, the last one to be an inquest in a few weeks' time. At the dismal mortuary behind Brecon Hospital, Richard Pryor confirmed all that was anticipated from the circumstances.

The gunshot had not caused an exit wound on the back of the head, as the small cartridge from a four-ten had not had the power to send lead shot and gas through the thick bone of the upper spine and base of the skull and still have enough force to penetrate the back of the head.

'Was it a contact wound, doctor?' asked Nichols, airing his forensic knowledge gleaned from his inspector's course.

Pryor looked closely at the front of the neck, below the chin.

'Yes, near enough, though there's a bit of soot and burning at one side, so there was room around the muzzle for the gases to escape sideways. But pretty tight, all the same, as there's a partial muzzle mark on the skin.'

The coroner's officer handed him the tape measure and Richard stretched it out from the wound down to the tip of the index fingers of each hand.

'Thirty inches from muzzle to trigger, doc,' quoted the constable from his notebook.

'That's OK, then, he could easily discharge it with these long arms.'

When Richard opened up the body, he found ample evidence of the prostate problem, with secondary growths beginning in several bones. The interior of the neck and the base of the skull had been shredded by the shotgun blast, and the skull bones at the back of head were widely fractured.

'I'll save a few lead shots for the lab, just in case anyone ever wants to check that they are the same as the ones that would have been in the spent cartridge in the gun,' he said.

'Doubt we'll need that, doc, but as you say, just as well to do things by the book,' agreed Crippen.

After he had sewn up the body and cleaned it as well as the basic facilities allowed, it was seven o'clock. After a decent wash in the hospital itself and a cup of tea and some sandwiches in the dining room, he was ready to set off for home in the advancing dusk.

'Thanks for everything, doctor,' said DI Crippen as the officers saw him off from the hospital car park. 'We'll see you again at the inquest, no doubt.'

As he drove the Humber across country, he felt rather sorry that tonight he could not expect to be greeted by Moira with a good meal and a warm welcome.

THIRTEEN

Monday was a routine but busy day for all those in Garth House, except for Jimmy Jenkins, who mysteriously disappeared, as he often did. Richard knew that he gardened for other people in the valley and, given the minuscule weekly pay that he received, Pryor had no complaints as long as he did what was needed here. Sian was happy playing with a new EEL colorimeter that had arrived, which, though a relatively simple instrument for measuring colours from chemical reactions, added a few more analyses to their repertoire.

Angela had come back from her weekend in a buoyant mood, which Siân and Moira put down to the shopping spree she told them about in Oxford on Saturday. Wartime austerity was rapidly fading, though it was only a couple of years since the end of rationing, and excursions to the big shops was now Angela's main indulgence. When Richard returned from Chepstow mortuary later in the morning, he put his head around the laboratory door but retreated quickly when he heard a three-sided conversation about A-lines, pencil skirts and peplums.

Back in the safety of his own room at the back of the house, he opened his notes and drew the telephone towards him.

Dialling the overseas operator, he gave her the number of the medical faculty of the University of Cologne in western Germany. He had found the telephone number during his researches in the medical library in Cardiff, in a large directory of all European universities.

The operator said there would be a delay of probably an hour, as on Monday mornings there was always heavy traffic on the lines. He settled back to write out rough drafts of the three post-mortems he had carried out earlier for Moira to type up. He thought again about getting one of the portable tape recorders that could be carried in a case, which would cut out the need for all this pen-pushing. He had heard that some operated off batteries, so they could even be used outdoors at scenes of crime or in mortuaries without mains electricity. He had done a post-mortem a month ago in a cemetery outhouse, where there was no light other than that coming through a small window.

The phone rang about forty minutes later with his call – it must have been a slack Monday in the Federal Republic, he thought wryly. The first problem was language, as all he could manage was '*Sprechen sie Englisch?*' There was some confused talking at the other end, then, '*Ein moment, bitte*', and soon another voice came on the line, asking in excellent English whether she could help.

'I would like to speak to Professor Wolfgang Braun in the Institute of Forensic Medicine, please,' he asked gratefully.

'Of course. I will put you through to his secretary,' came the well-modulated voice. As he waited, he wondered how many switchboard operators in British universities could reply so effectively in German.

Soon he was speaking to Braun's secretary, who had adequate English, though not so good as the first lady. It turned out that the good professor had just gone to lunch, as Richard had not appreciated the one-hour time difference in Germany. However, the secretary gave him her direct line number to avoid the main university switchboard and asked him to call back in two hours' time, presumably to allow Wolfgang Braun time for a good meal.

He decided to brave the fashion debate and went into the laboratory to tell Angela that 'the game's afoot', in true Sherlockian style. Moira had gone off to get their lunch ready and soon the quartet was in the kitchen, where the figure-conscious Siân was eating her salad sandwiches and Angela and Richard were tucking in to one of Moira's specialities, a shepherd's pie. Between mouthfuls, he told them of the outcome of the Ty Croes Farm affair, Moira staying back for a time from her usual return home for lunch and dog-walking to listen to the unhappy denouement.

'The whole thing is tragic,' she observed sadly. 'All that grief and trouble in two families, just because of some drunken man's lust!'

Richard saw Angela slightly raise an eyebrow at him and knew she was referring to Moira's strong sense of morality. He could have said that Betsan and Rhian needn't have gone along with Tom's importuning but decided to keep quiet and not contradict Moira's more puritanical feelings.

'What will happen now?' asked Siân.

'There'll have to be two inquests, I'm afraid,' said Richard. 'Hopefully, the coroner will try to keep much of the scandal out of the public eye, but he'll have to show the notes to the jury, so I can't see that the affair with the two wives can be kept quiet. The press will have a field day if they find out about it.'

'What will the verdicts be, d'you think?' asked Angela.

'Has to be suicide in Mostyn Evans' case. I'm not sure about Littleman,' he replied. ' I don't see how a coroner's jury could decide between murder and manslaughter with so little evidence available. Maybe "unlawful killing" would cover it, but Mostyn would have to be named as the perpetrator.'

'A sad business!' said Moira again. Richard thought that she was a genuinely sympathetic soul, perhaps a little too sensitive to be working in such a morbid trade as forensic medicine.

For dessert, they had junket, something Richard had not tasted since he was a child at home. The strawberry-flavoured milk, solidified with rennet, was new to Angela and she was not sure whether she liked it or not. Coffee soon took the taste away and they sat talking until Richard looked at his watch.

'Time to talk to Herr Professor!' he declared and went back to his room. Again there was a half-hour delay in getting connected, but eventually he was speaking to the secretary and then to the scientist himself.

Thankfully, Wolfgang Braun spoke good English, though heavily laced with a Bavarian accent. Richard explained who he was and what his problem was in the case of the veterinary surgeon.

'I heard you speak in Brussels and wondered whether you had published any of your research yet?' he asked.

Braun seemed very interested and rather pleased that someone was taking notice of his work.

'I have accumulated a lot of data but have not yet made it ready for publication,' he confessed. 'I have a draft of the paper but need some statistical work done on the results and am waiting for a colleague in the Department of Mathematics to supply that.'

He also told Richard that several other people were working on the same idea, and that he was in contact with them. One was in Chicago, another in Minnesota and both agreed with the general principles of the new idea but had varying experimental results.

Richard groaned to himself at the thought of trying to reach researchers in the middle of the United States, but Wolfgang Braun added: 'There is also another man in Denmark, who, since I read that paper at Brussels, has been working on the same problem.'

Richard spoke to him for another ten minutes, jotting down the names and addresses of the contacts Braun had mentioned.

'If necessary, professor, would you be willing to write a short statement for production in court? Our lawyers would arrange that, and I'm sure there would be an expert fee attached for your trouble.'

Again Braun, well used to legal processes, readily agreed, and they parted verbal company in a friendly manner. As soon as he had put the phone down, Richard looked up the number of the solicitor in Stow-on-the-Wold and dialled again. When he was put through to George Lovesey, he told him of his success in contacting Professor Braun.

'He's agreed to make a formal statement about his research concerning potassium – and he's given me further contacts of other researchers.'

'I'll get on to a law firm who organize affidavits abroad and get them to send a German advocate to see him,' replied Lovesey. 'The trial is only about a fortnight away now, so it will all have to be done by telex and telegram, apart from the actual deposition for court, which will have to be sent by courier or express mail. Anyway, that's our problem. Who are these other people?'

'I'm afraid two of them are in the States – the other is in Denmark. Do you want me to contact them as well?'

'Yes, we always need a belt-and-braces approach, doctor! Don't worry about the cost – compared with Prideaux's fees, that will be chicken feed.'

Richard dictated the phone number and address for Wolfgang Braun and told him who the other three experts were.

'Thankfully, one of our office staff downstairs is German; she married a British officer at the end of the war. I can get her to sort out any language problems when we do our telephoning and the like. Can't help with Danish, but I'm sure most people there speak English.'

'Got anyone in your office who speaks American?' said Richard facetiously, but thankfully George Lovesey laughed down the phone.

'You're on your own there, doctor. Best of luck!'

Though Braun had given Richard the addresses of the other researchers, he had no telephone numbers for them and thought this was more a job for the patient Moira. He called her into his room and explained the problem.

'Perhaps you could try the British Council or even the US Embassy in London. Someone must have the phone details of these institutions. There's an international directory of universities, so try one of the college libraries.'

As she was leaving the room, full of enthusiasm for this novel task, he called after her. 'Moira, make sure you ask the operator for the cost of each call – otherwise we'll be bankrupt before I can claim it back from the lawyers!'

Moira spent almost an hour on the telephone, cajoling various librarians and consular staff into giving her contact numbers for the three institutions where the overseas researchers were situated. She returned in triumph to wave the list at Richard and receive his sincere praise for her efforts.

'It's that seductive voice of yours, Moira – who could resist it!' he said, success making him a little flirtatious. She flushed, but looked even more pleased with herself. 'Now I've got more work for you! See if you can track down these chaps at those places, so that I can have a few words with them.'

Moira looked at her little wristwatch. 'It's gone four o'clock here. That means that office people in Denmark will probably have gone home, given the hour's time difference.'

'Right, let's try first thing in the morning. What about America?'

Moira did some calculations in her head. 'The middle part of the USA must be about eight hours behind us, so it's only about seven in the morning there.'

She made for the door with a purposeful air. 'I'll get on with making something for your and Dr Bray's supper, then I'll start phoning at about five o'clock. I don't mind staying on for as long as it takes.'

Moira eventually went home at about eight, after serving a mixed grill to 'her two doctors', as she had come to think of Richard and Angela. As they sat at the kitchen table, enjoying an unusually lavish dinner for their evening meal, Richard told his partner of his transatlantic conversations.

'Got both of them, thanks to Moira. She was like a terrier with a rat – wouldn't take no for an answer until she got hold of the right people.'

'And did you get anything useful?'

'Yes, both had been working on this potassium in the eye fluid idea since they heard Wolfgang Braun speak at that conference in Brussels.'

'They must have been there like us, among the hundreds who attended,' said Angela rather pensively. It was that congress that changed her life, as meeting Richard there had brought her down to Wales from London.

'Well, like Braun, they've collected a lot of raw data but not published it yet, though Gerald Stoddart in Chicago has a draft ready to send off to a journal. He's going send a copy to us by express mail today. It should get here within a few days.'

'What about the chap in Minnesota?' she asked.

'That's Donald Kaufmann. He's been doing the eye as part of a much wider study of body fluids, but the general trend is the same in the vitreous as Stoddart and Braun.'

'Are their results the same?'

Richard shrugged. 'Not numerically, though perhaps their methods are different. But the general thrust is similar, which is all that I need. They're working towards solving a specific problem, but we only want to show that the previously accepted assumptions have been wrong.'

They discussed this until their plates were empty and they had gone on to tackle the apple tart that Moira had left for them.

Forgoing tea or coffee for a celebratory gin and tonic in Angela's sitting room, she asked what would be the next move.

'I've got to get the solicitor to contact these two men tomorrow and get them to agree to make a sworn deposition, just like Braun.'

'Will they come in time for the trial?'

'I know the gist of what they will say and can write that

into my advice to the lawyers. The Americans can send their statements by telegram or teleprinter, so that we'll know what they're going to say. Then if the actual signed documents are sent by express airmail, they should arrive in time for production in court.'

'It all sounds one hell of a rush, but it seems the only chance this vet has of avoiding conviction. Anything else you have to do for him?'

Richard nodded. 'Find an eminent physiologist to confirm the other branch of our defence. That should be easier and a lot nearer than these foreign parts!'

He sat back contentedly after topping up their glasses. Angela was in her favourite place on the settee, having kicked off her shoes and drawn up her legs elegantly on to the cushions.

'That was a good meal tonight – beats our usual cold ham and salad. I don't know what we'd do without Moira to look after us,' he said.

Angela looked across at him with a slight smile on her face. 'You seem to be getting quite attached to the peerless Moira, Richard! I'm beginning to think that you have designs on her.'

She spoke lightly, but he thought he detected a touch of irony in her voice.

'Nonsense, she's years younger than me,' he protested. 'And still grieving for her husband. It's obvious how fond she was of him.'

'We all have to move on, Richard. You after your divorce, me after that swine jilted me – and Moira will have to do the same.'

She stopped and waved her glass at him. 'Though, in fact, I think she already is moving on. She's got her eye on you, my lad!'

Richard scoffed at her claim but was secretly intrigued by the idea. 'Go on, Angela! You'll be saying next that Siân has got designs on me!'

'No, I wouldn't go that far. I think she hero-worships you a bit, but you're old enough to be her father – just about!'

He gave her one of his wry grins, finished his drink and stood up. 'I think I'd better go before we get any sillier! A busy day again tomorrow, with these army lawyers coming to see us.'

As he went back to his office to write some notes about what he had learned from his expensive transatlantic phone calls, he pondered what Angela had said. This was the first time that she had mentioned her broken engagement to a superintendent in the 'Met', since he had unexpectedly turned up a few months ago at a scene of crime near Gloucester. He knew she was still bruised by the experience, but it was a topic that they both avoided. She was right, though, he thought. They had to move on, and living in a house with three women, all attractive in their different ways, constantly reminded him of what he was missing.

With a sigh, he sat at his desk and pulled a writing pad towards him.

FOURTEEN

Next morning Moira had her first failure, for when she got through to the Forensic Institute at the University of Copenhagen she discovered that the doctor to whom Richard wished to speak had gone to Greenland for two weeks.

'They said that the Danes cover it for forensic cases and he's had to go back there for a court case in a murder,' she announced despondently.

'Never mind. I think we've got enough with the German and the two Yanks,' Richard told her reassuringly. 'Now I'll have to get the solicitor in Stow to get his sworn statements from the States. That should keep him busy for a few hours.'

With no post-mortems to do that day, he felt at a loose end until the War Office wallahs came in the afternoon. He recalled that he was having trouble with the Humber's handbrake, which came to the top of its ratchet before the brakes gripped. Though Jimmy had offered to fix it for him, he preferred to have it looked at by a competent mechanic. Jimmy was adept at farm-style lash-ups, but Richard decided that though a plough might be mended by the use of binder twine and a few blows from a hammer, a brake problem was too serious to be dealt with in that fashion.

He drove down to Tintern and called at a small garage behind one of the pubs, which he had patronized before. It was little more than an oily shed, but the grizzled man who ran it, with the help of a teenager, offered to look at it straight away. As he vanished under the Humber, Richard was strongly reminded of another dungareed mechanic with a young assistant, who so recently had been under a vehicle fixing the brakes. However, this one soon emerged unscathed and, wiping his hands on a rag, announced his diagnosis.

'Your cable needs tightening, that's all, doctor. Leave it for half an hour and it'll be ready.'

There was an hour before Moira would have their lunch ready, so he decided to have a pint at the Royal George, almost opposite the abbey. The majestic ruin set against a backdrop of autumn-tinted woods was a calming sight, as he sat outside with a tankard of best bitter. Though he had enjoyed his years in the Far East, this beat sitting in the stifling heat of the bar in the Singapore Swimming Club, with the condensation running down the outside of a glass of Tiger.

As he sipped, he looked at the tall, roofless edifice opposite and wondered what it had been like in its prime, before King Henry had destroyed it because of his desire to change wives. This triggered another flashback, this time to his conversation with Angela the previous evening. They were both healthy, virile people with no outlet for their emotional or physical appetites, a state of affairs which was unsatisfactory, to put it mildly. True, both of them had been fully occupied for the past six months in setting up their new venture, but now that a regular pattern had been established for their work, it was surely time for some social life. As the level in his glass dropped, he went over the options – joining a golf club, perhaps. He was not an enthusiastic sportsman, apart from yelling for Wales at a few internationals at Cardiff Arms Park, but a club might be somewhere where he could meet people outside the tight medical-police-lawyer circle that now dominated his acquaintances. But the thought of seeking a new wife among the sturdy tweed-clad golfing fraternity was not all that attractive.

Was Angela just teasing him about Moira having a crush on him? He thought he had sensed a slightly caustic undercurrent in her voice, but it would be ridiculous to think that she felt that Moira was in any way a competitor. What nonsense! He chastised himself for even considering it and irritably swallowed the rest of his ale and stalked back to the garage.

'All done, sir! And I've topped up your brake fluid, radiator and engine oil as well.'

Impressed by the man's speed and efficiency, he happily paid the thirty shillings he was asked for and drove back to Garth House and his 'monstrous regiment of women'. Over a tasty casserole for Angela and himself, the conversation centred on why the War Office wanted them to look into a case.

'Don't they have any pathologists of their own?' asked Siân between bites at her Cox's Orange Pippin.

'Yes, I was one of them!' retorted Richard. 'But it sounds as if they want someone who's now outside the service, to appear independent if there's some sort of claim against the army.'

He was proved right when the visitors arrived soon after lunch.

They came not in a sleek staff car nor a green Land Rover, but in a private hire taxi which had met them at Newport railway station. The driver hesitantly slowed near the bottom gates, then drove up and stopped on the drive level with the front door.

This was hardly ever used, as everyone else went around to the back yard. Richard hurriedly found the key in his office and went to admit two men in sombre double-breasted suits and a middle-aged woman wearing businesslike spectacles.

He shepherded them into Angela's sitting room, the most comfortable place, with its superb view from the large bay window. She had suggested it, and, when they had settled, Moira came in to ask if they would all like tea or coffee. The niceties finished, the elder of the two men introduced themselves. He was a large man with a grey walrus moustache and pale, watery eyes. In true Whitehall style, he clutched a bowler hat.

'I'm Paul Bannerman, from the Army Legal Branch,' he announced in a deep, resonant voice. 'This is Gordon Lane, one of our Crown solicitors – and our lady colleague is Mrs Edith Wright, who will take any notes that are required.'

Gordon Lane was about forty, a slightly hunched man of slight physique but with an amiable, round face.

Bannerman hauled up his briefcase from the floor, a black leather one with a crown embossed on the flap. Taking a file from it, he launched into an explanation.

'I'm the only serving officer here, a half-colonel, though I rarely put on my uniform,' he said with an unexpected smile. 'We know that you were one of our pathologists during the war, leaving with the rank of major.'

Richard was surprised to learn that the army had kept tabs on him for so long, as it was almost a decade since he had returned to civilian status.

'That's partly why we sought your help, as you are familiar with service life and must have had considerable experience of gunshot wounds,' said Lane, the solicitor. His voice sounded shrill compared with Bannerman's base tones.

'The other reason is that you are now an independent expert, not beholden to any official institution,' added Bannerman. 'So no one can accuse you of any bias or partisan opinions.'

Mrs Wright sat stiffly on one of the harder chairs, her notebook open on her lap, but so far she had nothing to write.

Angela, whom Richard had already introduced as his forensic science partner, was anxious to know what this was all about.

'We wondered why you came to us, as there are quite a few experienced people in London,' she said.

Bannerman nodded. 'It was certainly the fact that Dr Pryor was a former army pathologist that attracted us. I'll tell you the problem, shall I?'

It had to wait a few moments, as Moira came in with a large tray and served coffee all around. 'Have you had lunch?' she asked solicitously, but was relieved to hear that they had eaten on the train from Paddington – no doubt all travelling First Class, thought Richard.

'This all stems from the death three months ago of a British soldier in one of the Gulf States,' began Bannerman. 'Herbert Bulmer, originally from the Duke of Hereford's Light Infantry, was a Warrant Officer, Class Two, in a Special Forces Training Unit. He was forty-four and had an excellent record in the war, serving in the Western Desert and Italy.'

He paused and looked at a paper in his file.

'Last year the War Office accepted a contract from the small Gulf state of Al Tallah to train a unit of their forces in counter-insurgency techniques. WO2 Bulmer was one of those sent out there for six months from our own training facility on Salisbury Plain.'

Richard and Angela looked at each other covertly, being still none the wiser as to the reason behind this visit, but clarification was on the way as Gordon Lane took up the story.

'We sent seven men out there on quite a lucrative contract, as Al Tallah is an oil-rich state. The instructors were all senior NCOs, apart from a former Black Watch major who was in administrative charge. They were to train six batches of men from the Al Tallah Defence Force, giving each of them one month's instruction. Unfortunately, four months into the programme, Bulmer died in an accidental shooting incident.'

'We say it was accidental,' cut in Bannerman. 'But his widow is not only suing the War Office for negligence but is trying to get the man who shot him charged with murder!'

There was a heavy silence as Richard and Angela digested this unexpected twist.

'So what were the circumstances and why is it so contentious?' asked the pathologist.

'The shooting occurred during a mock assault on an aircraft that was supposed to have been taken over by hijackers,' explained Paul Bannerman. 'It was a standard training exercise that had been carried out many times before with different groups. They used the grounded fuselage of an old Dakota that was dumped out on the perimeter of Al Tallah airport.'

He went on to describe the nature of the procedure, which was a live-fire exercise using real ammunition. Richard knew from gossip in the officers' mess years ago that some of these commando types indulged in very risky training scenarios, like the notorious 'killing house' used by the SAS near Hereford.

'What happened was that man-shaped plywood targets were set up in front of the cabin, near the cockpit. This first exercise was to accustom the trainees to the noise and confusion of an assault, with live-weapon firing and thunderflashes being thrown about.'

The colonel in barrister's clothing went on to describe what had happened. The two instructors were WO2 Bulmer and Staff Sergeant Leo Squires, with four local trainees in the first batch. They were to burst in through the cabin door with Bulmer in the lead and Squires behind him, immediately letting fly with their weapons at the targets. The other four followed and, after flinging thunderflashes up the fuselage, would also open up with their automatic weapons.

'How did they avoid shooting each other?' asked Angela, thinking that this sounded a bit like overgrown boys playing soldiers.

'Well, they didn't in this case, I'm afraid. The pre-exercise briefing told the trainees to spread out sideways and keep low. Not much room for that, as this old plane was a Douglas DC3, left over from the war.'

'So what happened that this man ended up dead?' asked Richard.

'There was the expected God-awful noise of weapons and explosives in that confined space. According to the witnesses, the confusion lasted a minute or so while they riddled the targets, then it was seen that WO2 Bulmer was lying in the aisle. When he failed to get up, it was found that he was dead, with a gunshot wound in the back of his head.'

'So who was behind him?' asked Angela.

Bannerman explained that the standard ploy was for the leader, Bulmer in this case, to advance up the aisle between the seats, firing as he went, with the second instructor behind him and the trainees spread out on each side of the back row of seats, everyone hammering away at the targets.

'What about the second trainer, right behind the boss?' asked Richard.

'He fires around him when he gets the chance and takes over in a real situation if the leader gets hit by the baddies.'

'God help any passengers!' murmured Angela. She noticed a quickly suppressed smile on the face of the secretary, proving that she was human after all.

Bannerman heard her as well and grinned. 'I don't think this particular exercise was meant to be a very realistic procedure. It's really to get the new trainees used to a hell of a lot of noise and confusion.'

Pryor wanted to get back to the actual event. 'So what happened next, when they saw he was dead?'

Bannerman sighed. 'It was a first-class cock-up, I'm afraid. Naturally they wanted to get Bulmer out in case he needed medical attention, though the staff sergeant said he knew straight away that he was dead. He said he'd seen enough battle casualties after D-Day to know a corpse when he saw one. They lugged the body out of the fuselage, then someone ran for an airport ambulance.'

'No photographs were taken of the body in situ, though I suppose that would hardly be the first thought in anyone's mind,' said the Crown solicitor. 'Of course, this was a foreign country. We had no other military presence there to organize things.'

The story unrolled, telling how the ambulance took the dead man to the civilian hospital about five miles away, where

'Did they keep the bullet after the investigation was over?' asked Pryor.

'It's still available in Al Tallah, as far as I know. Did you want to see it?'

Richard rubbed his chin, still staring at the photographs. 'It's possible, so perhaps you could make sure that they don't chuck it away. What about his clothing? Did they keep that?'

Bannerman looked nonplussed. 'Clothing? I've no idea. Gordon, do you know anything about that?'

The solicitor shook his head. 'We can find out from the major out there. He's still in Al Tallah. We sent a pair of NCOs out to replace Bulmer and Squires.'

The show must go on, thought Angela cynically – especially if the War Office is getting a nice fat fee for the training.

'So we don't know if he was wearing a hat of any sort,' continued Richard.

Bannerman pursed his lips. 'Again, I don't know. The usual kit for that part of the world is a khaki tunic and shorts and a bush hat with a floppy brim. Does it matter, doctor?'

'It might if the shot went through the hat. For a start, it might help with determining the range, if there was burning or propellant soiling from a close discharge.' He looked again at the photos. 'There's no chance of seeing anything like that on these fuzzy pictures.'

'Why do think it might have been a close discharge?' asked Gordon Lane.

'The wound is large and split, as far as can be made out. A direct distant shot wouldn't do that, but a near-contact one could. The gases from the muzzle can be forced under the scalp and, because there is unyielding skull underneath, it causes a blowback which can split the skin.'

The prim Mrs Wright paled a little at the description she had to scribble on her notepad.

'Is there any eyewitness evidence as to how close the two men were when the shooting started?' asked Angela.

The two War Office men looked at each other uncertainly.

'Not really. There are fairly sparse statements from the trainees. Some of them hardly speak any English and, given the hectic turmoil of the moment, I doubt their testimony would be of much help.'

'It's only now that these issues have blown up into such

Bulmer was pronounced dead and taken to the mortuary. The major in charge of the training unit was called from his office in the British Consulate, a villa in one of the suburbs, and he immediately reported the matter to the civilian police.

'They don't have a coroners' system there, I presume?' asked Richard.

'No, the police do it all, in a random sort of way,' said Bannerman. 'They took statements from everyone, as did the Al Tallah army people. The police eventually ordered a post-mortem, done next day by an Indian doctor at the hospital. I'm not clear whether he was actually a pathologist, but he was the chap who did the work for the police.'

Bannerman turned over a few pages in his folder and pulled out several black and white photographs, each half-plate size.

'The police took these, but they're not of very good quality, I'm afraid.'

Richard looked at the grainy, underexposed and slightly out-of-focus pictures, then handed them over to Angela. One showed the naked body lying on a mortuary table. From the background surroundings, it looked a fairly primitive place, not unlike some of the ones he was familiar with in rural places in Wales and the west. Two others were of the scalp wound and another one showed the interior of the head, with fracture lines across the back of the skull.

'Later, our major took a few pictures of the inside of the aircraft with his own camera – in fact they are much better than the police photos, as he had a Leica.'

He handed over a couple of smaller prints, which were indeed much sharper than the others. They showed the interior of a battered fuselage, with all the lining stripped out down to the bare metal. Many windows were smashed, and most of the remaining seat frames were devoid of upholstery. At the front, three crude silhouettes of men were leaning drunkenly, punctured by bullet holes.

'What happened to the body?' asked Angela.

'After the post-mortem, it was embalmed for transit and flown home to be buried with military honours in a cemetery near his home in Lewisham.'

'Was there a further post-mortem here?' queried Richard.

Bannerman shook his head. 'No, it was reported to the coroner on arrival, but he accepted the War Office account and declined to hold an inquest, allowing the death to be registered in the normal way.'

'So what went wrong, to bring you here today?' asked Pryor rather bluntly.

Gordon Lane leaned forward to explain. 'Naturally, the widow was awarded his full pension entitlement, and the War Office paid all expenses related to the death. She seemed resigned to the situation, as she was aware of other deaths these days among servicemen in Malaya, Kenya and Cyprus. But a month ago we had a writ served on us for a large negligence claim – and subsequently her solicitor has demanded that Staff Sergeant Leonard Squires be charged with murder.'

Richard's face showed his astonishment. 'Murder! I could understand some sort of negligent manslaughter, but murder's bit steep, isn't it?'

Bannerman agreed. 'We think it's nonsense, added to bolster up their civil claim for large damages. This solicitor is what the Americans would call an ambulance-chaser. He's got hold of this poor woman and brainwashed her into thinking there's a pot of money to be made, including him.'

'But how on earth can they sustain a murder charge?' asked Angela. 'The whole affair seems very risky, but I suppose that's what being in the army can mean. And why should it even be negligence, if that training routine is an accepted part of military practice?'

'Well said, Dr Bray,' replied Bannerman. 'We are naturally contesting the allegations, which is why we've come to you to see if there's anything in the medical aspects that are relevant.'

'The allegation of murder is based on undoubted bad blood between Herbert Bulmer and Staff Sergeant Squires,' said the solicitor. 'The wife has letters to show that her husband wrote home to her several times complaining about Squires.'

He went on to describe how the warrant officer had claimed that Squires was insubordinate and aggressive, even to the point that they came to blows in the accommodation provided for them by the Al Tallah military.

'It seems that the antagonism began even before they went out to the Gulf, as several of the unit members we interviewed back at their depot near Salisbury said it was well known that the two men didn't get on, to say the least.'

'What does Squires say about this?' asked Richard out of sheer curiosity, as it was no part of his medical brief.

'He readily admits that he couldn't stand Bulmer, who he claims was officious and overbearing, treating him as if he was a raw recruit rather than an experienced NCO who was only one rank below him.'

Bannerman added to this litany of dispute. 'Squires reckoned that Bulmer treated him with contempt in front of the trainees and often countermanded Squires' orders to the men. We couldn't get any confirmation from any of the officers, but a sergeants' mess is well known to be adept at keeping their own affairs under wraps.'

'So the allegation is that Squires took the opportunity of the firefight in the plane to put one in the back of Bulmer's head?' suggested Richard. When he was in the army himself, he had heard rumours of similar 'accidents' to junior officers or senior NCOs, when they were up at the head of a patrol.

He picked up the photographs again and studied them, even fishing a small lens from his pocket to look closely at the ones showing the head injury.

'A pity they're such lousy photos,' he muttered.

'Can you tell anything from them?' asked Bannerman.

'It's a big wound, slightly ragged around the edges, as far as one can tell. What weapons were being used?'

'Bulmer and the trainees had standard-issue Sterlings, b[ut] Squires used a Thompson sub-machine gun. God knows wh[ere] he got it from, but some of these Special Forces types in[sist] on having their favourite weapons.'

'There's no doubt, I suppose, that the fatal shot came [from] his gun?' hazarded Richard.

Bannerman shook his head. 'None at all! The Al [Tallah] police have virtually no forensic facilities, but they did[n't need] to. A Sten gun uses nine-millimetre ammunition, [but a] Thompson fires forty-fives.'

'So there was no microscopic matching of the bul[let and] weapon?' asked Angela. Although she was not a firea[rms exam]iner, a lot of knowledge had rubbed off on her [during her] years at the Metropolitan Police laboratory.

'No point, even if Al Tallah were able to get i[t,' said] Paul Bannerman. 'No one else there had a we[apon of that] calibre.'

importance,' said Lane. 'Before, it was a tragic accident three thousand miles away. Squires was put through the grinder when he was brought back to the depot, but of course he would quite naturally avoid saying anything that was to his disadvantage.'

'It's only since the wife and her stroppy lawyer came on the scene that we've had to sit up and take notice,' confessed Bannerman. 'Is there anything you can do or suggest that might take us further forward?'

'Have you got the post-mortem report from Al Tallah there?' asked Richard. The colonel delved into his black bag again and brought out a single sheet of paper. When he handed it to Richard, he saw it was poorly typed on a printed pro forma with 'Al Tallah Police Department' at the top.

'Pretty skimpy, but we get them just as bad in this country,' he commented as he began reading.

The brief report described a well-built man six feet in height. There was no mention of clothing or a hat. A fulsome description of rigor mortis and lividity was unhelpful, given that the time of death was known to the minute, but the actual head wound was given scant attention. It was described as being on the 'back of the head', and its dimensions were stated as 'about one and a half inches by one half-inch'. There was no mention of burning of hairs or the blackening of surrounding skin.

The rest of the body was dismissed in a few repetitions of 'NAD', an overworked acronym meaning 'nothing abnormal detected'. At the end was a terse summary: 'Death was due to skull fracture and brain damage due to a gunshot wound to the back of the head.' At the bottom, it was signed 'Dr Pradash Rao'.

'Pretty uninformative,' grunted Richard, always annoyed by skimped workmanship. 'He offers no opinion as to whether it was a close or distant discharge.'

'Is there anything you can tell us that might help us in challenging this claim?' asked Bannerman. 'They are saying that the army was negligent in not ensuring that the trainers were competent enough to avoid such incidents – which rather cuts across their other allegation that Squires deliberately shot Bulmer out of malice, though they also claim that the antipathy between the two men should have been known to senior

officers and that the two men should not have been posted to
the same place, especially if the opportunity arose to escalate
their quarrel through the use of firearms.'

Richard shrugged. 'I'm afraid the legal complexities are
outside my remit. But a couple of things occur to me about
the gunshot wound.'

He turned to Gordon Lane. 'There's absolutely no doubt
that the fatal shot came from Squires' weapon, which fired a
forty-five-calibre bullet?'

When the solicitor confirmed this, Richard tapped the photographs with a finger. 'Then I'm surprised that if a man was
hit in the back of the head at close range with a forty-five,
there was no exit wound. It's by no means inevitable, but a
big slug like that fired from a few feet away – or even much
nearer, for all we know – usually causes a through-and-through
track across the skull, with a messy exit wound on the other
side.'

'Why didn't this happen in this case, doctor?' asked
Bannerman.

'As we've got only lousy pictures and an uninformative
post-mortem report, I can't tell. If it was a long-range
discharge, the bullet may have been at the end of its trajectory and lost much of its energy, but this can't be the case
here, inside an aircraft. One other reason can be that the bullet
hit really dense bone inside the skull, but that's all in the base
and this impact is too high for that.'

He shook his head in annoyance. 'One way to take this
forward is to have the bullet for examination, but, really, the
only effective way is to have another post-mortem.'

There was a silence, then Bannerman reminded him that
the man had been dead for over three months.

'That's not a big problem,' replied Richard. 'You said the
body had been embalmed, so it will still be in reasonable
condition.'

The two lawyers looked uncomfortable. 'I see your
point, but it'll be a mammoth task to get permission for an
exhumation.'

Richard was too polite to say that that was their problem,
but he suggested that if the widow and her lawyer were that
keen on pursuing the claims, they would have to agree to it.

'Getting Home Office permission is the hardest part of

obtaining an exhumation,' he said. 'But, of course, you are in a different position, with your ministers in government able to oil the wheels of bureaucracy.'

They discussed the matter for a further half-hour, though much of the conversation was between the pair from the War Office, bemoaning all the work they would have to do to get these various suggestions put into practice.

'We'll have to get this major back from the Gulf to see exactly what he knew about these two men,' said Bannerman. 'We may have to send some SIB men out there to interview those trainees more thoroughly, too.'

Eventually, they got up to leave, with a promise that they would keep in touch about developments. The last welcome invitation Bannerman made as they went out to their hire car was for Richard to keep a note of his fee and expenses as he went along.

The driver went up to the yard to turn around. When they had passed back down the drive and out into the road, Angela and Richard went into the house and locked the front door.

'What did you think of that?' he asked her. 'A bit out of the usual run of cases, eh?'

'What was that SIB he mentioned at the end?' she asked.

'Special Investigation Branch – it's the army's version of the CID, part of the Military Police, under the Provost Marshal.'

They went back to the staffroom, where at teatime Siân and Moira were waiting impatiently to hear what the mysterious men from Whitehall had to say. Richard gave them a summary of the problem and said that unless more information could be found, there was little help he could offer.

'Do you think they'll get an exhumation?' asked Siân.

'Perhaps the thought of digging up her husband might persuade the widow to drop the case,' said Angela, recalling the unpleasant procedure at their last exhumation in Herefordshire a few months earlier.

Moira shuddered at the thought of disturbing anyone's final resting place, especially that of a soldier killed doing his duty. It was too soon after the loss of her own husband for this image to be anything but disturbing. She tried to put the thoughts aside and asked Richard if he felt there was anything he could do for the lawyers.

'Not unless they come up with something more definite.

But I'm not happy about that gunshot wound, even if that staff sergeant was so close that his weapon was virtually touching the victim.'

'Perhaps it was!' declared Angela. 'With that standard of investigation, anything could have happened.'

Richard Pryor finished his tea and stood up, ready to go back to work in his room. 'Well, there's nothing more to be done about it unless those War Office types can come up with some more information, especially consent for an exhumation.'

At the door he turned around with a last exhortation. 'Keep your fingers crossed that we get something soon from Germany and the good old United States of America, or our veterinary client from the Cotswolds is going to be in deep trouble!'

FIFTEEN

Early on Wednesday Richard Pryor was up at the crack of dawn again to catch the Beachley–Aust ferry across the River Severn, as he had to give a nine o'clock lecture to the medical students in Bristol. A weekly event during the Michaelmas term, it was sometimes difficult to arrange when attendance at court or an occasional police call interfered with the timetable. Thankfully, the pathology staff, in whose lecture allocation the forensic topics resided, were flexible enough to swap their hourly slots to accommodate his problems.

As he drove towards the medical school on the hill high above the Bristol Royal Infirmary where the Norman castle once stood, he savoured the task of talking to an audience who were keen to hear what he had to say. Students never showed any reluctance to attend forensic lectures, due to their intrinsic interest and the often gory slides that Richard showed to illustrate his teaching. In fact, with some of the more blood-thirsty or salacious topics, he knew that more than a hundred per cent of the class was facing him, as some students from other faculties crept in at the back. However, unlike some of his colleagues in other universities, he did not strive to be shocking or outrageous, but the very nature of the subject seemed to fascinate most people. He tried to tailor his talks to practical matters, especially the legal obligations of doctors, as he knew full well that probably not one of his audience would ever become a forensic specialist, the vast majority ending up as family doctors. Today was an example, as he was speaking about medical negligence, ethics and the General Medical Council, subjects of far greater relevance to doctors than cut throats or shootings, even though they were unlikely to attract any gatecrashers from the engineering or music departments. As he drove home in the late morning after the lecture, he wondered if Dr Pradash Rao had ever been taught much about gunshot wounds, as his report on the warrant officer was woefully inadequate. However, Richard sympathized with him, as he probably was a general-duties medical officer in the hospital, pushed into this extra job with little or no forensic experience.

He got back to Garth House just in time for one of Moira's welcome lunches, this time a pair of fresh trout from the nearby Wye, which Jimmy had produced, tapping the side of his nose to indicate that no questions should be asked as to how he had come by them

'I wonder when you'll hear from abroad?' asked Siân as she sat on the other side of the old table with her sandwiches and fruit.

'Give it a chance. It's only been two days,' chided Angela. 'I can't imagine anything getting here from America in under a week, even if they use airmail. Germany should be quicker, I suppose.'

'Couldn't they telegraph it?' persisted their technician. 'I'll bet they didn't wait a week during the war when there was military stuff to communicate.'

'If it's a scientific paper, it would be a hell of long telegram,' said Richard. 'And they couldn't include graphs and diagrams and things like that.'

'The newspapers send photographs by wire,' said Siân stubbornly. 'I don't see how written material is any different.' She was the keenest of the lot to see her chief getting his teeth into something that might save the vet from hanging.

'I know the Met used to get copies of fingerprints by wire from police forces overseas,' said Angela. 'But I've no idea how they did it.'

This topic exhausted, the conversation moved on, over a creamy rice pudding, to current events. Siân, an avid cinema fan, had been particularly upset by the news on the wireless that James Dean had been killed in car crash in California, especially as fellow actor Alec Guinness had met him less than a week earlier and had announced his premonition of Dean's death. Angela preferred discussing the new fashions in her latest *Vogue*.

Afterwards, they went back to work, Richard to his microscope and Siân to her fume cupboard, where she was digesting tissue in nitric acid to look for diatoms. Ever since their first success in helping the police with a homicidal drowning some months earlier, she had taken a great interest in these microscopic algae and was trying out different methods of extraction, described in some journals that Richard had passed on to her.

Angela was involved in a new procedure – at least new for the Garth House partnership, though she had dealt with hundreds at the Met lab. A solicitor had sent in an item of a lady's undergarments, provided by a suspicious husband seeking a divorce. An alleged stain was claimed to be evidence of adultery, and Angela had to determine whether it was, in fact, seminal and, if so, whether or not it came from someone with a different blood group from that of the husband. Like the growing trade in paternity tests, it opened up a new avenue for increasing their revenue, and she was keen to get a reliable report out as soon as possible to encourage the lawyer to recommend her to his colleagues in the divorce business.

Several days went by in the same pattern. Richard had postmortems in Monmouth and Chepstow, as well as being asked to go to Hereford for a 'special' case. This was a death under anaesthetic, which had to be reported to the coroner if it occurred within twenty-four hours of an operation. It was customary for the coroner to ask an outside pathologist to conduct the examination, rather than the resident pathology consultant, in order that no suggestion of a cover-up could be made.

In this case the issue was straightforward, as Richard Pryor found that the relatively young patient had severe coronary artery disease, which had been symptomless and impossible to foresee as a fatal complication – even a preoperative electrocardiogram had shown no abnormality.

On Friday still no word had come from Stow-on-the-Wold about receipt of the reports from abroad, but Richard was diverted by the arrival of a British Railways Scammell lorry. The three-wheeled 'mechanical horse' laboured up the drive to the back yard, where the flat-capped driver waved a delivery form at Jimmy Jenkins, who came out of his shed to see what was making the racket. By the time he and the driver were dropping the tailboard, Richard had appeared, beaming with anticipation.

'Your grape plants have arrived, doctor,' announced Jimmy ungraciously as he helped lift off the first of six large boxes from the lorry. As soon as the truck had gone, Richard insisted that they prise off the thin slats and inspect the contents.

'Bit small, ain't they?' growled Jimmy, holding up a foot-long twig with a piece of sacking wrapped around the root.

'They'll grow like crazy once they're established,' said Richard with a confidence born of inexperience. 'They'll need drastic pruning when they're bigger.'

'Are you sure you should plant them in the autumn like this?' grunted the countryman, who had an almost instinctive feel for what was right.

'Many vineyard owners prefer the spring, but this valley is one of the most frost-free places in the country,' said Pryor, repeating the wisdom he had gleaned from half a dozen books on the subject.

'You'd have been better off with bloody strawberries,' growled Jimmy, half to himself, but he went to work with a will and soon they had a hundred plants laid out on the yard.

'They look a bit dry, God knows how long they've been on the railway,' advised Jimmy. 'The sooner we get them in the ground the better.' After a dousing with the hosepipe, they barrowed the vines up to the plot and began planting. Jimmy dug a hole with a spade and threw in a shovelful of rotted manure, while Richard unwrapped the sacking from each plant and held it at the right level while Jimmy refilled the hole. They stuck at it for two hours, until Richard decided that he would leave the remaining fifty for next day.

They celebrated with a flagon of beer drunk on the seat outside the back door, Richard glowing with satisfaction and manual labour, though he suspected that with all that bending and crouching his back would be killing him in the morning.

'So when will we be drinking this wine, doctor?' asked Jimmy with thinly veiled sarcasm.

'Give the vines two years and we'll be picking a crop,' said Richard confidently. 'And the next year we'll be drinking Chateau Wye Valley!'

On Monday the usual routine held sway, as both Chepstow and Monmouth demanded Richard Pryor's services. A fatal two-car road accident on the A48 near Caerwent was a possible Section Eight, according to John Christie, the coroner's officer. He meant that the surviving driver might be charged with causing death by dangerous driving, contrary to Section Eight of the Road Traffic Act. This was a potentially serious offence, punishable by up to five years in prison, so often a Home Office pathologist was asked to carry out the post-mortem.

'He'd been drinking, doctor, no doubt of that! Our police surgeon was called to the nick late on Friday night to make him walk the chalk line.'

John Christie was the right-hand man of the local coroner, Richard's medical school pal, Brian Meredith, who was also a family doctor in Monmouth. The officer looked more like a prosperous farmer than a policeman, always attired in thorn-proof tweed suits with a matching trilby with a turned-down brim. He doubled up as the mortuary attendant in Monmouth, managing to assist in the dissection and restore the body without getting a drop of blood on his clothes – all with his hat firmly in place.

As Dr Meredith's coronial patch extended over most of east Monmouthshire, he also came down to Chepstow for post-mortems, but at that public mortuary there was a part-time assistant. Richard dealt with a sudden death from natural causes and a sleeping-pill overdose before going back to Garth House in time for his lunch.

Though Moira had cooked roast pork with apple sauce for Angela and himself, she was more concerned with giving him a message from Stow-on-the-Wold than with her culinary labours.

'Mr Lovesey rang to say that he had had some of the material you wanted from abroad,' she reported cheerily. 'Can you give him a ring as soon as you can, please?'

As he tackled his welcome meat and veg, Richard wondered what had arrived from foreign parts. As Germany was so much nearer than the centre of the United States, he thought it was more likely to be something from Wolfgang Braun in Cologne.

After his meal he hurried through their usual coffee session in the staffroom to get to the phone in his office and ring George Lovesey in Stow.

'Dr Pryor, I've had several responses from your requests for written material. One was from Germany, by mail – and another from Chicago.'

'That was quick work!' responded Richard. 'I didn't think anything could get here by mail that fast.'

'It didn't – at least only from London! Apparently, it was

sent by something called photo-telegraph service to a GPO office in London and they sent it on here by post.'

'That's extraordinary, but welcome. No sign of anything from Minnesota yet?'

'Afraid not, but I'll get these others to you as quickly as I can. If I sent them by taxi today, would you be able to study them tonight? Time is really pressing now.'

Richard readily agreed, and by the time that Siân and Moira had left for the day he had a large envelope delivered by a man driving a rather aged Austin Fourteen. He called Angela and they both sat in the kitchen with an extra pot of tea and some of Moira's home-made cheese straws, while they looked at what George Lovesey had sent.

The large envelope contained a smaller one with airmail stickers and West German stamps on it, together with another holding half a dozen pages of thin, rather brittle sheets covered in typescript and some graphs and tables.

'Funny-looking paper – the print is a bit blurred, but it's readable,' said Angela. The German envelope also had a few pages of regular paper, the typing obviously a carbon copy of an original. There were short covering letters from the senders, hoping that the accompanying material would be of some use.

'What happens next?' asked Angela as she began to read the missive from America.

'I've got to read it all and see if it helps to support my hypothesis,' he answered, looking intently at the pages from Cologne. 'Thank God it's in English. We'd be delayed again if we had to wait for a translation from German.'

They read steadily for ten minutes, then exchanged papers, absently drinking their tea between pages. 'Does it help?' asked Angela when they finally dropped the documents on the table.

Richard nodded. 'Just the job! I don't know how strong the evidence is for these chaps' own research – estimating the time of death – but that's no concern of mine in relation to our veterinary surgeon.'

'What happens next?' she asked again.

'I'll have to go through all this stuff carefully, then draft a summary of the aspects that we need for this defence. George Lovesey wants it urgently, to send to them and get affidavits

sworn and returned for submission to the court in Gloucester.'
'How's he going to do that in time? We haven't even had
the second lot from America.'
Her partner shook his head. 'That's his problem. I expect
he'll find a way – lawyers usually do, especially when they're
going to stick it all on the bill!'

Next morning Richard monopolized Moira and her typing
skills so completely that lunch had to be cold ham and salad.
He had spent all evening until midnight going through the
papers from Stow and roughing out drafts for affidavits. Now
Moira was banging out fair copies on her big Imperial as
Richard had arranged with the solicitor to take them to Stow
that afternoon.

For once, he was free, as there were no post-mortems at
his two regular mortuaries, though he had agreed to go next
morning to the big hospital in Newport. Here he had been
asked to act again as an independent pathologist over a death
in the operating theatre, as according to the coroner's officer
the relatives were unhappy.

When he had checked through the final copies, Richard
dropped them into his old oriental briefcase. 'Let's hope these
do the trick,' he murmured to Moira.

'You've got the other American one to deal with as well,'
she replied, getting up to start setting out lunch. 'I hope you
understand all that stuff. It's gibberish to me!'

'We've got to convince a court, so I'll have to put it over
as simply as I can,' he answered soberly. 'That's the problem
with our jury system. When it comes to technical evidence,
the jurors tend to switch off – or go to sleep!'

This led to an argument about whether the Continental
system of a trio of professional judges was better than the
Anglo-Saxon reliance on the good sense of a dozen solid citi-
zens. Angela was all for a jury, but Richard had his doubts.

'It's fine when it comes to straightforward facts, like whether
Bill was in the pub that night or whether Joe beat his wife,'
he argued. 'But start a long lecture about temperatures and
time of death or some obscure explanation about the concentration of some poison, then you've lost them. You really need
experts to evaluate expert evidence.'

Siân, always the champion of the common man, was

strongly with Angela, but Moira sided with Richard, saying that she had read in the newspaper about a fraud trial that was still going on after three months, with the bemused jury trapped under a welter of accounts and statistics. Soon after lunch, Richard decided he had better leave for Gloucestershire.

The Humber made good time across the full width of the big county, and he arrived at Stow soon after three o'clock. As soon as he was shown into the lawyer's chamber, George Lovesey rose to meet him, waving another sheaf of papers at him.

'Dr Pryor, the other American material has arrived! Almost as quickly as that telegraphed batch.'

Richard sat down on the other side of the desk and they exchanged documents. The lawyer began reading the draft affidavits that Pryor had written, while the pathologist pored over the notes that the researcher in Minnesota had sent. It was an outline for a future article to be submitted to the *American Journal of Forensic Sciences*, generally similar in concept to the ones from Chicago and Germany but with different experimental results in respect of timing death.

When he had finished studying his papers, the lawyer looked over his glasses at Richard Pryor.

'You've made it quite clear; even I can understand it!' he said warmly. 'But it seems that the three experts have come to somewhat different conclusions about the potassium levels. Is that going to be a problem for us? In cross-examination, prosecuting counsel will seize on any opportunity to discredit us.'

Richard nodded and tapped his own papers, the ones from Minnesota. 'I know what you mean, but happily that doesn't concern us. They can argue between themselves until the cows come home, about the implications of their findings, but that's not what matters to us.'

He explained at length what he meant, and eventually George Lovesey was satisfied. 'We'll have to have at least one pretrial conference with Nathan Prideaux to get this really sorted out,' he observed. 'Now what about the other prong of your attack on the prosecution case?'

'You mean Professor Lucius Zigmond? He seems the most authoritative person to fire that particular broadside.'

Lovesey waited for a few moments as one of his office staff had tapped the door and brought in the inevitable tray of tea and biscuits. When she had served them and left the room, he continued.

'As you suggested, I contacted him and he is quite happy to give a statement and attend court if necessary. He seemed quite tickled by the idea, especially when I mentioned the fee and expenses. I think you should go to see him, to explain exactly what is required. That seems to be the most effective way, given how short of time we are.'

Over the teacups, they discussed details of the affidavits, the solicitor suggesting a few editorial changes to fall in line with legal conventions. Then Richard settled down to write a version of the affidavit based on the new material from Minnesota. It was fairly straightforward, as it followed the others almost exactly, apart from substituting some of the different analytical data of the potassium concentrations in the eye fluids at varying periods after death. When they had agreed on final versions, Lovesey said that he would get his legal agents in London to send them by the fastest route, the one that the Chicago papers had arrived by.

'I hadn't realized that the GPO had this photo-telegraph service from London,' he said. 'Apparently, it's been there since 1935, but the place was bombed out during the war and they restarted it on the Victoria Embankment in 1948.'

'I've never heard of it either,' admitted Richard. 'Probably damned expensive, but useful.'

'It's used mainly for sending photographs for newspapers, but apparently it will accept text just as well,' explained George. 'Our agent can use it to send these drafts back to the three researchers, to save time. But, of course, the actual sworn statements will have to be airmailed back to us. The court would never accept anything but original signatures and the stamp of the attorneys who administered the oaths.'

Richard grinned to himself at the archaic language of the law, though he knew that medicine's vocabulary was just as mystical.

Before he left, he promised Lovesey that he would make arrangements to talk to Professor Zigmond in London and agree on a form of words that could be used in a deposition of the biochemist's evidence in court.

'Make it soon, doctor,' were the solicitor's final words. 'We'll be at the door of the Assize Court before we know it!'

SIXTEEN

The next day, Wednesday, was too busy with post-mortems for any expeditions to 'the Smoke', as Angela was fond of calling the city where she had worked for so many years.

However, Moira kept Thursday clear by phoning a couple of coroners' officers to postpone cases for a day, and by just after eight that morning Richard Pryor was on the up-platform at Newport Station waiting for the eight twenty-five to Paddington.

Thankfully, the crippling industrial disputes of the early summer, which had seen Fleet Street closed down and a total national rail strike for weeks back in June, were over, and the nationalized British Railways system was back to normal working.

He still found it thrilling to see the huge bulk of the Caerphilly Castle hauling the coaches of the daily Red Dragon as it rolled into the station, shaking the platform as it passed him. Brought up in a thrifty Welsh home, he usually travelled Third Class – not that he often went by train since he had returned to Britain and bought the Humber. However, as George Lovesey had pressed him to submit all his expenses, today he launched out with a First-Class ticket and settled back in one of the end coaches in relative luxury. He had thought of suggesting to Angela that she came with him and had a half day beating up the dress shops in the West End, but he could hardly claim for her on Lovesey's expenses, much as he would have enjoyed her company on a day out.

A copy of the *Western Mail* occupied him until Swindon, and as the great steam locomotive pounded along the second half of the journey he was content to look out of the window at the autumn scenery of the Thames Valley. He still found it slightly unreal, after some fourteen years of the lush colours of Ceylon and Malaya. Dead on time, the Red Dragon coasted into the smoky glass cupola of Paddington Station and Richard alighted, dawdling past the great engine as he walked up the platform. Like many of the men nearby, he gazed appreciatively at the huge driving wheels and massive connecting rods, sniffing the smoke and oil like some rare perfume.

He made for the Tube and took the Bakerloo Line to Piccadilly Circus. Richard was not all that familiar with London, but he had spent a few weeks there when he first joined the Royal Army Medical Corps, during hurried basic training at the RAM College at Millbank. That had been during the height of the Blitz, and his subsequent active service in the Far East had seemed like a holiday in comparison with London in 1941.

However, he knew some of the major teaching hospitals and was able to walk leisurely along the lower end of Piccadilly to Hyde Park Corner, where, on the other side of a daunting stream of traffic, the cream bulk of St George's Hospital stood. A solid early-Victorian building, it dominated the busy junction where Hyde Park, Green Park and Buckingham Palace Garden met.

Unwilling to risk his life crossing the road, he found a subway and came up near the hospital, where after a few enquiries he made his way to the medical school section and found the Clinical Biochemistry Department. Everywhere was cramped and overfilled with temporary cubicles for the ever-expanding staff, but eventually a secretary took pity on him and led him through corridors cluttered with equipment to a door hidden in a corner. A faded sign indicated that Professor L. Zigmond resided within.

Lucius Zigmond turned out to be a larger-than-life character, very Jewish and amiably rotund. Richard had spoken to him on the telephone when he had arranged this meeting, so he was prepared for his marked Central European accent, even though the medical directory had shown that he had been at St George's since 1937. A frizz of grey hair around a shiny bald head and a pair of small gold-rimmed glasses perched on the end of his large nose made him almost a cartoon version of an eccentric professor, aided by the crumpled white coat and a floppy bow tie. However, his keen eyes and direct manner were sharply at odds with his appearance.

As he shook hands and then dragged a hard chair out for Richard, he got straight to the point. 'Professor Pryor, nice to meet you. I gather you want my help in saving a man from the gallows?'

Richard went through his usual deprecating routine of saying that he had reverted to 'doctor' after giving up his university chair in Singapore. Though he had briefly explained the situation over the telephone, he now went through the problem in detail and described the two grounds on which he felt the prosecution medical evidence could be challenged.

Zigmond listened with genuine interest and seemed intrigued with the ongoing research from America and Germany that Richard described, especially when he produced copies of the papers obtained from abroad.

'It's not what you want from me, but fascinating all the same,' he enthused, peering keenly over his glasses. 'One works for years at a particular topic, without the faintest idea what other people might be doing by applying it to a new problem.'

This led them to despair about the 'compartmentalization' of science, where researchers beavered away at their own super-speciality, with no idea what others might be doing, which would have shed light on each other's problems.

Then Zigmond came back to the reason he was being asked for help. 'I'm basically a physiologist by training,' he explained. 'But I drifted into biochemistry by virtue of my interest in electrolyte balance – or more often imbalance!'

He handed back Richard's papers and picked up a letter he had been sent by George Lovesey. 'As a purely clinical biochemist, I've never been involved in any legal or forensic aspects of electrolytes, but there's always a first time.'

'You appreciate the task we have in defeating this allegation?' said Pryor cautiously. This man could run rings around him academically, and he didn't want to even hint that Zigmond was slow in grasping the problem. But the portly professor slapped his hand on a pile of three thick textbooks lying on his cluttered desk.

'With your idea, I think you've hit the nail on the head, Dr Pryor,' he said. 'That basic fact has been known for years, but no one had ever needed to attach much practical importance to it.'

He took the top book and opened it where he had stuck a folded envelope between the pages as a marker. Swivelling it around on the desk to face Richard, he jabbed a thick finger at a passage halfway down the page.

'Read that, will you?' he commanded. 'These other two standard texts on physiology and on electrolyte chemistry say the same thing.'

Richard read the passages, first in the book on the desk and then on the pages of the other two missives that Zigmond passed to him. When he had finished, he looked up. 'That seems cast iron to me,' he observed contentedly. 'If you can write a report to summarize the situation they describe, I'm sure our solicitor and counsel will be more than happy.'

He closed the last book and slid it across the desk. 'If you are called to give evidence, then naturally the court will want to see those books as corroboration.'

Lucius Zigmond nodded, his double chins wobbling above his spotted bow tie. 'Sure, as long as I get them back! The librarian here will have hysterics if they go missing.'

They talked for a time about the case and Zigmond also wanted to hear more details of the research from Cologne and the United States. He even wrote down the addresses of the authors, and Pryor suspected that he might well pursue the same line of investigation himself. St George's had a very well-respected forensic pathologist on its staff, Dr Donald Teare, one of the famous London three, the others being Keith Simpson and Francis Camps. Richard thought that Lucius would perhaps approach Teare to suggest some joint research, as it seemed well within his field of interest.

When they had talked the subject out, Richard rose to leave, knowing that the other man would be anxious to get on with his work – or possibly go to lunch, as it was now midday. Leaving with a promise to get George Lovesey to contact Zigmond over the details of the written statement, Pryor left and made his way out of the hospital. He had quite a few hours before he needed to get back to Paddington and decided to walk up to Wimpole Street, where he wanted to visit the library of the Royal Society of Medicine. He went back along Piccadilly to its famous circus, where the statue of Eros was back on its fountain, after its wartime evacuation. From there, he ambled up Regent Street, conscious of the mix of people he saw. Many were now smartly dressed, though there were some shabby figures and a few flat caps among the trilbies and occasional bowler hats. Though it was ten years since the end of the war, there were still some signs of bomb damage, behind builders' hoardings and cranes were now rebuilding the gaps.

The traffic was heavy and, being interested in cars, he recognized so many different makes, many of them still of pre-war vintage, as it was only now that new vehicles were becoming freely available. Most were British, though foreign ones were increasing in numbers, many of them unfamiliar to him.

On Oxford Street he decided he wanted something to eat and turned into one of Joe Lyons' Corner Houses, the famous white and gold facades welcoming hungry customers as they had for half a century. Upstairs, he found a table in the crowded restaurant and soon a 'Nippy' waitress took his order. Today's 'Special' was roast beef and Yorkshire pudding, with a plate of bread and butter, then 'spotted dick' and a pot of tea. He knew then that he really was back in Britain!

Sitting alone at the table made him wish again that Angela could have been with him, and he determined to bring her along next time he came to London. He sometimes wondered what had caused the drastic rift between Angela and her former fiancé that had made her so bitter about him. He recalled again the time when Paul Vickers, a detective superintendent in the Metropolitan Police had turned up at a post-mortem in Gloucester. Angela had frozen on the spot, then hurried out of the mortuary with no explanation. She had not mentioned it since, and he knew that the situation was a frequent source of speculation between Moira and Siân.

He poured himself another cup of tea, and his wandering mind seized on the unusual task that the War Office had given him. He wondered how far they had got with processing their case – perhaps the wife had given up, faced with the limitless legal resources of the government. Richard felt sorry for her and a little uneasy about being involved in the matter, but as with most other aspects of his work he was merely a technical adviser and had no part in the legal or especially moral aspects of any case. If he didn't apply his expertise to the issue and give his best shot at it, they'd soon find someone else who would. He had enough ego and professional confidence in himself to think that he would give as good as – and probably better – an opinion than someone else and at least it would be honest and unbiased.

He looked at his wristwatch, a genuine Eterna bargained

for in Change Alley in Singapore, and made his way to the cash desk.

Outside, he was temporarily disorientated but soon moved westwards down Oxford Street until he turned up to Henrietta Place and found the imposing Royal Society of Medicine building and the corner of Wimpole Street. He had become an overseas member when in Singapore and now was able to use their extensive library. He spent an hour searching 'Index Medicus', now a quarterly cumulative index of all significant scientific publications in the field of medicine. He had pored over copies in the medical school libraries at Cardiff and Bristol, but, in the hope that the RSM had a more recent copy, he thumbed through it again on the principle that he should leave no stone unturned in seeking anything new about potassium metabolism and toxicity.

He was out of luck, but while he was there he refreshed his knowledge of gunshot wounds from several forensic textbooks that he didn't possess himself. The time went by, and with a start he realized that he had better get himself back to Paddington. This time he launched out on a taxi, the noisy pre-war Austin weaving its way through the late-afternoon traffic to drop him off in Praed Street with a quarter of an hour to spare. The compartment he found was almost full, but First Class was still comfortable and he had a photograph of Torquay and a map of the Western Region to stare at when he was not looking out of the window at the Thames Valley rushing past. By the time he collected the Humber from the station car park at Newport and drove home, the October evening was drawing towards dusk. Angela had waited for him before having supper, though the table was already set.

'Moira was bustling about. She thought you'd be in need of a proper meal after your adventures in the big, bad city,' she said with a hint of sarcasm. 'So she's left a steak and kidney pie in the warming oven and there are peas and carrots in saucepans on the top.'

As she again broke her vow never to become domesticated by serving up their meal on to warmed plates, Richard found glasses and a bottle of their favourite cider that Jimmy obtained from someone he knew across the valley in the Forest of Dean.

They settled to eat, and Angela teased him again about Moira.

'I don't know if she's mothering you or whether she reckons the way to man's heart is through his stomach, but she certainly fusses over you like a hen with chicks.'

She speared a piece of kidney with her fork. 'I wish someone would fuss over me a bit more,' she said rather wistfully.

Richard rose to the bait, though he kept well away from the sensitive subject of her ex-boyfriend.

'You could have come with me, had a day in London. Next time, eh?'

He looked at her mane of brown hair as she bent over her plate and wondered if she was finding this new life in Wales too lonely, after the hustle and bustle of London.

'If this War Office job comes off, I'm sure we'll have to go up there to sort it out,' he said earnestly. 'We could stay the night – even a weekend if it's necessary.'

She looked up, her handsome face smiling at him. 'Are you propositioning me for a dirty weekend, Dr Pryor?' she demanded. 'Because if I can have a few hours window-shopping in Bond Street as well, I accept without hesitation!'

He grinned at her, feeling at ease with her over such light-hearted banter, though a part of him wished there might be some truth in her coquettish response.

'Better not let Moira hear you say that; she'd be shocked. You know how strait-laced she can be.'

Angela looked at him scornfully. 'Come off it, Richard! We've been sleeping in the same house without a chaperone for six months now. Do you imagine that Moira – or Siân, for that matter – hasn't been speculating every day about our relationship?'

He looked at her in genuine surprise. 'Never thought about it, to be honest.'

She shook her head in despair. 'Men! I think you mean that, Richard! Don't you ever think of anything other than dead bodies and your damned grapevines?'

She got up to take their plates to the sink, and as she passed him she ruffled his hair. 'You're like a big schoolboy, Richard Pryor. But you're not a bad chap, really.'

By the time she had brought cheese and biscuits as their dessert, the moment of relative intimacy had passed and he began telling her about his meeting with Lucius Zigmond.

'Not that there's all that much to report, apart from the fact that if he's needed he's quite happy to turn up in court and say his piece. He seemed quite tickled by the idea, actually.'

Richard told her about the textbooks that the professor had shown him. 'Apparently, it's all standard stuff in the physiology and biochemical world, been known for years.'

'Then it's a wonder that the prosecution hadn't cottoned on to it,' complained Angela. 'I suppose it would have torpedoed their case even before it started.'

Richard cut himself a slice of Double Gloucester and took a couple of water biscuits. 'Zigmond and I talked about this, the watertight boxes that science is divided into. You can be a Nobel Prize winner in one speciality and a complete ignoramus in another.'

They chatted away amiably over coffee in her sitting room as darkness fell over the quiet valley outside. 'What happens next in the vet case?' asked Angela. 'Are you going to meet this fancy QC again before the trial?'

'Yes, George Lovesey said we'd have to have a final conference once all the affidavits are in. He must be working his staff hard in Stow, getting letters and telegrams going hither and thither to Germany and the States.'

'Must be a bit of a change for a country solicitor,' observed Angela. 'He probably spends most his time conveyancing expensive cottages and writing leases on farms!'

They progressed from coffee to their usual gin and tonic, though Richard was beginning to feel ready for his bed after a long day in London.

'No news from the War Office chaps, I suppose?' he asked sleepily as he sank further into the comfortable old armchair.

Angela shook her head. 'Not a word yet, by phone or mail. I suppose they're trying to persuade either the widow or the Home Office to allow an exhumation.'

'Can't really do a thing without that,' agreed Richard. 'The poor woman can't win her case and the War Office can't defend one, so it seems a stalemate. I wonder if they're getting that bullet from the Gulf. The way that place operates, they've probably lost it down a drain by now.'

'I feel very sorry for her,' said Angela sympathetically. 'And our crusading Siân is a bit annoyed that we're acting on the side of the new Tory government, which she says is trying to sabotage the wife's claim.'

'I can see the woman's anger over the suspicion that it was a deliberate shooting by this staff sergeant,' said Richard. 'Not that that seems all that likely to me. But compensation for his death, over and above her normal pension, seems a bit out of order, unless it was due to some negligence on the part of the army.'

His partner bridled a little at this. 'Why not, if she lost her husband and his very good rate of pay as a warrant officer?'

Richard turned up his hands in defence. 'Sure, if there was any fault on the part of the War Office, such as bad training, or equipment failure or recklessness. But unfortunately soldiers are being killed every day in other parts of the world, like Malaya, Cyprus and Kenya. Their relatives are not suing the government, as being in the armed forces is a dangerous business.'

Angela didn't seem convinced, but, as Richard pointed out, their job was to establish the physical facts and leave the morals and the law to others. They finished their drinks, and Richard hauled himself out of the chair, leaving Angela to wait for the start of a BBC Symphony Orchestra concert on the Third Programme.

She was keen on classical music, especially Mozart and Vivaldi – a little over the top for Richard, who was more a male-voice choir and light opera fan. He left her to her large Marconi radiogram, which stood next to a rack of records, and went to his office, where he wanted to look at the day's mail before having a shower and going to bed.

However, he was seduced by a copy of the *Practical Viniculture* magazine which had arrived that day. Fifteen minutes later, he was sound asleep in his chair. He awoke two hours later with a crick in his neck and dragged himself off to bed, with the faint sounds of a recording of the *Jupiter* symphony coming from Angela's room.

SEVENTEEN

I t was the following Tuesday before the usual routine of the Garth House partnership was disturbed. The coroner's officer in Brecon phoned to say that a double inquest on the two deaths at Ty Croes Farm was to be held on Friday and that both Richard Pryor and Dr Bray would be required as witnesses.

'Why on earth do they want me, I wonder?' asked Angela. 'Apart from collecting some material for the Cardiff lab, I had nothing really to do with it.'

'It's a day out in beautiful countryside,' said Richard cheerily. 'And there'll be a fee – probably enough for a couple of cups of coffee, given it's only a coroner's court.'

For some time Siân had been dropping hints about wanting to visit a court of law, where she could see how her efforts in the laboratory were sometimes used. Angela suggested to Richard that the Brecon inquest might be a good introduction for her, as they were keen to encourage her enthusiasm for all things forensic. The young blonde was as pleased as if they had given her a salary rise – which they had not long ago, as it happened.

But before the great day arrived, more news came in about their other cases. A large registered envelope came from Stow-on-the-Wold, containing copies of the expert opinion written by Professor Zigmond and a copy of the sworn affidavit from Wolfgang Braun in Cologne. George Lovesey wanted Richard to make a careful check of the wording to make sure that there would be no hitches when they were presented in evidence.

'No sign yet of the American opinions?' asked Angela as he retreated to his office to go through the documents.

'Should be here soon, if airmail performs as well as last time,' he replied. 'I expect George is biting his fingernails every time he looks at the calendar.'

An hour later, satisfied that every word, comma and full stop was acceptable, Richard rang the solicitor in Stow and reassured him that the affidavits seemed in perfect order.

'You don't have to disclose these to the prosecution in advance, then?' he asked out of curiosity.

'No, but once we offer them in evidence, they could ask the judge for an adjournment to discuss the spanner we've thrown in the works. They could even ask for time for their experts to investigate our new propositions.'

Richard heard him clear his throat over the telephone and suspected he was in for a legal lecture.

'There's been unease about these "surprise defences", as they're called, among the law lords and the legal pundits in Parliament,' he explained. 'I suspect that one of these days there'll be a change in legal procedure to make advance notice of new evidence compulsory, but at the present time we can spring it on them.'

Lovesey confirmed that his leading counsel, the flamboyant Nathan Prideaux QC, had been kept abreast of Richard's efforts and was happy with the way in which things were progressing. 'He wants another conference before trial, but I haven't got a date yet. I'll be in touch with you again as soon as this material comes from the United States.'

After the call, Richard felt unsettled, as keeping track of several cases at once called for some mental agility. The murder-suicide near Brecon was now a straightforward clearing-up exercise, as there was no question of anyone being prosecuted, but the veterinary surgeon threatened with judicial execution, and the strange matter of the soldier shot through the head, seemed to be hanging over him like a cloud. To divert himself, he got up from his desk and wandered into the office and then through into the laboratory to take his mind off these problems.

'What are you doing this morning, Siân?' he asked as he stood behind his technician, who was seated before several rows of test tubes in racks.

'This is new, doctor! Water analysis, not exactly forensic, but it's all grist to the mill.'

Angela called across from her bench on the other side of the large room. 'Jimmy got that work, bless him!' she explained.

'Some of his farmer friends up near Trelleck have had bore-holes drilled on their land for a water supply and they want to make sure that they're not going to poison themselves or their cattle. It's mostly spot tests for dissolved metals.'

Siân swung round on her stool, a pipette in one hand.

'Jimmy says that there may well be a number of other farmers wanting an analysis, if we can do it cheaper than the big labs elsewhere.'

Richard moved over to his partner's section, where all the biological work was done. 'More paternity tests?' he asked.

'No, it's an insurance job,' replied Angela, looking up from a microscope. 'The owner of a fur shop in Bristol has claimed thousands for stolen mink coats, but their insurance investigator has sent in fibres from a suspect van belonging to the owner's cousin.'

'You've got to identify them, have you?'

She nodded. 'They're animal fur, right enough. I'll have to try to narrow it down to mink, if I can find the right references. Anyway, the cousin said he used the van only for carrying carpets, so it's obviously an insurance fraud.'

He squatted on a nearby stool, pleased to hear how they were diversifying their business.

'It's good to know we're expanding into the civil side, not just coroners' and police work. There must be lots of other problems out there that we can help with.'

Angela readily agreed. 'And the other good thing is that we're getting almost all our new cases by word of mouth – usually solicitors recommending us to one another. Nothing to beat the old boy network, is there?'

'Perhaps you'd better join the Freemasons and the local Rotary Club, doctor!' called Siân from her bench. 'My dad says that's where all the power lies these days.'

Richard grinned at Angela at the thought of getting business advice from a red-hot trade unionist like Evan Lloyd, then took himself back to his office to check the last batch of post-mortem reports which Moira had just typed.

Half an hour later his phone rang, switched through from Moira's office next door. When a few months earlier Post Office Telephones had extended the single line to the phone in the hall, they had put a simple switching device in her office, so that she could divert a call to either the laboratory or to Richard's room.

'It's the War Office!' she hissed in a conspiratorial whisper before connecting the call.

'Gordon Lane here, Dr Pryor.' The voice of the Crown

solicitor came across the ether. 'We've made some progress, I'm glad to say. The first thing is that the bullet has arrived from Al Tallah. We've got it in a jar in the office here, safely wrapped in cotton wool.'

'Good. I suggest you ask your ordnance experts in Woolwich to examine it, but I'd like to have a look at it first,' said Richard. 'What was the second thing?'

'That's the point of ringing, as we also have had consent from both the widow and the Home Office for an exhumation. I wanted to arrange a date with you.'

Richard Pryor was surprised at the speedy action, which normally could take weeks or even months. 'That's very quick work, Mr Lane! How did you manage that?' he asked, perhaps impertinently. The lawyer sounded a little evasive.

'There are ways and means within government, doctor. Anyway, the widow's solicitor saw that they were not going to get any further with their claim if they refused – and the coroner for Northolt, where the body came in by air, said that it was none of his concern as he had declined to hold an inquest.'

'So that left just the Home Office?'

'Yes, and even they were somewhat uncertain about their jurisdiction as this was an army incident that occurred abroad. However, to be on the safe side they rubber-stamped the appropriate forms, so we can proceed.'

Richard thought rapidly, as the Gloucester trial was now less that a fortnight away. He had the Brecon inquest this week, so that ruled out the next few days.

'I think it will have to be one day next week, Mr Lane. As far as I recall, the body is buried in south-east London?'

'Yes, in Lewisham municipal cemetery.'

'Where could we take it for a post-mortem, somewhere that has decent facilities?' asked Richard.

'I've discussed this with Paul Bannerman, who's leading this case. He suggests the Queen Alexandra Military Hospital in Millbank. Perhaps you know it, having been an RAMC officer?'

'I know where it is, certainly. Very near the Royal Army Medical College, with the Tate Gallery between them.'

'Paul Bannerman is still a serving officer, so I'm sure he can arrange matters with the hospital commandant. Which day would suit you best?'

Richard decided that Wednesday would be as good as any

other, and the solicitor promised to ring back to confirm a time.

'We'll have to make arrangements with the cemetery for the exhumation and also for transport from Lewisham to Millbank.'

After he had rung off, Richard went to report to his partner. 'Trip to London next week, Angela. Know anything about bullets?' He repeated what Lane had told him.

'I'm a biologist, not a firearms examiner,' she said. 'But I've picked up a bit of the jargon and mystique from listening to them in the Met Lab over the years.'

'Good enough. You can look at the thing with me next week. I've got a feeling about what could have happened, but first I need to look at that wound.'

At lunchtime he told Moira and Siân about the developments, but neither of them wanted to join Angela on a trip to London.

'Must be horrid, an exhumation,' said Moira with an expression of disgust. 'How long has the poor chap been buried?'

'Only a few months – and he was embalmed first, so he'll be almost as good as new.'

'I'm happy to be coming to that inquest with you, doctor,' said Siân. 'And I saw a couple of post-mortems when I worked in the hospital lab. But I draw the line at exhumations!'

That evening Richard talked to Angela about the arrangements for the following week. 'We're not going to get our dirty weekend, I'm afraid. But as the exhumation is bound to be in the morning, we'll have to travel up on Tuesday.'

Angela made a mock pout. 'Oh, and I was looking forward to a sinful Saturday night!'

His lean face broke into one of his famous grins. 'We may as well make a day of it, so we'll go up early on the Red Dragon and you can have the afternoon to hit the shops while I go to the BMA library to see if they've got anything I missed elsewhere.'

'Oh, you're so masterful, Richard! The romantic BMA library!' In a playful mood, she pretended to swoon.

'Stop taking the mickey, lady!' he commanded. 'We've got to decide on somewhere to stay. I suppose the Great Western Hotel at Paddington is the easiest, especially as we're not footing the bill.'

Serious again, she nodded. 'Sounds fine to me. Better get Moira to book a couple of rooms there. Knowing her, she'll make sure that they're on different floors at opposite ends of the building!'

On Friday they set off in the Humber at eight thirty, as the inquest was to start at half past ten. Siân arrived early and they left Garth House in almost a picnic mood, in spite of the sombre nature of the event. The technician sat in the back, enjoying the ride in a large, comfortable car, for there was no such luxury in her household. Though Siân was a very mature, self-possessed woman of twenty-four, for a few moments Richard had a fantasy that she was their daughter, with Mum and Dad sitting sedately in the front!

It was a nice day, getting cooler as the autumn took hold, but dry and sunny between breaks in the cloud. As they drove up to Monmouth, then along the A40 through Abergavenny and Crickhowell to Brecon, they all revelled in the lovely countryside of Monmouthshire, then the grandeur of the Usk Valley through the Beacons. Apart from her one visit to the crime scene, this area was new to Angela. She had been brought up in the flatter Home Counties and today she had the leisure to better appreciate the Welsh scenery. As for Siân, she was entranced, as being a child during the war, with all the shortages and restrictions – and no car in the family – her excursions had been mainly to Barry Island and Porthcawl, with a few holidays in Gower or Ilfracombe.

Brecon came all too quickly and soon they were driving up The Watton into the town, past the grim nineteenth-century barracks that was the depot of the South Wales Borderers.

'That's where that young lad who found the body is being called up to National Service this week,' said Richard. 'Let's hope he enjoys it, though he'll find it a lot different from mending tractors on a farm.'

'Won't he have to be at the inquest?' asked Siân.

'Yes, I'm sure he will. But he won't have far to go, for we're there already.'

On their left, at an angle to the main road, was another massive early Victorian building, the Shire Hall, with its classical portico of four fluted columns supporting a trian-gular pediment.

The coroner's officer was in the forecourt, and he waved them in to a parking place behind the iron railings.

'I kept you a place, doctor. There'll be a fair crowd here today. It's not often we get a murder.'

Billy Brown led them up the steps into the impressive building and into the main courtroom, a forbidding place panelled in dark wood, explaining as he went.

'The coroner usually holds inquests in the magistrates' court or even in his own office, if there are only a few witnesses. But today he's borrowed the courtroom. Normally, it's kept for sittings of the Assizes and Quarter Sessions.'

A high panelled bench dominated the front of the court, below which was a desk for the clerk and a large central table with benches for the lawyers. The witness box was to one side near a couple of rows of pews for the jury. On the opposite side there was more seating and a place for the press. The rest of the large, high chamber was filled with benches for witnesses and the public – Siân was reminded of the interior of her Methodist chapel in Chepstow.

Billy Brown shepherded them into a pew just behind the lawyers' table, where a florid middle-aged man in a dark suit and a wing collar sat with a thin file of papers. Three journalists were squeezed into a narrow space on the opposite side of the court from the jury benches. One was a bald man with a large red nose, another an anaemic-looking girl and the last a bored-looking young man with severe acne.

In the row behind the forensic team, the four members of the Evans and Morton families were sitting silently, dressed in their Sunday clothes, the men displaying black ties and Betsan and Rhian in suitably black or grey outfits.

The chamber was partly filled with some farming neighbours from Cwmcamlais, together with members of the public attracted by the morbid thrill of a murder-suicide in this usually peaceful area. There were several uniformed constables at the back of the court, and five minutes after the Garth House party arrived Detective Inspector Arthur Crippen and his sergeant slipped into the other end of their pew, nodding a greeting at the Garth House group. Just before the large old clock on one wall reached ten thirty, the coroner's officer shepherded in half a score of people to act as jurors. They filed self-consciously into the two rows of hard benches, eight men in their best suits and a couple of women in shapeless hats. Billy Brown vanished, then reappeared from a side door and came up to whisper to Richard Pryor.

'The coroner would like a word before we start, doctor.' He led Richard up to the front bench and lifted a flap in the corner. A few steps led up to the judicial platform, then through a door at the side into the judge's chamber.

The coroner was Charles Matthews – as usual, a local solicitor. A tall, thin man, he could only be described as 'grey', as he was grey-haired, had a grey walrus moustache and wore a grey suit. Even his complexion seemed grey, but he was a courteous and affable man. As he shook hands, he thanked Richard for his prompt and expert assistance in this matter.

'I just wanted to meet you and explain that I am keeping the inquest as low-key as possible, doctor. This tragic case has the potential to cause serious embarrassment to respectable people living in what is a very tight-knit rural community. I see no merit in offering the press a lot of irrelevant detail, given that there is no possibility of any further legal action.'

They chatted for a moment longer, Matthews expressing genuine interest in the new venture in the Wye Valley and promising to bear them in mind when he or any of his legal colleagues in the area had need of forensic advice.

Gratified by this promise of future work, Richard took his leave and got back to his seat before the inquest began.

Billy Brown appeared inside the side door and, in a stentorian voice that seemed loud for his short stature, demanded that all should rise.

The coroner hurried in clutching a sheaf of papers and sat himself in the large central chair, normally occupied by a High Court judge or the chairman of the Quarter Sessions. His officer then called the court to order with the traditional exhortation.

'Oyez, oyez, oyez, all persons having anything to do before the Queen's coroner for the County of Brecon, touching the deaths of Thomas Littleman and Mostyn Dewi Evans, draw near and give your attendance!'

Before anything else was commenced, the lawyer at the table rose to his feet and announced to the coroner that he was Maldwyn Prosser, a solicitor holding a watching brief for the Evans family. As his practice was directly across the street

from Charles Matthews' own law office, the coroner was well aware of his identity, but the professional niceties had to be maintained.

The next task was to swear in the jury, and Billy walked along the two rows of benches, giving a battered copy of the New Testament to each juror as he came to them.

'Take the book in your right hand and read the words on the card.'

A piece of pasteboard stuck out of the book and, in either halting words or more confident bravado, each person stood up and swore by Almighty God that they would diligently 'a true presentment make according to the evidence'.

When they had settled down again, the coroner leaned forward and regarded them over his half-moon spectacles.

'Ladies and gentlemen, there are two inquests to be dealt with today, but as they are inextricably linked I am taking them together, though at the conclusion you must provide me with two separate verdicts.'

He then asked the jury to choose their foreman, and a portly, red-faced local butcher was appointed.

'Undoubtedly, all of you must have heard about this sad occurrence in Cwmcamlais, but you must put out of your mind anything you have heard or read and consider only what yo' will hear in this courtroom today.'

He leaned back and shuffled his papers unnecessarily b' continuing.

'A coroner's inquest is concerned with only fou' Who, where, when and by what means someone ca' death. In addition, I have the power under the la' any person you consider guilty of criminally c death for trial in a higher court. However, I c that this will not arise today, so it is only need consider.'

He nodded at Billy Brown, who mov' witness box, his trusty New Testamer

'The first witness is Shane Willia' turned to watch the former apprer the court and step up into the w' wood.

He wore an ill-fitting khaki ba' days of service in Her Majesty's arm'

Shane had been sitting halfway up the chamber, alongside the impressive figure of a sergeant major in the uniform of the South Wales Borderers, and the general impression was that it was with reluctance that the army had let such a raw recruit escape his penal servitude for an hour or two.

The youth mumbled his way through a different oath printed on the same card, swearing by the same Almighty God that he would tell the truth, the whole truth and nothing but the truth.

Richard glanced past Angela to look at Siân and saw that she was transfixed by the proceedings, which brought to life all she had read about courts in newspapers and novels or heard on the radio.

'Wait until we take her to the Assizes,' he whispered to Angela. 'She'll be in ecstasy then with wigs and gowns!'

His partner banged his knee with hers to shut him up, as the coroner began questioning Shane Williams. The former worker at Ty Croes stumbled through a description of when and how he had found the body, and confirmed that it was indeed that of Tom Littleman. Matthews avoided any probing into Shane's knowledge of any disputes between the dead man and any other persons at the farm. There was little else to be said and, after a short description of the barn and its contents and the position and state of the Fordson tractor, the coroner finished with Shane. He invited the family solicitor to ask any questions, but this was declined and Shane left the witness box with obvious relief. As he came back into the body of the court, the immaculate sergeant rose and reclaimed his recruit, marching him off as if he was under arrest.

At this stage the coroner instructed his officer to hand a im album of photographs to the jury, to be passed around ong them.

These are not very pleasant, but I'm afraid you need to w what was found in this barn at Ty Croes Farm, as will scribed by the next witnesses,' explained Matthews.

y huddled over the pictures as they went along the two s. Although the coroner had excluded the more gory several of the men looked queasy at the sight, though women did not turn a hair, studying the details with relish.

Crippen was called next and, scorning the card, held

the Testament high in the air and rattled off the oath with the familiarity of thirty years' experience in the courts.

He then described the scene in the barn when he was called by the uniformed officers and, with the jury following his account on their photographs, led them through the relevant points of the tractor, the scattered wooden blocks and the position of the chain hoist hanging from the roof.

The next witness was Aubrey Evans, who was dealt with quite briefly but sympathetically by Charles Matthews. He formally confirmed that the dead man was Thomas Littleman and, on being further questioned, said that he knew almost nothing of the man's background, except that he had been an army mechanic and had worked at Ty Croes Farm for several years.

The coroner then explained to the jury that efforts by the police to trace any relatives had failed.

'Military records showed that he was born in London and had joined the Regular Army at the age of eighteen. His parents were dead and he had no brothers or sisters. No other family has made themselves known, so that disposal of the body has been left to the local authority.'

After stating that the dead man had last been seen alive on the previous evening, Aubrey Evans left the witness box, the coroner having carefully avoided any questions about his own family, and the next witness was Richard Pryor.

Angela had been in court with him previously, but she listened again to see how he conducted himself. Siân was on the edge of her seat, enthralled by her boss being the centre of attention for a few minutes.

After taking the oath in a steady, serious voice, he identified himself and gave the Garth House address.

'Your qualifications are a Doctor of Medicine and a Bachelor of Surgery?' asked Matthews. Richard agreed and added that he also held a Diploma in Clinical Pathology.

'You are also a consultant pathologist to the Home Office?' added the coroner, to make it clear to the jury that the witness was an expert.

After these formalities, Richard explained how he had been called to the scene and what he had found there.

'The dead man had severe injuries to the neck region, but these were caused after death. They were insufficient to conceal

a ligature mark on the neck which indicated that he had actually been hanged.'

There was a buzz of astonishment in the court, and the three
reporters suddenly jerked themselves into more rapid scrib-
bling in their notebooks.

This was further increased when he then calmly announced
that even that was not the cause of death, but that the victim
had been manually strangled before being hanged.

The coroner led him into an explanation of the proof of
these remarkable deductions, and Richard described the
settling of the blood in the legs and arms which showed that
the body had been in a vertical position for a considerable
time after death, which had probably occurred during the
previous night.

'And you ascertained where this hanging had taken place,
doctor?' asked the coroner.

'It seemed likely that it was from the hook of that hoist
you can see in the photographs. There would have to have
been something like a rope as well, which was confirmed by
laboratory examination.'

After a few more questions about the lack of natural disease
as a contribution to death, Richard stood down, the coroner
indicating that he would recall him later. Then Billy Brown
invited Dr Angela Bray to the witness box. In a trim navy-
blue suit and a small tilted hat, all dark enough for the sombre
occasion, she stood calmly erect and took the oath with practised ease. Charles Matthews, who seemed very taken with this
elegant scientist, invited her to be seated, but she gracefully
declined. He then got her to declare her professional qualifications and the fact that she was a former senior scientist in
the Metropolitan Police Laboratory, which again stimulated
some whispers and more rapid note-taking on the press bench.

She explained that she had been present at the scene in the
capacity of a professional colleague to Dr Pryor and that
she was not the official forensic scientist.

Matthews rather brushed this aside and said that no doubt the
investigating officers were very glad to have someone of such
experience and expertise at the scene. Angela then said that she
had removed some fibres from the neck of the dead man and
caused them to be sent to the Cardiff laboratory for examination, together with various samples of rope from the barn.

The coroner nodded wisely and followed this up. 'I have not thought it necessary to bring anyone from that laboratory up to Brecon today, given that you are present, Dr Bray. So perhaps you could read out the report they prepared on the samples you had recovered.'

He gave his officer a sheet of paper, which Billy handed to Angela. She studied this before reading it verbatim, then explaining its significance for the benefit of the jury.

'It means that the fibres I recovered from the skin of the neck were examined under a microscope and by various other tests and were found to be identical with fibres from two of the lengths of rope that were recovered from the barn.'

'Does that indicate that one of those lengths was used to hang the deceased, doctor?' asked the coroner.

Angela shook her head. 'One can't be definite, sir. Sisal rope varies widely in type, but no doubt there are many other coils in this county which are identical. The ropes from the barn were examined at Cardiff for any traces of skin, but none were identified. It would be very difficult to find such tiny fragments on long lengths.'

Matthews nodded wisely. 'But it shows, does it not, that a rope of this nature had been wrapped around the neck?'

Angela agreed. 'Also, the laboratory applied sticky tape to the hook of the hoist you described and found identical fibres caught on the rusty surface. Of course, they may have come from previous legitimate use in the workshop, but it seems to point to the use of that hoist to suspend the body.'

'Is there anything else you can tell us, Dr Bray?'

'We analysed samples of blood and urine retained from the body and found that there was a moderate amount of alcohol present. It was enough to hamper a person's ability to drive a vehicle safely, but in my opinion well below the level likely to make him obviously inebriated.'

The coroner seemed rather reluctant to let this elegant witness leave the box, but, after receiving profuse thanks, Angela stepped down.

'He seems quite taken with her,' Siân whispered to her boss. 'But I don't think he's her type!' she added with a grin.

The coroner then explained to the jurors that he would move on to the second part of the double inquest, so that they could

understand the sequence of events. He recalled Arthur Crippen
and reminded him that he was already on oath.

'Detective inspector, I understand that you made extensive
enquiries into this matter over the course of the next few
days?'

Crippen related how his officers had interviewed all the
family members and neighbours within a reasonable distance,
without making any progress.

'Enquiries were also made in Brecon, at the flat where the
deceased lived, as well as with the army authorities in relation to Littleman's past history,' he added.

As Arthur had also had a pre-inquest chat with the coroner,
he avoided mentioning the revelations about the victim's
amorous relations with the two women in the family. At this
point, Betsan and Rhian sat immobile in the court, hardly
daring to breathe, even though Crippen had explained to them
that the coroner had decided that in view of subsequent events
he saw no reason to parade embarrassing family matters for
the delectation of the press.

Charles Matthews then led the detective through the finding
of Mostyn Evans' body in the same barn and the obvious
supposition that he had killed himself.

This time it was Jeff Morton who was to identify the body.
He was called to nervously relate how he had heard a distant
shotgun discharge and gone to investigate.

'One look was enough to know who it was. And I recognized the four-ten as belonging to Uncle Mostyn,' he said. 'So
I shut the door and ran back to ring the police.'

Both he and his cousin Aubrey testified that they had
no idea of Mostyn's actions and that he had not given the
slightest indication of committing suicide, so the coroner then
recalled Richard Pryor, again reminding him that he was still
on oath.

The pathologist gave a brief summary of his findings,
describing death as having been caused virtually instantaneously
by a shotgun wound to the throat which had penetrated the
brain.

'Mr Evans also suffered from an advanced cancer of the
prostate gland, which had already spread into his bones,' he
added.

Matthews followed up his report with a few additional

questions. 'Doctor, is there any doubt in your mind that this gunshot was self-inflicted?'

Richard shook his head, feeling on safe ground given that a suicide note had been left.

'None at all, sir. The position of the wound was one of the prime "sites of election" for suicide. The gun had been resting against the skin, leaving a partial muzzle impression. I measured the length of the weapon from muzzle to trigger and it could easily have been fired by the deceased.'

The coroner turned over a sheet of paper on his desk and nodded. 'I see that only the fingerprints of Mostyn Evans were found on the shotgun.'

Richard Pryor finished his report by confirming that the body contained no alcohol or drugs and that the time that Jeff Morton heard the gunshot was consistent with the time-of-death examination that he himself had made on arriving at the farm later that afternoon.

Once again, the family's solicitor had no questions, and Richard went back to sit with Angela and Siân.

The coroner then applied himself to the jury, peering at them over his glasses. 'The only remaining evidence is what you might well consider the most important and revealing,' he began, holding up a couple of pages of pale blue notepaper.

'This letter was found on the ground near the body, addressed to me. I have no intention of making it public, as it contains very personal family issues which I see no reason to divulge, as the rest of the very full description of the circumstances seem to me to be more than adequate for the purposes of this inquest.'

There was again a low buzz around the court, and one of the reporters hurriedly turned over a page of his notebook in preparation for his scoop of the month.

'In this letter, Mr Mostyn Evans acknowledges that he had a terminal illness, which, incidentally, he had concealed from his family. He then admits that he had killed Thomas Littleman on the night before the body was discovered, the motive being a personal dispute about which I do not propose to elaborate. Suffice it to say that Mostyn Evans knew that he had only a short time to live due to his fatal illness and decided that he would settle his dispute with Littleman and then kill himself.'

Again the coroner peered intently at his jury as if defying

them to challenge his decision. 'Of course, if this was a murder trial in the Assize Court, every scrap of information would have to be presented in the cause of justice. But again I emphasize that this is an inquest, not a trial. We are here to determine who, where, when and by what means these two men came to their deaths – and I feel you have ample evidence before you to come to a conclusion.'

Aftei delivering this homily, he briefly summarized the evidence they had heard about the two deaths and then charged the jury with providing verdicts on each victim, offering them the choices of natural causes, accident, suicide or unlawful killing.

The result was never in doubt, and within minutes, after a muttered consultation between the ten stalwart Breconians, the beefy butcher rose and provided Charles Matthews with what he wanted.

After expressing his sympathy to the families from Ty Croes and thanking the jury and witnesses for their help, Billy Brown asked the court to rise and the coroner gathered up his papers and left through the door at the side of the bench.

Outside, Arthur Crippen and Detective Sergeant Nichols were standing talking with the two couples from the farm, but broke away for a moment to say goodbye to the Garth House team.

'Thanks for your help, doctors, you did a grand job for us,' said Crippen. 'If the opportunity to use you again comes up, we'll look forward to seeing you!'

As they walked towards the gates, the coroner's officer also thanked them and recommended the Wellington Hotel if they wanted some lunch. This was a large Georgian building just up from the Shire Hall, one of the focal points of the small town. As it was now noon, Richard steered his colleagues towards it and treated them to a celebratory meal.

As they sat over their oxtail soup in the old-fashioned dining room, Angela asked Siân what she thought of her first visit to a court.

'Great, it's all so medieval!' she enthused. 'That business of the coroner's officer chanting the "Oyez" bit! Do they always do that?'

Richard grinned. 'It's dying out, but often in the country courts the coroner's officer likes to have his say. Wait until you go to the Assizes, then you'll see scarlet robes, wigs and velvet breeches!'

'Can I come to the Gloucester trial when you go, doctor?' she asked, almost like a child wanting to visit a funfair.

'I think Moira has booked a visit there, but I might have to go for more than one day, so be good and I'll see what I can do!'

Over their gammon steaks with egg and pineapple, a treat that had only come back on the menu in the last couple of years, Angela remarked on the skilful way in which the coroner had avoided the embarrassing background to Littleman's death.

'I'll bet the jury were bursting to know what was in that suicide letter,' she said. 'There'll be some tongues wagging in the neighbourhood tonight, all with their theories about what was really going on at that farm.'

Richard speared a chip with his fork. 'I think he cut a few legal corners this morning – but who's to stop him? Coroners are almost a law unto themselves, especially out here in the sticks. Unless a family challenges his verdict and takes it to a Divisional Court for appeal, what he says, goes.'

'Well, this family certainly won't object,' said Angela. 'No doubt they're desperately relieved that their dirty washing hasn't been hung out in public.'

After apple tart with custard for dessert and a cup of coffee, Richard paid the bill and they walked back to their car. He drove leisurely back through the sunlit countryside, Angela noticing that on the main roads traffic was noticeably greater than it had been a few years earlier, now that new cars were freely available after their scarcity during the immediate post-war period.

There were still plenty of pre-war cars about, but now the sleeker Fords, Austins and Vauxhalls abounded, with foreign cars like her own Renault becoming too common to be curiosities any longer.

For Siân, the Wye Valley appeared all too soon, and after the last few miles down the side of the river from Monmouth, they finally pulled into the yard at Garth House satisfied with a day away from their usual routine.

EIGHTEEN

An early start on Tuesday took Richard and Angela to Newport Station, from where the Red Dragon hurried them eastwards. As he had little doubt that the two War Office bureaucrats always travelled first class, he again overcame his Welsh parsimony and settled his partner and himself in a similar coach on the London train.

Angela, with the prospect of half a day parading around Bond Street, was dressed in a very smart A-line suit of pale blue under a long swing-backed coat of a darker blue, with a matching pillbox hat. Richard appreciated her elegance, but hoped that the suitcase he had carried for her contained something more suitable for attending an exhumation. He had another reason for being glad that she looked so good, as he intended to surprise her by taking her to a theatre and a good meal that evening.

After they had left their overnight cases at the Great Western Royal Hotel at the end of Paddington's huge station, they took the Tube to Oxford Circus. Here they parted company, Angela heading to the shops and Richard saying that he would walk up to the Royal Society of Medicine and then to BMA House in Tavistock Square However, he diverted somewhat, going to West Street, off Charing Cross Road, where he managed to get two tickets at the Ambassadors Theatre for that night's performance of Agatha Christie's *Mousetrap*. It had already been running for three years, and some time ago, during a coffee break at Garth House, Angela had expressed a desire to see it before its run ended.

They had arranged to meet back at the hotel at five o'clock, and Richard found his partner sitting in the foyer lounge with a tray of tea and pastries. Alongside her low armchair were several expensive-looking carrier bags, though the names on them meant nothing to him except to suggest that Angela had just spent a lot of money.

'Have you checked on our rooms?' he asked as she poured him tea. When they had arrived that morning, the rooms were not ready for them and they had left their cases with the porter.

Angela smiled at him mischievously.

'You maligned Moira's intentions to keep us apart, Richard. We've got adjoining rooms!'

Richard smiled back rather weakly at her, not knowing how to take this. 'Jolly good! What do you think we should do to pass the evening?'

Handing him the plate of rather sickly-looking cakes, she suggested a cinema, if there was a decent film to be found.

'Oh, no, we're not!' he announced with a hint of triumph. He dipped into his inner pocket and waved a pair of theatre tickets at her. 'We're going to see *The Mousetrap*, and then I'm taking you for a decent meal! It's time to celebrate six months of hard work and the success of our partnership.'

The play was as enjoyable as they had expected, including the exhortation of the management not to divulge the final twist, so as not to spoil the surprise for other prospective patrons.

After the show, Richard's other surprise was to take Angela to Shaftesbury Avenue for a meal in a Chinese restaurant, a novelty for her and a bit of nostalgia for him, after all his years in Singapore. Though there had been a couple of Chinese restaurants in London for many years, they were still unknown to most people. Angela tackled king prawns in oyster sauce and sweet-and-sour chicken with some trepidation, abandoning chopsticks for a fork, in spite of Richard's attempts at rapid tuition. However, she enjoyed the new experience, and a bottle of Italian white wine helped to make the occasion go with a swing.

It was late when they took a taxi back to Paddington. Both feeling pleased with life, she slipped an arm through his as they lolled in the back of the big Austin.

'Thank you, Richard, that was a really lovely evening,' she said. 'You're a nice old chap, aren't you?'

He was not sure how to take this and wondered if he should put an arm around her shoulders, but a sudden lurch of the taxi as the driver decided not to jump the traffic lights in Edgware Road spoiled the moment and soon they were at the hotel.

On the first floor, they stopped outside their bedroom doors, which were side by side. After a couple of gins and half a bottle of wine, Angela fumbled a little with her key and her partner came to help in finding the keyhole. As the door opened, she grinned up at him in the dim light.

'Somehow seems a bit naughty, this!' she giggled. 'Staying in a London hotel, in adjacent rooms!' He avoided reminding her that they had slept almost every night for the last six months alone in an otherwise empty house, and bent to give her an affectionate kiss on the cheek. She hesitated in the open doorway, then responded with a full kiss on his lips, before slipping inside and, with a whispered 'Goodnight, Richard, and thanks again for a lovely time!', she firmly closed the door.

He stood for moment looking at the blank panels and then with a sigh hauled out his own key and went to bed.

The Queen Alexandra Military Hospital was squeezed into one of the most densely built-up areas of London, on the north side of a rectangle of roads that abutted on to Millbank, not far from the Houses of Parliament. A classical red-brick building on Bulinca Street, it faced the Tate Gallery, on the other side of which was the Royal Army Medical College. As a taxi dropped Angela and Richard on Millbank next morning, his nostalgia was stimulated once again as he looked back at the RAMC Officers' Mess on the corner of Atterbury Street, where he had spent some weeks during the war before being posted abroad. He still remembered the Blitz and the fire-watching duty that occupied many of the nights.

They walked around the block to the hospital and when Richard enquired at the porter's lodge to introduce themselves, a staff sergeant shepherded them towards a nearby side room.

'Colonel Bannerman wants a word with you, sir, before you go to the mortuary.'

He opened the door and ushered them into a bare interview room, normally used for talking to relatives of patients in the hospital. Bannerman was sitting at a table and rose as they entered, greeting them both and shaking hands.

'I wanted a quick chat before we start, doctors,' he said. 'Since we last spoke, the lawyer for the wife has engaged a medical expert and wants him to attend the examination.'

Richard nodded. This was the usual procedure in criminal cases, where the defence could engage their own expert to either attend the first autopsy or perform one of his own later, as he had done on a number of occasions.

'Where is he?' he asked. 'And who is he?'

'A surgeon, apparently, not a pathologist,' replied Bannerman. 'He's waiting in the mortuary for us, a chap named Lorimer. It seems he's a general surgeon from Farnborough Hospital, down in the direction where the widow lives.'

'Do we know what his opinion is on the case?' asked Pryor. 'I presume he's seen the same material as I have – the photographs and the background story?'

The War Office man fished in his black document case and pulled out a thin folder, which he handed to Richard. 'Their solicitor sent me a copy of Lorimer's report. It's quite short, if you want to look at it before meeting him.'

Pryor sat on the edge of the table and scanned through the two stapled pages. 'I see he was a doctor in the RAF towards the end of the war,' he observed. 'I'm not sure they saw a great many bullet wounds from small arms.'

He read through the brief opinion and handed the papers back to Bannerman. 'Let's see what he has to say when we both look at the actual wound for the first time.'

The staff sergeant led them through some corridors and then out through a door at the back of the ground floor. As usual, the mortuary was hidden in the nether regions, next to the boiler house. Thankfully, it was little used, as the hospital catered mainly for young and often otherwise usually fit service personnel, so there were few deaths in peacetime.

'Small, but well formed!' murmured Angela as they entered the featureless concrete building, externally resembling a large garage. Inside, it was spartan and spotlessly clean, with a small refrigerated body-store and a post-mortem room with a single table. An RAMC corporal, a technician from the pathology laboratory in the college, was waiting to act as mortuary assistant, and the body of Herbert Bulmer was already on the table, decently covered with a white sheet. As they entered, a tall man came forward to introduce himself as Steven Lorimer.

He still had a bushy moustache, which used to be referred to as the 'Flying-Officer Kite' style, even though he had been an RAF surgeon rather than an aviator.

Richard and Bannerman chatted to him for a few moments,

partly to cover the slight stiffness than often existed when two strange experts met, who may have potentially opposing opinions. The presence of the handsome Angela helped to ease the moment, as she was adept at social lubrication.

Then they got down to business, and the corporal handed the two doctors rubber aprons and gloves before he removed the sheet from the corpse. The smell of formalin and other preservatives confirmed that the body had been embalmed, which was obligatory before it could have been flown home from the Gulf. Although dead and buried for several months, this had kept it in fairly good condition, apart from the unnatural grey-green colour and the waxy texture of the peeling skin.

'It's really only the head wound that concerns us, would you agree?' asked Richard courteously. 'I doubt looking at what's left of the internal organs is relevant, especially after a previous autopsy.'

Steven Lorimer readily agreed, as, not being a pathologist himself, he was not keen to go groping through the debris that lay beneath the long stitched incision down the front of the body. 'Let's have a look at his head, then. I've only seen the photographs, which weren't all that brilliant,' he said.

With the head propped up on a wooden block, they stooped to stare at the back of the scalp. Another line of stitches ran over the head from ear to ear, but Richard wanted to see the outside before he opened this up.

'Of course, the hair has been washed after the first post-mortem, so there would be no signs left of any propellant or soot deposit from a close discharge,' said the surgeon.

Pryor agreed, but pointed out that the record stated that the man had been wearing a bush hat at the time. 'They didn't think to keep that or even take a photo of it,' he added. 'So we'll never know if it was soiled or scorched.'

'Given the size of the wound shown in the photographs, I feel sure this was a very close discharge,' said Lorimer rather stubbornly. 'Can we have a good look at it in the flesh, so to speak?'

Richard carefully parted the brown hair that lay over the back point of the head. It was short, as was to be expected in a serving soldier, and when moved aside revealed a roughly oblong wound in the scalp. The edges were ragged and inverted. Thankfully, the previous doctor in Al Tallah had not stitched it up at the end of the examination, so it was in its original state.

'Certainly no sign of burning or blackening,' said Richard. 'The hairs aren't clubbed, either.'

Angela noticed that Lorimer looked slightly bemused by this and she explained for his benefit, as this was marginally within her expertise. 'The keratin of the hair can melt under intense heat and then re-solidify, so you get little beads on the ends like the head of a match.'

'I see. But, again, if a hat was interposed, we wouldn't expect heating effects on the surface.'

Richard began to carefully shave the hair from a rim around the wound, to be able to see the margins more clearly. As he did so, he questioned Lorimer. 'So why do you feel this was a close, almost contact wound?'

'Because of the size of the wound,' answered the surgeon confidently. 'It must be over an inch long and half that wide. If it was a more distant discharge, a forty-five-calibre missile would have punched a clean, round hole of about that diameter. This big hole is due to the gas from the muzzle blasting into the tissues.'

Richard suspected that the surgeon was repeating the usual mantras from the standard textbooks, rather than from his own experience, and had several reservations about that claim. He kept his thoughts to himself and turned his attention to the scalp wound again. When the hair was removed from around it, it was seen to be a wide slit, with tearing at the left end and some brown scuffing at the other end.

He stood back to let Lorimer have a good long look, then suggested to Bannerman, who was waiting well back in the doorway that they should get some close-up photographs.

'I'd anticipated that, doctor. There's a photographer from the RAM College outside now.'

While the man came in and began taking some flash photographs, Bannerman invited the three doctors out into the body-store, where there was a desk against one wall. Again he rooted around in his leather case and pulled out a glass tube with a screw top.

'While we're waiting, perhaps you'd like to look at the bullet. It was flown back from Al Tallah after our liaison officer retrieved it from the police.'

He placed the tube on the table. Richard Pryor opened it and carefully unwrapped a wad of cotton wool to reveal a badly deformed bullet. It was heavy and bent, like a small banana. The two doctors studied it for a long moment, then Richard carefully turned it over to look at the whole distorted surface. When he had satisfied himself, the other doctor prodded it rather aimlessly and then nodded his agreement to having the missile put back into its protective wrappings.

'I think you should send it to your army experts in Woolwich to examine it fully,' said Richard, looking at the man from the War Office.

He didn't actually wink at Bannerman, but the astute colonel got the message that there was something significant in this suggestion.

When the photographer had finished, Richard went back to the head and cut the stitches that had secured the scalp after the original post-mortem. Pulling the tissues back, the two doctors studied the exposed skull, which had several fractures running up from the area of the bullet wound. Carefully lifting off the skullcap, which had been sawn around its circumference by the Al Tallah pathologist, Richard placed it on a dissecting table that the mortuary assistant had placed over the legs of the corpse. He then removed a large wad of crumpled bandages that had been used to stuff the cranial cavity after the first examination.

'They cut through just below the point of impact,' observed Pryor, 'so bits of skull have fallen out, where the fracture lines cross his saw line.'

The back point of the skull had been shattered, and Richard retrieved several loose fragments and fitted them together as best he could, like the pieces of a jigsaw. This produced a defect with jagged edges, roughly the size of the external scalp wound.

'Is there any point at looking at what's left of the brain?' asked Lorimer, looking askance at the front of the cadaver, where the long line of string stitches stretched down the middle of the chest and belly.

Richard shrugged. 'I very much doubt it. It was pretty mashed up by the bullet, according to the first autopsy report and the poor photos we have. Since then, it's been dissected, then no doubt stuffed back into the abdominal cavity and then buried for three months.'

'Where exactly was the bullet found, d'you recall?' asked the surgeon.

'It was up against the inner wall of the skull, on the left side, just above the inner ear.'

The two doctors spent a few more minutes exploring the inside of the cranium and studying the defect in the back of the skull, from which fracture lines ran in several directions, including across the base of the skull. Angela watched silently, leaving medical matters to the other two, as there was nothing that her specialism could offer, apart from the working knowledge of firearms examination that she had picked up from her years in the Met Lab.

Eventually, Richard and the defence expert had seen all they wanted of the body, and Richard indicated to the technician that he could restore the head, ready for return to the grave in Lewisham. They removed their gloves and aprons and washed up in a sink in the corner, where with true army efficiency there was a new tablet of soap and clean towels.

'Different from the usual public mortuaries I have to work in,' observed Richard. 'In some of them you're lucky to have running water!'

The surgeon, used to spotless operating theatres and nurses anxious to offer sterile gowns and instruments, failed to follow Richard's appreciation of military organization, but he courteously motioned Angela out of the mortuary as they left to speak to Bannerman, who had gone out into the outer room.

'All finished?' asked the War Office man. 'Any conclusions yet?'

Lorimer seemed to stiffen at this. 'I don't think it proper if we discuss the outcome at this stage,' he said rather pompously. 'It might prejudice any later disputes between us.'

Richard raised his eyebrows at Bannerman. It was usual for medical witnesses to exchange an informal impression of their examination and to indicate where they agreed and disagreed. It was for the lawyers and the courts to sort out the eventual decisions.

However, he had met a few expert witnesses who played their cards close to their chest and it was within their right to do so, if they were that way inclined.

'Fine, I'll just go off with the colonel here and have a talk,' replied Pryor. 'We can leave you in peace, if you want to make some notes or anything.'

The surgeon had left his dark overcoat and homburg in the outer room, together with a slim briefcase. He drew a writing pad from that and laid it on the small desk. 'Thank you very much for your courtesy, Dr Pryor.'

He shook hands with Angela, Richard and Bannerman, who left him to write whatever conclusions he had come to about the examination.

'Stuffy sort of chap, that!' observed the colonel as they walked back into the hospital. 'Seemed a bit out of his depth to me.'

Richard grinned. 'I don't think he cottoned on to what I was suggesting, but if he doesn't want to talk about it, that's up to him.'

They went back to the small interview room, where the helpful reception sergeant had organized a pot of coffee and some biscuits. Angela handed round the cups as they sat at the table and Richard explained his thinking about the injury. He spoke for a couple of minutes, Bannerman nodding sagaciously at intervals.

When the pathologist had finished, the War Office man tapped the side of his briefcase. 'So I gather from your expression in there that getting this bullet examined at Woolwich might be an important part of the exercise?'

Woolwich Arsenal, a name perhaps better known for its football team, was the long-established military centre for anything to do with arms and ammunition, being founded back in the seventeenth century.

Richard nodded. 'Get them to have a good look at it, especially on the outside. I'll wait for their report before firming up on my opinion.'

Bannerman nodded. 'I'll twist a few arms to get it done as quickly as possible and let you know on the telephone.'

A few minutes later the bowler-hatted bureaucrat said farewell and strode off towards Whitehall, leaving Richard and Angela to find a cab to take them back to Paddington.

'Do you really think that's the answer, Richard?' she asked, referring to the provisional explanation he had just given to Bannerman.

'I can't fault it and, if their laboratory in Woolwich confirms what I think, then it has to be accepted. A pity they've since destroyed the fuselage of that old Dakota out in the Gulf; that would have really clinched it.'

They had lunch in the Great Western Hotel, then caught a mid-afternoon express back to Newport, arriving home in the valley tired but pleased with their trip to the big city.

After one of Moira's casseroles left for them in the Aga, and a couple of relaxing gin and tonics, they talked over the events of their spree in London, feeling more than usually comfortable with each other's company. Eventually, they went to their separate rooms and, when in bed, both spent some time staring at the ceiling and thinking about the previous evening, which had been so different from their usual routine.

NINETEEN

Colonel Bannerman telephoned the following Monday, when Richard Pryor was away at Hereford County Hospital, the local coroner having asked him to perform a post-mortem on a patient who had died during an abdominal operation. Moira took the call and when Richard returned at lunchtime she passed on the message from the War Office, checking the actual words from a note she had made.

'The colonel said he had had a report from the Woolwich place and would like to talk it over with you. He has to come to Bristol tomorrow on another matter and wonders if you could meet him at lunchtime at his hotel, as he would prefer to speak to you personally, rather than over the telephone.'

Richard had no commitments on that Tuesday and readily agreed. Moira had the name of the hotel in Clifton and he asked her to phone Bannerman's secretary to confirm that he would be there.

'You must come too, Angela,' he said over lunch. 'You were at the examination last week, so you need to see the thing right through with me.'

Next morning they drove down to the Beachley–Aust ferry, which intrigued Angela, as she had never seen it before. When they trundled the Humber off the ungainly vessel on the Somerset side, she declared that the sooner they built a bridge, the better she would be pleased.

They found Bannerman's hotel, a large, Edwardian building in Whiteladies Road, and discovered the War Office man waiting for them in the bar. His tall figure hovered over them as he invited them to sit at a small table in the corner and signalled to a waiter to take an order for drinks. When Angela had been served with a gin and tonic and Richard with a half of bitter, Bannerman raised his own glass of whisky in a toast.

'To your good health and my thanks for your able assistance,' he said genially. 'I think the report from Woolwich will confirm what you outlined to me when we last met in London.'

He pulled out a thin folder from his black briefcase, which seemed as much a part of him as his pinstriped suit and old school tie.

'Perhaps we can look at this now, then we can have lunch in peace. I have to be at a conference with counsel at two, over a legal problem with a procurement contract, but I've booked a table in the dining room, if you would care to be my guests.'

Angela obviously appreciated his old-world courtesy and Richard covertly felt that his partner came from the same social stratum as the rather upstage colonel.

Bannerman opened the file and put it on the table so that they could all see it. 'They sent this photograph as well,' he began, tapping a long finger on a large black and white print.

It showed a much-magnified image of the distorted bullet, the sharp focus emphasizing a pale streak on the least-damaged side.

'That was the thing you were interested in, doctor. They concentrated on that and sent this short report that confirms what you suggested to me.'

He slid the photograph to one side and displayed a single sheet of typewriting, beneath an official letterhead that bore the logo of a crowned lion over crossed swords.

Richard and Angela bent over the form with their heads almost touching and read through the somewhat terse report. The pathologist skipped the preliminaries, then read out the significant part aloud.

'"The item submitted was a .45-inch-calibre bullet consisting of a copper jacket over a lead core. It was badly damaged from impact and had a discoloured streak on one side consistent with a glancing impact during its trajectory. Metallurgical analysis of this artefact indicated that it was an alloy of aluminium, containing copper, magnesium and manganese, commonly known as Duralumin."'

Richard looked up at Bannerman and grinned. 'Looks as if that clinches it, colonel!' he said.

Following a good lunch, Angela could not resist another hour's delay for her to investigate Clifton's main shopping street, where there were several smart boutiques. Her partner stayed in the hotel lounge, where he treated himself to a leisurely

pint of bitter while he read *The Times* and the *Telegraph*. After
they left Bristol, they were fortunate with the ferry at Aust
and arrived back at Garth House before Moira and Siân had
left for the day, both anxious to hear what had transpired.

Deciding that this justified an extra cup of tea, Moira brought
a tray into the staffroom and they settled down to listen to
Richard's explanation. He briefly recapped the story for Siân's
benefit, as she had not had Moira's knowledge of the War
Office call.

'It's all about the family's claim that this warrant officer's
death out in the Gulf was either due to negligence or even
might have been deliberate,' he began. 'There's no doubt that
the fatal shot came from his sergeant's weapon during this
practice assault in the fuselage of an old aircraft, but it's the
way he was shot that has given rise to all this controversy.'

'How did the widow come to start this claim?' asked Siân.

'I suspect she went to a solicitor to see about demanding
compensation and he started the hare running. He got a medical
opinion but really didn't understand what sort of expertise
was needed. A hospital surgeon may know a lot about treating
wounds, but he's not the best person to decide how they're
caused.'

Angela nodded her agreement. 'I've seen this in the forensic
science business – there are too many instant experts around.
They know a bit about everything, but not enough about the
issue in question.'

Siân still looked dubious. 'But you say that no one is
claiming that the sergeant didn't shoot the poor chap! It was
his gun, so what's the controversy about?'

Richard took a Marie biscuit from the tea tray. 'The widow,
or rather her lawyer, is claiming that the shooting was deliberate, under cover of the exercise. The alternative is that it
was caused by negligence on the part of the sergeant – and
perhaps also by the army itself for having faulty procedures.'
As he bit into his biscuit, it was Moira's turn to question him.

'Why on earth should the sergeant want to kill him?'

'Because it's admitted that there was bad blood between
the warrant officer and the staff sergeant. They had even come
to blows not long before, over disputes about how to run the
training programme and claims that the senior NCO was
bullying the sergeant.'

'So he took the chance to aim one of his shots in the wrong direction?' summarized Siân. 'It seems a damned dangerous business to me, firing off guns inside an aeroplane.'

Richard shrugged. 'War and fighting terrorists is a dangerous business. You can't learn it from a book, that's why the War Office hired these chaps to this place in the Gulf, to train their own fellows.'

Moira wanted to get down to the denouement. 'So how did you sort it out, Dr Pryor?'

She was already proud of him, even though he hadn't yet explained anything.

'Having studied the original post-mortem report and the poor photographs, the medical expert the family had hired was convinced that the wound on the back of the head came from a direct shot at close quarters. He based this on the large size of the hole, claiming that a more distant discharge would have made a small round hole, but that because it was much bigger it must have been due to the gases from the end of the gun barrel bursting into the tissues.'

'Is that right, doctor?' asked Siân, determined to see fair play.

Richard nodded. 'Up to a point. The gun would have to be very close indeed, so that the hot gas blasts through the skin, hits the hard skull underneath and bounces back, splitting the skin. It can't happen over soft areas, like the belly.'

'So why do you disagree?' demanded Siân, determined to be devil's advocate.

'There was no burning or propellant residue on the hair or skin which you would get with that close a discharge, though I admit straight away that if he had been wearing a bush hat covering that part of his head, it would have filtered off any of those signs.'

'But they didn't mention a hat in the Al Tallah reports, and no one there thought to keep the clothing, so we don't know one way or the other,' explained Angela, determined to get a little forensic science into the discussion.

'So where's the proof to the contrary?' demanded Siân, doggedly. Richard thought she would have made as good a lawyer as she was a technician. He held up three fingers and ticked them off with the index finger of his other hand as he spoke.

'First, the scalp wound didn't look right for a gas burst. It was roughly oblong and the edges weren't torn badly enough. There was a gouged slope at one end and I felt that the bullet hadn't penetrated nose first but had hit sideways on. Second, there was no exit wound – the bullet hadn't gone right through the head and was still resting against the inside of the skull on the left side.'

He tapped his third finger as he made his last point. 'And though badly distorted, the bullet had this pale streak down the one side.' He held up a copy of the photograph that Bannerman had given him at lunchtime.

'Those bullets have a copper jacket, but the laboratory confirmed that this pale stripe is mainly aluminium, with traces of other metals which make up the alloy Duralumin.'

Siân and Moira looked blankly at their employer. 'So what does that tell you?' demanded Siân.

Richard held up another photograph, a view down the length of the Dakota's interior, with the foreground slightly out of focus but showing a double row of rather dilapidated seat frames, partly covered with the remains of ragged upholstery.

'Nearly everything you see is made of aluminium alloy. It's been shot up by repeated previous exercises, but the walls of the fuselage, stripped of their lining, are Duralumin, as are the seat frames. I'm convinced that one of the bullets fired by the staff sergeant must have hit a seat frame with a glancing impact and ricocheted away to hit Bulmer in the head.'

'Why a seat frame and not the walls of the plane?' asked Moira.

'The skin of the plane is so thin it would probably have gone straight through. The seats are much more substantial,' he replied.

'Does that fit with the nature of the wound?' asked Siân.

Richard Pryor nodded. 'It explains it very well. The bullet would have been knocked off its direct trajectory and would probably have started tumbling, perhaps end over end. It hit the scalp sideways on, and even the scuffing at one end of the wound suggests that it was a tangential impact.'

'Anything else?' asked Moira.

'The bullet didn't go right through the head, probably because it had lost much of its energy by hitting the seat frame. Even high-velocity missiles like that can get stopped inside the skull if they strike the thick bars of bone in the base, but this one hadn't done that. It just didn't have enough momentum to break out at the front of the head.'

'I suppose we should have excluded carbon monoxide in the tissues under the scalp,' added Angela. 'Though maybe the embalming would have obscured it if it had been there.'

Siân pricked up her ears at this, as carbon monoxide estimations were part of her job. 'What's that got to do with it?' she asked.

'Where the gas from a close discharge is blown into the tissues, the carbon monoxide from the explosion in the cartridge combines with the blood and muscle in the tissues,' explained Angela. 'It persists a long time. I recall finding it in a case we had in the Met Lab six months after death.'

Moira looked satisfied that Dr Pryor had proved his case. 'So the sergeant didn't deliberately shoot his boss!'

Richard shook his head. 'I don't think so. He fired some rounds past the warrant officer at the dummies down the far end of the plane, but for some reason one bullet hit the top of a seat and went pinging off at an angle, tragically hitting the victim on the back of the head.'

'So the poor widow won't win her claim?' said Siân rather truculently. 'It seems a bit hard. Are you really sure about this?'

Richard grinned at his technician's crusading spirit. 'Hold on. I'm not a judge or a court of law! I was asked to give an opinion on how that wound came about, and I'm quite sure that what I think happened, did happen. It's not for me to say what is done with my opinion, but I reckon there's no justification for suggesting that it was a deliberate attempt to kill the warrant officer. No one could arrange a ricochet that just happened to hit the poor guy!'

'So she'll get no satisfaction at all out of this?' grunted Siân.

'I didn't say that, did I? It may well be that she can sue the War Office for employing a faulty, dangerous practice – though I suspect that Crown Indemnity might mean that you can't sue the government, but I'm not a lawyer.'

'What a stitch-up!' exclaimed Siân. 'That's what we get for electing another Tory government this year!'

Pryor sought to head off a political argument. 'Hold on a

minute! Bannerman, the chap from the War Office, mentioned to me at lunchtime that they would probably make an ex gratia payment to the widow, as a matter of good public relations. So she wouldn't have to try to bring any legal action or start campaigning for justice in the *Daily Mirror* if the army coughed up a reasonable sum in addition to the pension she will get as of right.'

This seemed to mollify Siân, and she joined in the general self-congratulations that the Garth House forensic consortium had triumphed once again.

Richard finished his tea and got up. 'Right, I'd better start writing a full report for the dear old War Office, so that Moira can type it up in the morning and get it off to London. It will mean a few more shillings to keep us all out of the workhouse!'

TWENTY

Siân had accompanied Angela and Richard to the inquest in Brecon, so it was tacitly agreed that it was Moira's turn to have an outing to the Assizes when her employers were warned for the 'veterinary case', as it became known in Garth House. As a former clerk in a local lawyer's office, she was not unaware of the archaic system of solicitors, barristers and Queen's Counsel, but she had never experienced the almost medieval rituals and costumes of the English legal establishment and looked forward to her day in court with almost adolescent expectation.

Richard had made another trip to Stow-on-the-Wold for a conference with George Lovesey and his junior counsel, Leonard Atkinson. Their colourful QC, Nathan Prideaux, had not been present as he was busy making a fortune in the London courts, but his junior was an able deputy.

'Nathan will want another "con" with you on the day you go to Gloucester, Dr Pryor,' he explained. 'But I'm keeping him abreast of all the details we discuss here.'

As well as this visit to Stow, where all the evidence was gone through in minute detail yet again, the solicitor was on the telephone several times to Garth House. Richard sensed that he was very anxious about the outcome of the case, as he told the others over a coffee break a few days before the trial was due to start.

'Lovesey says that it will hinge almost totally on the conflict between the medical evidence. Even though it's admitted that Samuel Parker was having a long-term affair with another lady, virtually all the rest of the evidence is circumstantial and not very convincing.'

Angela put her cup down in its saucer, looking serious.

'So it's all down to the cause of death, then,' she said soberly. 'It's a heavy responsibility for you, Richard, challenging the prosecution's expert.'

He shrugged. 'All I can do is tell the truth as I believe it, based on this research about potassium,' he said. 'I can only provide the bullets for Nathan Prideaux; it's up to him to fire them as effectively as he can.'

The analogy with bullets reminded them all of the recent case in the Gulf, which ended in a sudden death. Another sudden death was a possibility if Richard's hypothesis was not accepted, this time at the end of a hangman's rope.

'What will happen if you fail?' asked Moira almost tremulously.

'Our vet will be found guilty!' he answered succinctly.

'They won't hang him, will they?' asked Siân, a keen opponent of capital punishment.

Again her boss shrugged. 'Unless Prideaux could plead for clemency by playing the mercy-killing card, it seems very likely. It couldn't be an accident and it can't be manslaughter, so there's only murder left. Unless some powerful mitigating circumstances can be dredged up, then a death sentence is almost mandatory.'

'The poor man!' whispered Moira, looking quite upset.

'If he did it, then he should be found guilty,' said Siân, stubbornly. 'Though he should be locked up, not thrown down a hole with a rope around his neck!'

Like the bullet analogy, this again recalled the Brecon farm murder, but Moira was casting around for some less awesome solution.

'But what about manslaughter, doctor?' she asked. 'If she was already dying of cancer, surely that's a factor.'

'I'm not clear what's murder and what's manslaughter,' added Siân.

Richard looked across at Angela. 'These ladies certainly ask some difficult questions, don't they?' he complained, but he did his best to answer them.

'Look, I'm not a lawyer, but as far as I know, murder is when someone in their right mind unlawfully kills another, with the intention to either kill or seriously injure them. The death must follow within a year and a day of the attack. It's the intention that's the crucial factor, because manslaughter is where the first person kills another during some unlawful or negligent act but did not intend that to happen. There are all sorts of caveats about the definitions, but that's the general idea for simple folk like me!'

'So if he did inject potassium chloride into his wife, there's no way he could plead manslaughter, unless he was so off his head that he didn't know what he was doing,' supplemented Angela.

Richard was thankful that this explanation seemed to satisfy the two women, but they moved on to the logistics of the forthcoming trial.

'What will happen when they come to argue over the medical evidence?' asked Moira. 'Do you take it in turns to put forward your points of view?'

Richard nodded. 'The prosecution get first go, by calling their witnesses one after the other. The defence then cross-examine them and when the prosecution have finished, the defence have their turn.' He paused and rubbed his chin thoughtfully. 'At least, that's the usual batting order, but George Lovesey hinted that, typically, Nathan Prideaux may make an application to the judge to call witnesses out of order. We'll just have to wait and see what happens.'

Moira looked at her boss with her big eyes. 'Aren't you nervous at having to stand up in an Assize Court in front of all those people and argue about things that might mean a man's life?'

He smiled at her reassuringly. 'You get used to it – it happened often enough in Singapore; they get far more murders there than we do. The secret is not to chance your arm, just to stick to what you know without embroidering anything. If you don't know the answer, just say so – not bluster or wriggle or exaggerate. If you do, the opposing counsel will nail you to the wall!'

He said this with the slightly uneasy feeling that this particular case would be stretching medical science to the limit. But with Moira looking at him as if he was God's gift to jurisprudence, he thought that he had better look as confident as possible.

The following week the newspapers carried detailed accounts of the first day's evidence from the Assizes in Gloucester, which had even attracted the notice of the national press. Like naughty vicars in the *News of the World*, a professional man such as a respectable veterinary surgeon became an object of prurient interest, especially when his neck was in jeopardy – particularly with the added bonus of a secret mistress in the background. The Garth House contingent were glad that the lady had not so far been named, as it seemed that both prosecution and defence, once both had admitted that such a woman existed, saw no particular advantage in identifying her.

The *Gloucestershire Herald*, which covered the whole county including Stow and nearby Eastbury, quite naturally carried the most detailed account, a blow-by-blow record of almost every word that was said in the courtroom. That Tuesday morning, Siân bought a copy in Chepstow and brought it to the house, where it was pored over at coffee time.

'This opening speech they've printed,' said Siân, jabbing her finger at the report of the first day's proceedings. 'Only the prosecution made one. That doesn't seem fair to me.'

Angela, herself no stranger to the criminal courts, pacified the firebrand technician. 'They get their turn later, after the witnesses have been heard.'

The papers reported the evidence of a number of people, some of whom seemed to have only a tenuous connection with the main issue, such as the farmer's wife who made the phone call asking Samuel Parker to come and deal with the injured goat. More relevant was her husband, who described how the vet had arrived and given two injections into a vein of the animal, using the same syringe but two different fluids.

Then the District Nurse, Brenda Paxman, related how she had made a routine visit to Mrs Mary Parker in the late morning of that day. She had done her nursing duties of washing and bedmaking, then administered the first of two daily injections of morphine into the left arm. The patient was extremely drowsy, but certainly conscious and spoke a few words to her.

When asked in cross-examination, the nurse said that Mrs Parker's condition was deteriorating from day to day but was not markedly different on that morning.

This was confirmed by the vet's housekeeper, Mrs Cropley, who said that she gave her some warm milk from a feeding cup at breakfast time but could not coax her to eat anything. Her mistress, as she called her, spoke a few words to her, but she only wanted to fall back on the pillows and sleep, as she had done for the past week.

Nathan Prideaux confirmed with the housekeeper that

Samuel Parker was most concerned and solicitous about his wife's condition and spent much of his time when he was not working sitting by her bedside, often holding her hand.

The deceased woman's sister, the pharmacist Sheila Lupin, was called next and, even through the dispassionate print of the newspaper, it was obvious that she had a quite different outlook on the situation.

'She's got it in for him alright!' observed Siân as she read out the passage aloud for the others as they sat drinking their elevenses.

'"Miss Lupin described how she had gone across to her sister's house at about one o'clock, as she visited the sick woman several times a day. She found her unmoving in the bed, and there was a fresh injection mark on her forearm, from which a bead of blood was oozing. As she cleaned this off, she realized that her sister was dead and she then ran into the veterinary surgery to fetch the husband, who hurried to the sickroom and confirmed that his wife had passed away."'

Further down the news report, Siân read out the part where the sister said that her suspicions were aroused when she saw a used syringe and containers of sodium Pentothal and potassium chloride lying on the examination table in the surgery. Being a pharmacist, she knew the significance of that combination and confronted her brother-in-law with the accusation, given that there was an injection mark on the arm still oozing blood and that there had been no sudden change in her sister's condition that day to suggest that she had died of the disease from which she had been suffering for over a year.

'What did he say to that?' asked Moira, riveted by every word of the account.

'It says that this was strongly denied by Samuel Parker and they had a few strong words about it, but she was not satisfied. She later spoke personally to the doctor who was called, and he shared her concerns and reported the death to the coroner.'

Siân folded the paper up and laid it on the table. 'That's all there is for the first day. The judge isn't sitting today: something about a series of applications in other cases to be dealt with.'

'They don't work very long hours in these courts, by the sound of it!' said Moira in a disapproving tone.

'It's not that easy, running a court,' countered Richard. 'They can't start too early each day, as witnesses have to get there, often from a distance. And the judge may not like starting to hear an important witness who may go on for a long time, if it's towards the end of the day. Better to hear him out in one go.'

Siân nodded at this. 'It said at the end of the report that the judge commented that the case turned heavily on the medical evidence and he didn't want to start on that until tomorrow.'

She looked across at Richard. 'So does that mean you'll have to go up there in the morning, doctor?'

'I don't know yet, Siân,' he replied. 'No doubt they'll call the GP first, then the hospital pathologist, then the Home Office chap – all prosecution witnesses. Normally, the defence can't call their people until after the prosecution have finished, but I suspect that Nathan Prideaux will want me to sit behind him and listen to all the medical evidence the other side produce.'

Moira sat up at this. 'Don't forget you promised to take me this time, doctor!' she said earnestly.

Angela made a face at Siân. 'Looks as if you and I will be stuck here alone tomorrow, while these two go off enjoying themselves!'

Later that afternoon the expected call came from the solicitor in Stow, asking Richard to present himself at Gloucester Shire Hall at nine thirty in the morning. He was wanted well before the court began, as Nathan Prideaux wanted a last-minute conference about the vital medical evidence.

Soon after eight the next day, Moira was waiting in the kitchen for Richard to finish breakfast with Angela. Neither were hearty fry-up enthusiasts and usually cereal and toast were the starters for the day, so soon Moira was climbing into the passenger seat of the Humber and they were on their way.

'We both look very professional today, don't we?' he said as they hauled up Tutshill, the steep slope into England on the other side of Chepstow Bridge. Richard wore his double-breasted pinstriped suit, which the women of Garth House had badgered him into buying instead of the belted tropical linens that Siân disparagingly called his 'big-game-hunter outfit'.

Moira wore a business-style suit of charcoal grey with a prim white blouse – perhaps a little austere in these days of the New Look, but Richard thought she looked very smart.

'It was my office outfit when I worked for the lawyer in Chepstow,' she explained. 'So I thought it was legal-looking enough for attending the Assizes!'

When they arrived in Gloucester, they found a parking space for the car in a lane off Bearland and walked through to Westgate Street, where the imposing Shire Hall was situated. Moira knew the city slightly, but the classical building with its four massive Ionic columns flanking the main entrance was new to her. She followed Richard inside with a feeling of awe and expectancy.

The hall was a hive of activity, people either hurrying across it or standing in groups talking. Police officers, clerks in schoolmaster gowns and barristers in wigs were mixed with members of the public who stood around uneasily, especially if they were jurors or witnesses, unsure of what lay before them this day.

Richard made his way across to a set of heavy varnished doors.

When he pushed through they found themselves in a small panelled antechamber like an airlock, with another door ahead, which took them into the court itself.

Moira gazed around the high chamber, a huge room panelled in dark wood. It was almost empty, and on the high platform at the front which stretched the width of the court, seven chairs stood unused. The largest one in the centre was directly below a huge gilt model of the Royal Arms.

'Are you sure it's all right for me to come in?' she whispered to Richard as she trailed him down towards the front of the court, where three men and a woman stood talking.

'I'll get you tucked away somewhere where you can see what's going on,' he said reassuringly as he approached the group.

Two were in black robes, but they held their wigs in their hands, white tabs at the throat completing their archaic costumes. The other man was the rotund solicitor, George Lovesey, who came forward now to greet the pathologist.

'Morning, Dr Pryor. We'll be going to one of the small rooms in a moment to talk things over.'

Richard introduced Moira as his secretary and asked if she could be found a place in court. The portly lawyer shook her hand warmly, and Richard suspected that he still had an eye for an attractive woman.

'Sit on the end of this row here, behind your boss,' he said, indicating the third row of what looked to Moira like long church pews. 'My own secretary will be alongside you when we get started.' He nodded towards the middle-aged woman who was talking to the barristers. Moira settled herself on the padded bench and looked around the court, picking out the empty jury benches on her left and the witness box between it and the high palisade that stood below the judge's domain.

Nathan Prideaux detached himself from the others and came forward to shake Richard's hand. 'Good to see you, doctor. We'll go off and have a chat, shall we?'

Leaving Moira to absorb the atmosphere, Richard made his way out of the court with the barristers and solicitor, the secretary lugging several box-files under her arm. They went a few yards down a dark corridor to a small windowless room, furnished only with a table and some plain upright chairs. A couple of tin lids lay on the scarred tabletop to act as ashtrays, and as soon as they were all seated the QC lit up a small cheroot and promptly had a good cough.

He held out a hand to the secretary and, without prompting, she slid one of the files across the table to him.

'Today, the prosecution are calling their four medical witnesses. They will have to rely almost totally on their evidence to get a conviction, as what they've led so far wouldn't convince a monkey!' he said disparagingly.

His junior, Leonard Atkinson, looked slightly less sanguine.

'But if we can't crack their expert evidence, we're in the same boat. So it's largely up to you, Dr Pryor.'

Nathan nodded ponderously. 'Make or break, this looks like being one of the shortest murder trials of the year!' he growled. 'So I want you to sit right behind me, doctor. You know the drill; listen to every word they say – and if there's the slightest chink in their evidence, I want you to let me know.'

He looked across at the secretary. 'Mrs Armitage, make sure that Dr Pryor has plenty of sheets of paper so he can pass notes to me, please.'

He winked at Richard. 'Nothing like the sound of a defence

expert tearing paper to unnerve another medical man in the witness box! We need absolute rebuttal of their medical evidence, or we're sunk. I can deal with all the other circumstantial stuff, but if we can't torpedo Dr Angus Smythe, our client is going to be left in a very grave situation.'

'So what's the batting order, Mr Prideaux?' asked Richard. 'Are you going to pick Angus apart in cross-examination before I get to say my piece?'

The London QC gave a crafty smile. 'That should be the normal procedure, as you well know. But I'm going to try to get the judge to let me defer my cross-examination until after I've called you, as you would be the next witness anyway. I think it would make a bigger impact on the judge and the jury if you blew his conclusions out of the water first and then I'll come back and put him through the wringer.'

George Lovesey tapped his wristwatch and suggested that time was pressing, so the procession went back into court, where they found it far busier than when they had left it. The public benches were now almost filled, ushers and police officers were standing around and a gaggle of reporters were gossiping in the press benches on the right-hand side.

Richard Pryor went to sit with George Lovesey in the second row of pews, immediately behind the two defence barristers.

Behind him, the solicitor's secretary slipped in to sit alongside Moira, a friendly woman who introduced herself to Moira as Doris and proceeded to explain various aspects of the procedure to her.

'The defence team are on the left side of the benches, so the prosecutors are over there.'

She covertly pointed at another brace of bewigged barristers on the right side, with the acolytes from the Director of Public Prosecutions sitting behind them.

Both leading counsel had erected their small folding tables on the wide ledge in front of them, to hold their papers and give themselves something to either grip or lean on. The juniors had a collection of legal textbooks in front of them with bits of coloured paper marking relevant pages.

Moira watched as Nathan Prideaux flipped his wig on to his head with a practised gesture and shuffled over to have a word with his opponent, the prosecuting counsel. Rather to her surprise, they seemed to be cracking a joke together and she heard the words: '. . . a handicap of three and he still lost!'

Bemused by this strange system of English law where a man's life hung on a contest between two apparent friends, she now saw another man in a wig and gown seat himself behind a table below the judge's chair. The clerk of the court, an important cog in this elaborate drama, faced the courtroom, and almost on the stroke of ten thirty Moira heard a sudden susurration of whispers from the public gallery. Turning round, she saw that two prison officers had appeared in a box a few rows behind, one with a brass rail around it. Between them she saw the pale face of a man in a sober blue suit.

'Is that the vet?' she whispered to Doris and got a nod in return. Any further exchange was stopped as a portly man dressed in a morning suit appeared alongside the judge's chair up on the high dais and called out 'All stand!' in a voice that brooked no dispute. As everyone lumbered to their feet, he stood aside, and from a door behind the chairs Mr Justice Templeman appeared.

Though Moira had many times seen judges in photographs and films, the actual thing was much more impressive. A tall, lean figure with a severe face below a high forehead, he was resplendent in a scarlet gown with a black belt, cuffs and sash.

She had rather expected a long wig coming down to his collarbones, but his wiry grey hair was partly covered by the same compact headpiece as worn by the barristers below. More sinister was the square of black silk which he carried along with his gloves; she fervently hoped that this 'black cap' would not be needed and she mentally willed her employer to do all he could to save the life of the haggard man in the dock behind her.

The judge bowed to the counsel as a small procession followed him from the door hidden behind the large central chair. Moira was surprised to see two august-looking ladies shepherded in by two gentlemen. They wore expensive dresses and elaborate hats, their gloved hands clutching large handbags.

'Who are they?' she whispered to her friendly informant.

'The wives of the High Sheriff and the Lord Lieutenant,' hissed Doris Armitage. 'Those are the chaps in the fancy outfits!'

One man wore breeches and a black velvet jacket with frilled lace at the throat, the other a dark blue military-style uniform with gold epaulettes and red collar-tabs. As the judge settled himself in the large central chair, the others seated themselves two on either side, at a slightly lower level.

When Mr Justice Templeman had arranged his pens, magnifying glass and notebooks before him, the clerk of the court rose and opened the proceedings, directing the ushers to bring in the jury. From another door in the panelling, a dozen men filed in self-consciously and took their places in the two rows of the jury box. The judge greeted them courteously and reminded them that they were still under the oath that they had sworn the previous day. Then he turned to the prosecuting counsel.

'Mr Gordon, I believe you are ready to call your medical evidence today?'

Lewis Gordon, a tall, heavily built man with a rugged face, looked more like a retired rugby international than a Queen's Counsel. He had a deep, sonorous voice to match. Rising to his feet, he grasped the front edges of his black silk gown.

'Indeed, my lord, I have four doctors for the court to hear. I first call Dr John Anthony Rogers.'

There was some creaking of doors as an usher went outside and returned with the regular family physician of the Parker household. He ascended the three steps into the darkly varnished witness box and stood looking slightly uneasy to be the subject of such public scrutiny.

The judge's associate, who to Moira looked like a stage butler, stood up at the end of the upper bench to administer the oath.

'Take the book in your right hand and repeat after me,' he ordered. The GP, a benevolent-looking man of sixty, wearing large horn-rimmed glasses, held the battered Testament and spoke the well-known words which made him liable for a perjury charge if he strayed from the truth.

The evidence that the QC extracted from him was to the effect that, about eighteen months previously, Mary Parker had been diagnosed as having cancer of the pancreas and that there had been steady deterioration of her condition ever since, no effective treatment being available.

'When did you last attend her, doctor?' asked Lewis Gordon.

'Four days before her death, sir. I usually went in on alternate days, though there was nothing I could really do, except check that she was getting sufficient painkillers and proper nursing care. Unfortunately, I was on holiday when she died.'

No one took him up on why he considered his absence 'unfortunate'.

'And was she any different on that last visit?'

Dr Rogers thought carefully, as he knew the significance of his reply, but had no thought other than to tell the truth as he saw it.

'Not really. Her condition didn't change much on a daily basis, but she was certainly worse than she had been a week or two earlier.'

'But you had no reason to think that she would have died from the cancer four days later?' persisted the barrister.

Again the careful doctor thought before he spoke. 'No, but equally I had no reason to exclude that possibility. Patients in the terminal stages can die at any time.'

Gordon tried several more times, asking what was basically the same question in different ways, but Rogers stuck to his guns. Even though she was already partisan in this issue, Moira silently applauded him for his refusal to be pressurized into qualifying his opinion to suit the QC.

Gordon's court sense soon told him that the judge would get restive if he persisted in his repetition and, knowing that he had obtained all he was likely to get from the family doctor, sat down to leave the field to his defence colleague.

'Have you any questions for this witness, Mr Prideaux?' asked Templeman.

Nathan rose slowly to his feet and wrapped his gown around his stomach as he leaned against his document stand.

'I will be very brief, my lord.' He turned to the witness box.

'Dr Rogers, you indicated to my learned colleague just now that you had no reason to exclude the possibility that Mrs Parker might have died within days following your last visit. How strong would you rate the word "possibility"?'

Again the experienced GP hesitated before he replied. 'I think it impossible to quantify, sir. I have been in practice for over thirty-five years and seen many patients die in similar circumstances. I think it virtually impossible to forecast when death will occur. In fact, I sometimes deprecate the too-dogmatic opinions of some of my colleagues, which can lead to distress for both patients and their relatives when their estimates prove markedly incorrect, in either direction.'

Nathan Prideaux nodded wisely, to emphasize to the jury what a sensible fellow this witness was. 'So you were not surprised to hear that Mary Parker had died on that day?'

Dr Rogers shook his head. 'Not at all, though I was sorry that it occurred when I was away on holiday – especially when I learned of the allegations that arose later.'

Prideaux shied away from this aspect, as it was outside this witness's sphere of knowledge. He tried another tack. 'So why, medically speaking, would you not be surprised that this patient or any other in similar circumstances might die suddenly and unexpectedly?'

John Rogers looked down at the front of the court through his thick glasses and saw what he correctly took to be a pathologist in the second row. 'I expect you will get a more authoritative answer to that from other experts, sir, but as a mere family doctor I can say that a widespread cancer like that suffered by Mrs Parker can lead to a variety of fatal pathological events. She had secondary growths in her bones, her liver and her lungs. These could cause internal bleeding or clotting of the veins, which could cause sudden death by blocking the circulation in the lungs. Her liver impairment can reach a point where the whole chemistry of the body is irreparably damaged. But even apart from those specific problems, any patient with very severe disease of many kinds can just give up on life. We all have to die from something at some time – it used to be called "giving up the ghost"!'

Prideaux felt that this rather philosophical statement was an ideal point to leave with the jury and, being a canny advocate, he knew when to stop pushing.

He sat down with a sincere, 'Thank you, doctor.'

The judge asked Gordon if he wished to re-examine, but the prosecution barrister politely declined. Mr Justice Templeman offered his own thanks to the family doctor and released him from any further attendance.

As the next witness was being called from outside the court, Moira whispered to her new friend from the solicitor's office. 'How did that go, do you think?' she asked anxiously.

Mrs Armitage, who had attended many courts with her own boss, gave a little shrug. 'Neither helped nor hindered, really. Probably more helpful than not,' she said. 'It's the next chap who might be a problem.'

The 'next chap' was Dr Roger's locum, the man who had been called to the vet's house on the day of her death.

Moira took an instant dislike to Dr Austin Harrap-Johnson from the moment he strutted importantly down the side of the court to take his place in the witness box. Though rather short, he stood ramrod straight to take the oath, holding the New Testament dramatically high in the air. His voice was loud and imbued with a plummy accent that went well with the Old Harrovian tie that set off his immaculate pinstriped suit. His fair hair was Brylcreemed back from his round, pink face as he attentively faced the judge to respond to prosecuting counsel's request to state his name and confirm that he was a registered medical practitioner.

'I am a Member of the Royal College of Surgeons, a Licentiate of the Royal College of Physicians and also hold the Licentiate in Medicine and Surgery of the Society of Apothecaries of London,' he declared, inclining slightly towards the judge, as if to impress him with the notion that these qualifications were among the highest accolades in the British medical profession. In his seat on the second row of benches, Richard Pryor grinned to himself, as he knew that Mr Justice Templeman would be well aware that these 'Conjoint' qualifications and the LMSSA, though eminently respectable, were the basic requirements to get on the Medical Register. In fact, some medical students used them as a 'safety net' in case they failed the final examinations of their own universities.

Responding to further questions from the QC, Harrap-Johnson confirmed that he had acted as Dr Rogers' locum for three weeks at the material time and that he had attended Mrs Mary Parker during that period.

'And were you called urgently to the Parker household on April the seventh this year?'

'I was indeed – but unfortunately the patient was deceased when I arrived, and all I could do was to confirm the fact of death.'

The young doctor spoke with a degree of gravitas that suggested he was used to attending the deathbeds of royalty.

'You say that you confirmed the fact of death, doctor,' said Lewis Gordon, tugging his black gown more closely across his chest. 'But did you not certify the cause of death?'

Harrap-Johnson shook his head gravely. 'I did not, sir. I felt unable to do so for several reasons.'

'And what were they?'

'First, although I was of course fully aware of Mrs Parker's serious medical condition, I had seen her only two days previously and considered then that she was in no immediate danger of dying. Her notes compiled by Dr Rogers indicated that her condition had not deteriorated since his last visit.'

'And the second reason?'

'When I attended the house, I was met by the dead lady's sister, Miss Lupin, who immediately conveyed her concerns about the nature of the death. She told me that she was a qualified pharmacist and that she suspected that her sister had been given an injection of a toxic substance.'

At this, the murmur of excitement that came from the public seats was almost palpable and the judge looked up sharply, a frown of annoyance on his face.

Lewis Gordon pressed on with his questions.

'This must have come as something of a surprise to you, doctor?'

Harrap-Johnson managed to give the impression that such events were not uncommon in his practice and that he could take them in his stride. 'Well, it was rather! But I was already uneasy about finding the lady dead so unexpectedly.'

'What happened next?'

'After I had done all I could at the bedside and confirmed that there was nothing to be done by the way of resuscitation, Miss Lupin insisted on taking me through to the veterinary clinic, where she showed me a large syringe still containing some liquid, a bottle labelled as potassium chloride and a carton of vials of sodium Pentothal.'

'Was the defendant present when you arrived at the house?'

'Not at first, sir. The housekeeper who admitted me said that Mr Parker was very shocked and was in the sitting room where she had given him strong tea, while he telephoned a funeral director to start making arrangements.'

'So he was not present when his sister-in-law expressed her concerns about the nature of the death?'

'No, but before I left I naturally sought him out to express my condolences and to tell him that I feared I was not in a position to provide a death certificate.'

'How did he respond to that?' asked Lewis Gordon.

For the first time, the locum doctor looked a little uncomfortable, and Moira wondered if there had been some strong opinions exchanged at the time.

'Mr Parker expressed surprise and consternation at my inability to certify the death, especially when I said that I had no option but to inform the coroner.'

'Did you mention the suspicions of Miss Lupin at that point?'

'I did not. I thought it was not my place to do so; that aspect was up to the coroner.'

'So the possibility of some sort of poisoning was not mentioned?'

Harrap-Johnson again looked uneasy, and Moira thought he might be recalling some terse words from the veterinary surgeon.

'Not by me, but Mr Parker raised the allegations of his sister-in-law and forcefully rejected them.'

The prosecutor did not want to go further down this path and backtracked in order to get further details. This was boring stuff, and Moira could almost feel the restlessness of the court in having sheered away from more the dramatic revelations.

When he came to the end of these more mundane matters, the judge offered Nathan Prideaux the opportunity to cross-examine, which he accepted with an almost casual grace.

Leaning with one elbow on his little table, he started by investigating Austin Harrap-Johnson, rather than the facts of the case. 'Doctor, how long have you been qualified?'

The young man frowned; this was not what he expected – he was here to show off his forensic acumen to the court.

'Three years – and ten months,' he added defensively.

'How have you been employed during that time?'

Again Harrap-Johnson looked nonplussed.

'Employed? Well, as soon as I qualified I became a house surgeon at Guy's and then a house physician at the Royal Berkshire Hospital. Then I was called up for National Service for two years as a doctor in the Royal Army Medical Corps. Eastbury was my first locum after returning to civilian practice.'

'What were your duties in the army, doctor?'

'I was a Regimental Medical Officer to the Coldstream Guards. At first with the rank of lieutenant, then captain.'

Richard again grinned to himself – he knew that RMO postings to the posh regiments usually went to those with double-barrelled names who had been to Eton, Harrow or Marlborough.

The defence counsel nodded complacently. 'I assume that most of those in a Guards regiment were pretty fit chaps, eh?'

Mystified, Harrap-Johnson agreed. 'Most of my work was dealing with injuries of various types.'

'So you have had little experience of middle-aged ladies dying of cancer?'

The discomfited doctor huffed and puffed a little, but had to agree. 'But of course I had spent a year in two large hospitals before that – and as a student I had been trained in the full range of disease process.'

'But had you even managed a case of terminal pancreatic carcinoma before?'

Harrap-Johnson, for all his pomposity, was an honest young man and had sworn to tell the truth, so he agreed he had not.

'And had you ever seen a patient with that awful disease?' pursued Prideaux relentlessly.

The locum wriggled a little, saying that a case had been demonstrated by a consultant at Guy's and that he had seen other types of advanced cancer.

'So doctor, it comes to this, doesn't it?' concluded the QC. 'You have no personal experience of how and when a sufferer from terminal cancer of the pancreas might die. It's right, isn't it, that if Miss Sheila Lupin had not made her allegations about the possibility of a fatal injection, you would have taken your pad of certificates from your black bag and signed one on the spot?'

Harrap-Johnson pulled himself up in a last-ditch expression of defiance. 'I don't know about that. I was still not happy about the case.'

Nathan Prideaux gripped each side of his table and jutted his head forward towards the witness box. 'But why not? You were quite entitled to certify, under the law which states that if a doctor has attended a patient within the previous four-teen days before death, excluding the final visit, he is entitled to issue a certificate. You fulfilled those criteria and were also locum to Dr Rogers, who had been treating Mrs Parker for many years, let alone fourteen days!'

Deflated, Austin Harrap-Johnson mumbled something and attracted the notice of the judge, who glared at him over his half-moon spectacles.

'Doctor, please speak up! The jury need to hear what you have to say.'

Chastised, the doctor flushed and repeated what he had muttered. 'I said that I was playing safe, my lord, given that I had only seen the lady on one previous visit.'

Prideaux gave something suspiciously like a snort as he came to his last question. 'Come along, doctor! I put it to you that if Miss Sheila Lupin had not made the initial accusation to you that her sister had been poisoned, you would have been happy to issue a certificate – instead of dashing off to the coroner with this hearsay claim?'

As the flustered locum made a final half-hearted denial, Prideaux barked, 'No further questions, my lord,' and sat down with a flourish that suggested that the whole issue must now surely be settled.

The prosecuting barrister declined an invitation to re-examine, and Mr Justice Templeman released the witness from further involvement. Harrap-Johnson descended from the box and walked out, covered in less glory that he had expected. Moira's initial feelings had changed to sympathy as he looked embarrassed and deflated.

'That went better for us, didn't it?' she whispered to Mrs Armitage, who nodded then looked at her wristwatch. 'I expect we'll just about get the next witness in before lunch. That lot up there are keen on their food at the judge's lodgings.'

She nodded at the five august personages sitting up on the high bench – Moira irreverently thought that they looked like the characters in a Punch and Judy show, dressed in their colourful outfits.

This time, no witness was called from outside the court, but when Lewis Gordon called his name an elderly man, who was sitting at the end of the second bench furthest from Richard Pryor, rose to his feet and went towards the witness box. Moira knew from her reading of all the papers that had come to Garth House that he must be the local coroner's pathologist. He was a thin, dried-up man of at least seventy years of age, his dark suit hanging on him, his shirt collar too large for his leathery neck.

After taking the oath, he said in a faintly foreign accent that he was Dr Rupert Stein and that he was a semi-retired doctor, now living in Stratford-upon-Avon. Moira decided that he must be a pre-war immigrant from somewhere in Central Europe.

Rupert Stein haltingly explained that he had retired from his hospital post as a pathologist seven years earlier, but still did post-mortems for several coroners in the Cotswold region. One of these post-mortems was on Mrs Mary Parker, though his tone suggested that he now wished he had kept well clear of such a controversial case.

'On the day following the death, you performed an examination at the request of the local coroner. Did you know the full circumstances of the death before you began?'

'Only in the broadest terms. I had wondered why the death of a sufferer from advanced cancer, under medical care for many months, should have been reported to the coroner.'

The old doctor's voice was as dry as his appearance, but he seemed perfectly alert and competent as he dealt with the questions.

'And what were these "broadest terms", doctor?'

Dr Stein frowned and looked uncomfortable for the first time.

'The coroner's officer told me that a close relative had made an allegation that the deceased may have been given an injection of potassium chloride shortly before death. On hearing this, I considered declining to proceed with my examination, as I am not experienced in forensic procedures, but as the medical history seemed so strongly in favour of the cancer as the cause of death, I decided to carry on. I felt that any doubt could be resolved later.'

Junior counsel then led the pathologist through his post-mortem report, detailing all the relevant findings. These amounted to a catalogue of the effects of the malignant tumour in the abdomen, which had spread widely to many of the major organs and to the bones.

'Was there any additional condition that may have precipitated sudden death, doctor? Such as haemorrhage or thrombosis?'

Rupert Stein shook his head. 'No, I found nothing of that nature.'

'Was there anything that could have substantiated this allegation of an injection of potassium chloride?'

Again the pathologist answered in the negative, but added a caveat. 'Of course, I would not expect any signs of that. Potassium chloride stops the heart; there are no visible manifestations.'

'There was a fresh injection mark on the arm, was there not?'

'Yes, but she was being given frequent intravenous morphine,' countered the doctor. 'There were injection marks on both arms, of varying ages.'

The prosecution barrister did his best to bring the questioning to an advantageous conclusion.

'So the situation is this, is it not? You found no sudden pathological event that could have caused sudden death and you had no evidence to exclude potassium poisoning?'

The old pathologist looked steadily down at the advocate. 'That's true, but equally I had no evidence to confirm or even suspect potassium toxicity, especially in the presence of very advanced cancer.'

The barrister sat down and Nathan Prideaux rose to his feet at the judge's invitation.

'Dr Stein, you have really already answered all the questions I had for you, but just to summarize: this was an examination that was rather sprung on you, was it not?'

'Looking back, I suppose I should have told the coroner that I would have preferred him to have sought a forensic opinion. But at the time the attitude of the coroner's officer was that this allegation was not to be taken all that seriously. It was the day following the death and I understand that investigations had not got very far by that time.'

Prideaux nodded understandingly.

'You took no blood samples for analysis to check for potassium?'

'It would have been pointless. Potassium is a natural constituent of the body and leaks out rapidly from the cells into the blood after death.'

'Then, doctor, the situation surely is this – you did a post-mortem on a lady with very advanced cancer and found no objective evidence whatsoever that this was not the sole cause of death. Do you agree?'

When the pathologist accepted this, the defence QC had one last question.

'You may not be a forensic pathologist, but you have been an experienced hospital consultant for many years and must have seen many cases of advanced cancer. Given the medical history of this lady and in the light of your own findings, have you any reason to think that the cancer could not have killed her?'

When the doctor gave a firm 'No' as his answer, Prideaux gathered his gown about him and sat down with a confident thump.

Behind him, Richard Pryor, who so far had not had occasion to tear up any paper for notes, could almost hear the rumble of stomachs on the judge's bench. Sure enough, Mr Justice Templeman began gathering up his pens and notebooks as he declared a recess for luncheon. After warning the jury that they must not speak to anyone about the case, he announced resumption at two o'clock and the whole court dutifully stood as he led his colourful procession out of the court.

Much as Moira liked Doris and appreciated her whispered explanations, she was eager to talk to Richard to hear how he thought the case was going. In spite of the life-and-death seriousness of the matter, she was as partisan over the case as if she was rooting for Wales in a rugby international.

As soon as the court broke up, she waited for him to have a quick word with the defence lawyers until he caught up with her at the door of the court.

'Let's go and get something to eat first,' he said, taking her arm. 'We've got almost an hour and a half before the big guns come on this afternoon!'

He grinned at her, and she suddenly felt that she was in danger of falling in love with him. Ignoring a couple of greasy spoons, he steered her into a hotel in Westgate Street where they were settled at a corner table of the dining room. It was an old-fashioned establishment, which seemed a throwback to the thirties or even the twenties, with dark furniture and a waitress in a cap and apron. However, the menu looked acceptable. Before they started talking about the case, Moira ordered

Brown Windsor soup followed by a beef casserole, while
Richard chose lamb and mixed veg after his soup.

'So how do think it went,' she asked anxiously as he poured
glasses of water for them both, studiously avoiding any alcohol.

'As good as can be expected,' he replied. 'But this is the calm
before the storm. So far all the prosecution have is the accusations of that poisonous sister-in-law. The rest of the evidence
is neutral – doesn't prove or disprove that she died of either
cancer or potassium chloride.'

'So it all rests on Dr Angus Smythe this afternoon – and,
of course, you!'

'Battle of the giants!' he said cheerfully, which made her
shake her head in wonder.

'I don't know how you can be so calm about it, with probably the life of that poor man in your hands!'

Richard shrugged as the waitress approached with their
soup.

'Maybe he did it, maybe he didn't, but that's not my concern.
All I can do is state the scientific evidence as I see it. It's up
to the jury to decide who they want to believe.'

'Do you think they'll understand this chemical business?'
asked Moira, picking up her spoon.

'I'll do my best to put it in plain language – and no doubt
Nathan Prideaux will rub it in as hard as he can.'

In spite of her apprehensions, Moira enjoyed her meal, and
Richard Pryor's appetite seemed unaffected by the prospect
of him taking centre stage in an hour or two. Over the coffee
that followed a Pear Helene, they talked about the court and the
various personalities, Moira being fascinated by the grim
theatre of it all. She seemed particularly taken by the fact that
the wives of the High Sheriff and the Lord Lieutenant wanted to
attend such events.

'Never turn down a free lunch, Moira! That's their motto,
part of the perks of public office.'

She wanted to know why Dr Harrap-Johnson and Dr Rogers
had not been allowed to sit in court, unlike Dr Stein and
Richard himself.

'Because they were witnesses to fact, being directly involved
in the care of Mrs Parker. Theoretically, if they sat in court
and heard other evidence from the other witnesses, they might
be influenced by it.'

'So what about you?' she demanded.

'The pathologists are classed as expert witnesses, there to offer opinions, as well as fact. You'll see Angus Smythe sitting there when we get back. We're supposed to be indifferent to anything other than the scientific facts of the issues. Actually, the distinction is a bit blurred, as you heard the other two doctors being asked about whether Mrs Parker could have died of her cancer, which is really an opinion.'

He grinned at her again. 'There are higher rates of pay for expert witnesses, but I doubt that young Lochinvar-Johnson or even Dr Rogers will hold out for a rise!'

At half past one they walked back to the Shire Hall, in case the QC wanted a quick conference again, and by the time the court reconvened they were sitting back in their places. This time, as Richard had prophesied, a new face was present on the further end of the second bench. Dr Angus Smythe, a Home Office pathologist from Oxford, was a burly Scotsman with a big red face and short, fair hair showing a hint of ginger. During lunch, Richard had said that he was a competent pathologist, though inclined to resent contradiction, being quite dogmatic in his opinions, sometimes unwilling to accept another view.

'Fancies himself as another Sir Bernard Spilsbury, that allegedly infallible operator who dominated the business for forty years.' Moira was not sure if Richard's criticism was a touch of sour grapes, though she thought this would be foreign to his nature.

The butler appeared and, as the court rose, the now well-fed quartet followed the judge into their places. After the jury and the defendant had been settled, Lewis Gordon rose from his bench to call his last witness.

Angus Smythe stumped to the witness box and took the oath in a loud, gruff voice with a pronounced Scots accent. After it had been established that he was a consultant pathologist at the John Radcliffe Hospital in Oxford and was on the Home Office list of approved forensic pathologists, the prosecuting QC cut straight to the chase.

'Dr Smythe, you were asked by the coroner for North Gloucestershire to carry out a second post-mortem on the body of Mrs Mary Parker, were you not?'

Smythe agreed and there was a brief confirmation of dates and places connected with the autopsy.

'Why was this unusual procedure requested?'

'Because neither the locum GP nor the coroner's pathologist were willing to offer a cause of death, due to certain
allegations that had been made by a relative,' was the bluff
response.

More questions elicited that he had been informed of the
nature of these allegations and of the contents of the used
syringe and the two containers found in the veterinary surgery.

'And what was the result of your examination of the body,
doctor? Were you able to determine the cause of death?'

The Scotsman gripped the edges of the witness box as if
he intended to tear it apart.

'I reviewed the dissections made by Dr Stein and agreed
with all his findings. This did not assist me in arriving at a
cause of death, so I took a variety of samples for examination back at my own laboratory.'

'Did you perform these investigations yourself?' asked
the QC.

'I did some of the analyses, and the rest were performed
by my technicians under my direct supervision. The results
led me to an unequivocal opinion as to the cause of death,
which was cardiac failure due to the intravenous injection of
potassium chloride.'

There was an excited buzz of murmuring from the public
gallery, and the pencils of the reporters scurried across their
notebooks.

'In plain language, can you explain what led you to this
conclusion?' asked Lewis Gordon.

'The samples I took included blood, urine and the fluid
extracted from the eyeballs, called "vitreous humour",'
explained Smythe. 'I ran analyses for barbiturates, as there
was a vial of sodium Pentothal recovered from the premises,
but none was discovered. There was a substantial amount of
morphine in the blood, consistent with the painkilling use of
that drug, but it was not in a lethal range. As to potassium, it
was useless to seek it in the blood, as that substance leaches
from the cells after death and a high value would be mean-
ingless, even if extraneous potassium had been injected.'

'So how did you arrive at your conclusion that an excess
of potassium had been administered?' asked Gordon, though
he knew the answer full well.

'I said that the blood is useless because of rapid contamination from potassium in the body cells – but there is a place in the body which is insulated from this effect, where potassium remains at the same level as during life. This closed-off place is the fluid within the eyeball – and I found very high concentrations of that substance in the samples I took from both eyes.'

Again sibilant murmurs ran around the court, causing the judge's head to jerk up in disapproval.

'You are sure about this, doctor? Absolutely sure?' asked the prosecuting counsel, wishing to fix the vital point in the minds of the jury.

'I am in no doubt at all, sir,' grunted Angus. He shuffled some papers on the edge in front of him and stabbed a big finger at one page.

'The normal potassium level during life is about twenty milligrams in each hundred cubic centimetres, but my analyses revealed an average of no less than fifty-eight!'

He looked up and glared at the jury defiantly. 'The tests were run in duplicate on the fluid from both eyes and all four results were within the expected limits of analytical error.'

He tapped his papers together into a neat sheaf and waved them at the court. 'There can be no doubt at all that high potassium level – three times the normal amount – could only have been attained by a considerable amount of the substance being injected into the bloodstream, thus finding its way into the eye fluid.'

Just to seal the fact in the minds of the jury, Lewis Gordon added a supplementary question. 'You say that the only way potassium could get into the eyeballs would be from an injection. Do you exclude any other means, such as taking potassium by mouth?'

'Absolutely!' snapped the pathologist. 'Potassium is present in all kinds of food, especially fruit. It is even given as a medicine for bladder and kidney infections, but it is selectively absorbed and excreted, and its concentration in the blood is regulated within a very tight range, so that it could never reach these very high levels that I found in the eye fluid.'

'How does potassium chloride cause death, Dr Smythe?'

'It poisons muscles, causing irregularity of contraction. The most immediate effect is on the heart muscle, disturbing the rhythm of its beat.'

The prosecuting barrister pursued these matters in more detail, to emphasize the serious and indeed lethal effects of the substance. He led Angus Smythe to confirm that death from an injection of a large amount of strong potassium chloride solution would kill within minutes.

'That is why vets use it to put down animals,' he said gruffly. 'They usually precede it with an injection of Pentothal or some other barbiturate, to literally put the animal to sleep, as the effects of potassium, though very rapid, can be distressing as the heart fails.'

Final questions elicited the fact that Dr Smythe discounted the presence of the advanced cancer as the cause of death. 'There were no catastrophic complications, like an internal haemorrhage or a pulmonary embolism – that's a clot passing to the lungs. And given the potassium findings, there is no need to invoke the general effects of cancer, advanced though that was.'

Lewis Gordon spent a few more minutes questioning the dogmatic Scotsman, though what he was really doing was covertly going over the same ground, intent on impressing on the jury that this was the crux of the evidence, that Mrs Mary Parker was virtually awash with potassium, which could only have been the sole cause of death. He pressed this point as far as he dared, until he sensed that the judge was beginning to get restive with his attempts at repetition.

'That is the prosecution case, my lord. I am calling no other witnesses,' he said, with an air of finality that suggested that nothing else was required for a guilty verdict.

Mr Justice Templeman peered down over his glasses at the defence counsel.

'You wish to cross-examine, Mr Prideaux?'

Nathan rose to his feet and smiled almost ingratiatingly at the judge.

'I do indeed, my lord, but I would like to crave your indulgence concerning the order in which we proceed.'

Templeman looked suspiciously at the Queen's Counsel, who continued. 'As your lordship must be very well aware, the whole thrust of the prosecution case lies with the evidence of this witness. It would greatly facilitate my cross-examination – and indeed the course of justice – if I could call my only witness first, so that the evidence of Dr Smythe could be put into context with that of my expert.'

There followed some minutes of complicated legal argument, before which the jury were led out and Angus Smythe, looking irritated at the delay, stood down from the witness box to sit at a nearby empty chair. The judge and the two leading counsel engaged in an almost private debate, phrases such as 'natural justice', 'facilitating proper understanding' and 'outwith normal criminal procedure' were bandied about.

'What's going on?' Moira whispered to Doris. 'Why have the jury been chucked out?'

'This is all a bit irregular, as the prosecution normally have to finish completely before the defence have their turn,' murmured the lawyer's secretary. 'The jury mustn't be influenced by any goings-on that might affect their verdict.'

However, they soon returned, shuffling back to their places, as it seemed that with the judge's acquiescence the prosecution barrister had shrugged his agreement to Nathan's request.

Templeman turned to the jury to soothe them.

'That was nothing to do with the facts of the case, gentlemen, it was a legal discussion about a procedural matter.' He nodded at Prideaux and, pleased with his manoeuvre, the defence counsel called Richard Pryor to the box. Moira watched with mixed excitement, pride and foreboding as her hero mounted the steps, took the oath and identified himself in response to Nathan's questions.

'Dr Pryor, for how long have you been a pathologist?'

'About sixteen years. I began before the war, then I was a Senior Specialist in Pathology in the army until 1946.'

'And since then, you have been a full-time forensic pathologist?'

'Yes, I was Professor of Forensic Medicine in the University of Singapore until last year, when I entered private practice in that speciality, recently being appointed to the Home Office list.'

Richard said all this in a matter-of-fact way, free from any hint of aggrandizement. Nathan leaned forward against his table, as if reaching out to the witness.

'You were engaged by the defendant's solicitor to review

the medical evidence in this case, doctor. You have heard what Dr Smythe said, what do you say in response?'

Richard faced the jury, paused and then began speaking with careful deliberation. 'Much of what my colleague said would have been perfectly true according to generally held medical and physiological knowledge – until recently.'

'Which implies that you feel it is no longer correct?' prompted Prideaux.

'There is very recent and still-ongoing research from several parts of the world which reveals a fundamental flaw in Dr Smythe's interpretation of his findings concerning potassium in the eye fluids, on which this case largely rests.'

Down in the well of the court, Angus's red face became even ruddier, but he had had his say for the moment.

'As part of my review of the evidence, I discovered that several pathologists have independently done research in Germany, Denmark and the United States, which shows incontrovertibly that the potassium level in the eye fluid rises progressively after death – to a lesser extent than blood, but still unrelated to externally administered potassium.'

Nathan held up a sheaf of papers in his hand. 'Are these copies of publication drafts and personal responses to your enquiries by those researchers?'

Richard nodded, lifting his own copies briefly from the shelf in front of him. 'Yes, I contacted Professor Braun of Cologne, Dr Stoddart in Chicago and Dr Kaufmann in Minnesota. They all kindly sent me the results of their work.'

The judge made a gesture and an usher took the papers from Prideaux and handed them up to the bench.

'I have a number of carbon copies of all this work, my lord. No doubt my learned friend and his expert would like to see them. I also have spare copies for the jury, if you feel they would derive sufficient understanding from what is undoubtedly a very technical subject.'

There was a delay while papers were being handed around the court. Angus Smythe was given a set as he squatted on his chair, and there was a long silence as everyone scanned the flimsy carbons. After about ten minutes, with the court beginning to get restive, Prideaux began speaking again.

'Dr Pryor, could you just summarize, in a way comprehensible to us laymen, the import of this work? First, can you tell me why this research was done in various parts of the world? Surely there has not been a global epidemic of potassium homicides?'

Richard risked a grin, in spite of the fraught circumstances.

'Not at all, sir! This was done for a totally different purpose. Estimating the time since death is a very important forensic problem, because of alibis and the like. Most methods are notoriously inaccurate, but these gentlemen discovered the fact that potassium in the eyeball fluid rises progressively after death. They have been trying to use this as a measure of time since death by making a graph of potassium level against the number of hours – or indeed days – that have elapsed since death.'

'So what is the relevance to this case, doctor?'

'The second post-mortem on Mrs Parker was not carried out by Dr Smythe until the third day after death. Though the results of the three researchers are not identical, it is patently obvious that the concentration of potassium found by Dr Smythe is well within the expected levels for that period of time, some seventy-eight hours. So the interpretation that this level must have been due to the injection of extraneous potassium is now quite unacceptable.'

Nathan Prideaux wanted to nail this idea down firmly in the minds of the jury, who by now were looking bemused at this sudden turn of events.

'Dr Smythe claimed that the eye fluid is immune from the changes after death that make the blood levels of potassium useless. What do you say to that?'

'I'm afraid it's just not true. This was assumed, but until now no one has actually investigated it. Admittedly, it is much slower than in the rest of the body, but this new research shows that potassium leaks out of the cells in the retina – the inner lining of the eye that allows vision – and this is why they hope it will provide a new method of determining the time of death.'

Richard Pryor, at Nathan's request, went on to quote facts and figures from the research papers to consolidate what he was claiming, while the judge, barristers and prosecution expert followed it on the documents they had been given. From the glazed look on the faces of some of the jury, it was obvious that they had no idea of what he was talking about, but soon Prideaux put them out of their misery by diverting on to a new tack.

'Dr Pryor, I think you also have a second reason for disputing Dr Smythe's conclusions?'

'Indeed, though I admit that I, too, was unaware of it until I began researching all aspects of potassium and eye fluid. Unlike the new discoveries in Germany and America, apparently this has been known to physiologists and biochemists for a long time. I'm afraid it's a problem with all sciences, that there is so much knowledge available, but it tends to be kept in separate boxes, until someone actively seeks it out.'

'And what was in this particular box, doctor?'

'Dr Smythe quite correctly said that death occurs very rapidly on injection of strong potassium chloride solution – which is the allegation in this case. The heart stops very quickly, perhaps not instantly, but within a few moments. That is why it is used by vets to dispatch animals.'

'And what is the significance of that?' asked the QC.

'When substances such as potassium are injected into the bloodstream, it takes up to three hours for the substance to reach its maximum concentration in the eye fluid. This "equilibration" as it is called, cannot proceed if the heart has stopped, as there is no circulation to drive the substance around the body to reach the eyeball. So if an injection of potassium is sufficient to cause rapid death, there is no way that this extraneous amount can get into the eye fluid! Any rise in potassium must therefore be due to post-mortem leakage from the cells in the retina.'

He lifted up another document from his collection. 'Though I said this has been known for years, I sought advice from clinical biochemist Professor Lucius Zigmond of St George's Hospital in London, who is an expert in what are called "electrolytes" such as potassium. He has provided a statement in which this delay in equilibration is positively confirmed, and which is also contained in a number of standard textbooks.'

This statement was again handed around the court as a sheaf of carbon copies, the sworn original going to the judge for his inspection.

Nathan Prideaux took over again and asked the judge to accept all these papers as sworn evidence, entering them with exhibit numbers into the trial record.

There now seemed to be a hiatus in which the whole court was holding its breath, waiting to see what was to happen next in this drama.

Mr Justice Templeman finished reading the last of these documents, then looked down at both the leading counsel. 'Where does this leave us now, gentlemen?' he asked evenly. 'Do you want to cross-examine Dr Pryor first, Mr Gordon? Or do you wish to have Dr Smythe back in the witness box, Mr Prideaux?'

The prosecuting counsel shook his head almost helplessly as he declined the invitation. He would dearly like to have had the chance to discuss this turn of events with his expert, but once any witness began giving evidence no communication was allowed between him and counsel.

'If it pleases your lordship,' replied Nathan, in the traditionally obsequious language of the courts, 'I would like to hear Dr Smythe's reaction to these propositions.'

There was a general shuffling about, as Richard came down to sit on Angus's chair, while the Scot hauled himself back up into the witness box. As they did so, the two prosecuting barristers engaged in an animated, muttered discussion, while their defence counterparts sat back impassively until the judge invited Prideaux to begin his cross-examination.

'Dr Smythe, you have heard what Dr Pryor had to say and you have seen the various sworn statements of the other forensic experts. Is there anything in them which you do not accept or wish to dispute?'

Richard, sitting below the high witness box, fully expected the fiery Angus to begin a staunch counter-attack and was amazed when the man from Oxford immediately capitulated, contradicting his reputation for doggedly fighting off any opposition to his opinions.

'I have no option but to agree with all Dr Pryor's propositions,' said Angus. 'These are reports from reputable scientists – in fact I know of Dr Stoddart from other work. The publications have been accepted by well-known international medical journals. I did not know of this new work – and I very much doubt if the majority of my colleagues know of it. The delay in equilibration seems to be a long-accepted fact, but again I confess that it had never come to my knowledge, as I had never had occasion to seek it out.'

He nodded an acknowledgement down to Richard Pryor.

'I can only compliment Dr Pryor on such a diligent search of recent research and literature, and I unreservedly accept the conclusions which he has put forward. I withdraw my previous interpretation, which I now admit to being erroneous.'

Amid another buzz of excitement in the court, Nathan Prideaux turned to the judge.

'My lord, at this juncture I would like to make a submission to you.'

Doris hissed in Moira's ear. 'He's going to ask the judge to consider directing the jury to return a verdict of not guilty.'

But for once, Doris was wrong, as Mr Justice Templeman held up a hand towards the defence counsel.

'I think, Mr Prideaux, that will not be necessary. I am sure that Mr Gordon will not contest the fact that his witness has withdrawn virtually all his expert opinion which goes to the heart of this case. In my view, there is nothing left that can go to the jury for their decision. I therefore intend discharging the jury and also discharging the defendant forthwith.'

That evening Siân stayed behind to greet the victor, Moira having been unable to resist ringing Garth House from a phone box near the Shire hall with the news of the collapse of the prosecution case.

When they returned, an impromptu celebratory party was held in the staffroom, with a couple of bottles of Lutomer Riesling and a flagon of Buckley's Ale for Jimmy, who came in from the garden for the occasion. Moira related the dramatic scenes in Gloucester and extolled the triumphant success of Richard in the witness box.

'I should have let you go to the Brecon inquest and gone to the Assizes instead,' said Siân, wistfully.

Richard was as diplomatic as usual. 'Next time, Siân! There'll be plenty more opportunities, now that our reputation is spreading!'

He held up his glass in a toast. 'To our team, folks! I just fired the shots in the witness box, but you all were involved – everyone played a part! Angela is the brains and keeps me from the worst of my wild excesses, Siân is our queen of the laboratory and without Moira we'd not only starve but wouldn't have any reports to flash around. And Jimmy calms me down, hoeing weeds from my vines, as well as nagging me about bloody strawberries!'

Amid the celebrations and good humour, two pairs of eyes viewed Richard Glanville Pryor speculatively, as both Angela Bray and Moira Davison wondered what the next six months might bring. But fate was not willing to wait that long – indeed, it was the very next morning that the settled routine of Garth House was upset.

'There's a personal call on the line for you, Dr Bray,' said Moira, calling through from the office to where Angela sat at her bench.

As Angela came through to pick up the phone, Moira tactfully moved into the laboratory to be out of earshot and hovered over Siân in the biochemistry section.

'It must be her father,' she murmured to the technician. 'He asked to speak to his daughter.'

Siân looked up in concern. 'Neither of her parents has ever rung here before. I hope it's not bad news.'

They waited for Angela to finish her call and come back into the lab, but after a few minutes they heard the phone go down and her heels clicking away down the corridor.

'She's gone down to Richard's room,' whispered Moira. 'I wonder what's going on.'

Ten minutes went by before both Angela and Richard came back to speak to them.

'Unfortunate news, I'm afraid,' said Richard gravely. 'We're going to have to do without Dr Bray for a while.'

Angela, looking pale and strained, explained the problem. 'My mother has had a stroke. It's not life-threatening, thank God, but she's lost her speech and is partly paralysed down one side. I'll have to go home to stay with her for a while. My poor father is hopeless at looking after himself, let alone a sick wife. Just to complicate matters, my sister's just gone to New York on a three-month design course, so I've drawn the short straw, I'm afraid.'

The two other women clustered around full of sympathy and commiseration, asking if there was anything they could do to help.

'You'll have to go home straight away,' said Richard. 'Don't worry about things here, we'll cope somehow.'

He offered to drive her to Berkshire, but Angela said she was fine to drive herself.

'I'll just finish this batch of bloods,' she said, waving a hand towards her bench. 'Then I'll pack a suitcase and be on my way. With luck, my mother will recover quickly and I'll soon be able to get back.'

Within two hours she had gone in her little white Renault, leaving the house and its occupants strangely forlorn.

'How are we going to deal with her cases, Dr Pryor?' asked Siân over a consoling cup of coffee. 'There's no problem with your post-mortems, and I can handle the histology and the chemistry, but I haven't much idea of these paternity tests and bloodstains that she does.'

'Depends on how long she's likely to be up in Berkshire,' observed Moira. 'If it's only a few days or a week, I suppose things can wait until she gets back. But if it's going to be a lot longer . . .' There was a silence as her voice tailed off.

'Haven't they got a housekeeper or something?' asked Siân. 'They must be pretty well off, all that business with breeding horses and the like.'

'I'm sure they'll get in a private nurse,' said the ever-practical Moira. 'But it's not the same as having your own daughter, at least in the early stages. Pity her sister is abroad just when she's needed.'

Richard was philosophical about the crisis. 'Nothing we can do or even plan for until we hear how long Angela is likely to be away. She did mention to me, before she left, that she might know of a former colleague of hers who might be available as a locum. But let's not cross our bridges until we come to them, eh?'

When the phone rang later that evening it sounded ominous to Richard, now alone in the large, empty house. It was Angela, reporting that her mother, though in no danger, was very incapacitated. She had been taken to hospital in Reading the previous night, but later in the day a consultant advised her husband to have her back at home, as there was little they could do for her, except wait for the expected gradual improvement.

Their family doctor had arranged for a nurse to come in twice a day, and their daily woman from the village had agreed to increase the number of hours she put in and to add cooking skills to her duties.

'But I'm rather saddled with organizing things and keeping Mother company,' admitted Angela. 'My father is great with horses but clueless when it comes to anything inside the house.'

Richard took this as a coded message that his partner was going to be stuck a hundred miles away for some time to come. 'You must stay there for as long as you're needed,' he reassured her. 'We'll cope somehow. I'll just have to divert any serological requests to one of the university departments in London or Scotland who've got the proper facilities.'

Privately, he was quite anxious, as Angela had built up quite a clientele among solicitors in respect of paternity tests and other biological investigations. It brought in an appreciable part of their income, and to be deprived of it just when the Garth House consultancy was beginning to take off was a serious blow. However, his partner had a glimmer of hope to offer him.

'There's no way I can get back within a month or so, Richard, but remember that I mentioned the possibility of finding a good locum for us?'

Angela went on to say that she had already made a phone call to locate the person she had in mind. 'She wasn't there, but I've left a message and hopefully she'll call me back very soon.'

'Who is this Good Samaritan?' he asked.

Angela explained that several years ago she had had a junior colleague in the Metropolitan Police Laboratory, doing the same work as herself. 'She's called Priscilla Chambers. Has a London degree in physical anthropology and worked in the Natural History Museum for a bit, but then took a master's in serology and came to the Met Lab for a few years.'

Richard pricked up his ears at the mention of anthropology – a useful speciality when it came to identifying skeletal material. 'Why might she be available as a locum?' he asked.

'Priscilla left the Met about three years ago, as prospects of promotion were grounded by budget cuts, as I well know! She took a job in a forensic institute in Australia but came back about six months ago.'

Angela paused. 'I think she had a bad experience with a

man – another broken engagement,' she added rather bitterly. 'We forensic biologists seem to be prone to that sort of thing!'

'Is she free at the moment, then?' he enquired.

'She's been doing short-term work at a couple of archaeological digs, but at the moment she's "resting", as they say in the theatre!'

Before she rang off, Angela promised to let him know as soon as she had contacted her former colleague, leaving Richard to tramp up the stairs in the echoing house, wondering what a former museum employee and itinerant archaeologist might look like – a mannish suit and rimless glasses, or long straggly hair and projecting teeth?

He gave the news to Moira and Siân next day and they all anxiously awaited another call from Angela Bray. Like Richard the previous evening, the two women wondered what any new locum would be like, if she materialized.

'Why can't Dr Bray find us a handsome young man instead?' said Siân wistfully. 'All these biologists seem to be women!'

It was almost the end of the week before Angela rang Richard again. Her mother had slightly improved in that she could speak a little in a slurred way, but her arm and leg showed no sign of recovering, so there was no chance that Angela could leave her.

Her main news was that she had tracked down Priscilla Chambers and in principle the lady was quite keen to help out on a temporary basis. Richard and Angela agreed on a salary regime for the locum, Angela insisting on paying most of it from her share of the profits of the partnership.

'She can come down next Monday, Richard, and start immediately on a one-month agreement if she likes the look of the place. She doesn't have a car, but she can use the train.'

'Where can she stay? In that bed and breakfast you were in down in the village?'

'That's up to her, I suppose. She could use my rooms in the house, but that would cause another scandal in the valley!'

When Richard relayed this to Siân and Moira, they were relieved to hear that someone could take over Angela's work, but rather apprehensive at a stranger invading the cosy little world of Garth House.

'I'd better check with Mrs Evans that she's got a vacancy at her B&B,' said the efficient Moira.

'Dr Bray mentioned that she could stay here in her rooms upstairs,' said Richard mischievously.

This went down like a lead balloon with the two women, and Moira went straight off to telephone the lady who ran the bed and breakfast in Tintern Parva.

Angela rang again on Sunday evening to say that Miss Chambers intended catching the twelve o'clock express from Paddington next day. Richard offered to drive to Newport Station to pick her up, and just after two o'clock Siân and Moira heard the Humber roll up the drive and stop in the yard.

They hurried to the back door in time to see Richard opening the passenger door, from which a shapely pair of nylon-clad legs emerged, followed by a willowy redhead of about thirty.

With Richard grinning like a Cheshire cat behind her, she advanced towards them, elegant in a slim A-line suit under a swinging green topcoat, a tiny hat on her auburn curls.

Miss Chambers pulled off a glove and held out a hand, her perfectly made-up features breaking into a smile.

'Hello, I'm Priscilla! What a lovely place you have here.'

As the two residents went out to meet her, Siân whispered in Moira's ear, 'My God, she's gorgeous!'

'When Angela gets back,' hissed Moira, 'I'm going to kill her!'

AUTHOR'S NOTE

Though the forensic and legal procedures are broadly correct for 1955, some literary licence has had to be used, both because of the constraints of space and the need to offer an interesting story, as this was intended to be an entertaining novel, not a textbook! For instance, the research into changes into eye fluid potassium has been brought forward a few years, as the first mention was in 1958 and most of the published papers appeared from the 1960s.

Similarly, the military use of a Thompson sub-machine gun was unusual after the Second World War, though it was employed in Korea and Vietnam and some Special Forces members had an affection for odd weapons.

Until the highly controversial death of the nurse Helen Smith in Saudi Arabia in 1979, coroners had no obligation to investigate deaths occurring abroad. This has now changed, as the long-delayed inquest into the death of Princess Diana showed.

The order of court proceedings described at Gloucester Assizes has been manipulated somewhat for the sake of length – the Assizes are now the Crown Courts.

Agatha Christie's *Mousetrap* opened in London on 25 November 1952 – and is still running!